# Aggie Lichen; Pilp Collector

# Hero Required

## Debra J Edwards

PurpleRay Publishing

Published by PurpleRay Publishing

PurpleRay Publishing is the book imprint of
Debra J Edwards
info@purpleraypublishing.co.uk
www.purpleraypublishing.co.uk

A CIP Record for this book is available from the British
Cataloguing in Publication Data Office

ISBN 978-0-9550192-2-7

Printed in Bookman Old Style by
York Publishing Services Ltd
www.yps-publishing.co.uk

For Alfie, my beautiful boy.


And for believers everywhere ...

# Chapter One

It was the revolting stench that first aroused the sleeping pilp donor, a female human child of about ten years – that along with the constant pushing and shoving beneath its head. It started as a slightly unpleasant pong – the type often associated with mild foot odour. If it had stayed at that smell level then perhaps the events that followed wouldn't have followed!

As the first whiff arrived, the child pulled the pink flowered bed covers up close to her face and turned over. Her eyes remained tightly shut as the night's sleep consumed her still, her breathing deep, long and unaffected. Then as the tiny winged creature moved nearer, the smell it emitted grew stronger and more powerful. The human child gave a gentle cough causing her freckled nose to wrinkle as the invasion of her nostrils began. A stronger cough followed then a splutter. Like a snake, her tongue slipped from her mouth as she tasted the vile air. Her head was bumped around on the matching pillow as the creature rummaged underneath for its reward. As the child's eyes shot open there came a sudden awareness that all was not right in her world.

'MUM! MUM! Come quick! There's another one under my pillow.' Maddie, as the human child was called, leapt out of bed and grabbed the strategically placed plastic fly swatter from her chest of drawers. She turned back catching sight of the creature's hairy legs as it scrambled around, still searching. Maddie crept up to the edge of the bed, moving slowly towards the pillow from which a thin piece of string protruded and dangled over the side. She heard her mum climb the stairs and enter the room but, following a familiar routine, never turned round. With mum now positioned on the opposite side of the bed, they waited patiently for the string to wiggle, a sure sign that the bait had been taken. They didn't have to wait long!

As the string moved, mum swung into action lifting the pillow high in the air creating a large space which allowed her daughter to swoop down with a mighty whack. The creature, now sandwiched between the swatter and the bedsheet, made no attempt to move, partly because it was trapped and partly as it had been rendered unconscious by the force of the blow.

'Get the jar, mum. There's one on the dresser,' Maddie whispered. 'Quick, before it wakes up.' She turned to point, keeping the pressure on the fly swatter as she spoke.

Mum swung round and grabbed the large glass container. 'Here,' she said, passing it to Maddie with the lid already flipped open. Placing the jar directly over the creature and pushing down on the sheet, Maddie slid the swatter out carefully.

'Hurry, dear. It's stirring!' Seeing the creature's eyes flicker, mum shoved a piece of card directly under its body and flicked the creature into the jar. Snap! With the lid secured and a few air holes punched in, the capture was complete. Mum sighed with relief. 'Put it downstairs, Maddie, with the others.'

The child ran out of the room and leapt down the stairs to the basement. 'There,' she said proudly, pushing the jar onto a long wooden shelf full of similar looking containers.

Maddie stood back and admired her growing collection then shook her head. 'Oh dear, that won't do!' She moved her latest captive along slightly then took the last two jars that were already on the shelf and changed them around. 'Height order, that's how I like it! You must have grown,' she said to the creature in jar six. 'We'll have to cut your food down!'

She took a step back again and after nodding in approval, returned to the shelf. 'One, two, three, four, five, six, seven, eight!' She tapped each one noisily as she spoke startling each of the seven imprisoned creatures in turn. 'And now, number eight!'

She picked up jar number eight, turning it this way and that for a full minute. It was only a question from her mother that stopped the girl from completely flipping the jar over in her effort to fully awaken its occupant.

'Eight,' she answered, putting the jar back into its position. 'We've got eight altogether.'

'Wow!' shouted mum, her head appearing round the basement door. 'That'll make them believe us. Then we'll be on T.V. and everything.'

'Yep! But that reporter said to call him back when we had ten. Well, we're almost there, mum.' Maddie made her way towards the stairs counting on her hands as she climbed up and out of the basement. 'Just two more will do it,' she said, slamming the door hard behind her.

Since the demise of the pilp collector – or tooth fairy as humans call them – the capturing of Grublin-fairies had become a daily occurence in this household. Maddie and her mother had quickly realised that these strange little creatures could be worth a small fortune – if they could get someone to believe them! Several of the bigger newspapers had turned their story down flat dismissing them both as loonies and time wasters. Even the tabloids had ridiculed their story, bearing in mind that they ran stories like, 'A greenfly ate my gerbil!' In fact, it had become increasingly difficult to find anyone who would even answer their phone calls, until one small monthly magazine finally agreed to run the story, but there was one strict condition – ten captured creatures. The magazine was doubtful, just like the other publications, but by insisting on much greater evidence, there was a possibility of a news story. And now with just two more creatures to go, it finally looked as if fame and fortune were smiling down on Maddie and her mum, and their dream of going to Disneyland Paris could soon come true.

In truth, the Grublin-fairies were such easy prey as they were fundamentally ill-equipped to do the job of the tooth fairy. They were much heavier, smelt really bad and tended to flump – a cross between jumping and flying – rather than fly. Yet all was not as it seemed. A Grublin was indeed just that, a Grublin – an inhabitant of Grublin City which lay far to the north of Pilpsville, land of the tooth fairies, which in turn was part of the world of Mirvellon. Generally speaking, Grublins did not venture much into the human world and certainly did not collect pilps – teeth. The occupants of the glass jars that stood carefully upon the wooden shelf were, therefore, not true Grublins at all. They were, in fact, part Grublin, part pilp collector – Grublin-fairies.

At the bottom of the stairs, the jar filled shelf trembled slightly, knocking glass against glass. In jar number six the tiny creature steadied itself by pressing its grey chubby hands and feet against the sides, then once the rocking had stopped, it slumped despondently to the bottom. It scraped the remains of the mouldy scraps of bread off the inside of the jar into its hands, hungrily gobbling them down. The bulging eyes surveyed the extent of their prison. A piece of ragged green cloth served as a make-shift bed while a less than fluffy cotton wool ball posed as a pillow. The creature sighed, flicking thin strands of long black hair behind its shoulder. The screwed up face portrayed a mind in turmoil as it tried deperately to remember what it had been told to forget.

'II wass inn aa squaree, butt whatt wass II doingg theree?' The creature picked absent-mindedly at a black thread on its tatty skirt. 'Theree weree otherss.'

It reached into its bag, tossing an empty grey bottle over its shoulder. How it longed for one more drop of its tasty contents. It had been two long days since the last dregs of juice had been drunk. Now, the only liquid came in the form of water sprayed in the top of the jar by the human child.

'Onlyy aa feww dayss agoo II wass freee. Nott stuckk inn somee crummyy jarr withh noo properr foodd andd drinkk. Poorr mee!'

A sudden tapping made the creature look directly to the left into the jar of captive number seven, a grey skinned beast not unlike itself. On its face, a pair of thick framed glasses fought with its nose to stay in position. Dark tufts of hair were scattered across its head like clumps of grass, making it look quite ridiculous. The creature was jumping up and down like a furious froglet. The third nostril it possessed flared wildly as it tried deperately to catch the attention of creature six.

'Aaaaahhhh, over heree look att me,' it screamed – not that creature six could hear much through the thick barrier of glass walls.

Creature six, having no idea what this creature wanted, hurled a nasty remark then added, 'Ohh, justt goo awayy. I'mm veryy busyy beingg miserablee andd wouldd ratherr nott bee disturbedd!'

With that, it turned its back on creature seven, choosing to dwell a lot deeper into self-pity than it had originally intended. After all, things were getting worse not better so what was the point in trying to communicate with something that also had no future.

'II meann, II havee beenn heree twoo wholee dayss andd noww itt wantss too talkk.'

But the banging continued, and as hard as creature six tried, it could not ignore the thumpity-thump noises that kept pounding its eardrums. Cotton wool from the pillow, stuffed into the ears, had filtered some of the noise out. However, the vibrations on the glass from the banging were most disturbing and terribly irritating. It was no good; creature six had to concede defeat.

'Whatt iss itt? Whatt doo youu wantt withh mee?' it screamed.

Creature seven pointed to its left, tapping madly on the glass trying make its neighbour follow its gesture. Through the layers of glass creature six, still sitting on the base of the jar, cast its eyes, squinting to make a clearer picture. 'Ohh greatt! There'ss anotherr onee justt likee youu andd mee. Whichh meanss lesss foodd, youu stupidd idiott! Noww leavee mee alonee.'

To say the last few days had been hard for this pathetic little creature was really a bit of an understatement. It was driven by food and drink – especially the drink, and was used to having regular meals in return for collecting teeth. Going without food was one thing, but not having the special juice from the grey bottle gave the creature acute withdrawal symptoms. There were the mood swings, the cold sweats, the shivers and of course the big thirst where it ached to have just one tiny drop. But at this moment in time it was the former symptom, mood swings, that was dominating the arena.

'Sorryy, didn'tt meann too shoutt,' it said, apologetically. 'Justt havingg aa bitt off aa badd dayy!'

The creature in glass seven was having a bit of a bad day too. Having been in the jar two days longer than creature six, it had already gone through the withdrawal symptoms from not having had regular juice. It was now just hungry and thirsty, but with the constant influx of new arrivals it seemed that the human child was forgetting that her other captives still needed to eat and drink.

And then, creature eight had arrived. There was something about the new captive that stirred up memories in creature seven's mind. It didn't have thoughts like this before, yet now faces and ideas were darting around its brain like an FFP.

What's an FFP? it thought, determined to find out about it later. As its thoughts thinned and refined themselves over the last two days, it started to remember things. The first thing it remembered was that it was a Grublin-fairy! Then it started to remember faces. And today it started to remember who the creature in jar eight was. Then it had sighed as it remembered who creature six was too. It realised, as the only one of the three who probably remembered anything, that it would have to get the attention of both creature six and eight. Perhaps through them, it thought, there may be a way out of all this. Which is where the constant banging came in! But the creature in jar six was just being impossible and all his attempts to direct its attention to jar eight had been in vain.

'Youu know herr,' it screamed again. 'Look againn.' It banged on the glass with the empty grey bottle it had been using as a pillow. 'Lookk, you stupid creature, lookk!'

In jar six, the mood swing continued. 'Whatt noww? Can'tt youu leavee mee inn peacee, huhh?' Its occupant pulled up the green cloth over its face. 'I'mm asleepp, can'tt youu seee?'

*Bang! Bang! Bang!*

'Okayy, okayy. II givee upp!' Creature six threw the make-do bed cover on the floor of the jar and marched over to the left side. 'I'lll havee aa lookk, youu patheticc idiott,' it bellowed and then pushed its face up closely to the glass, taking in the distorted features of creature eight as best it could.

In the jar next door but one creature eight was starting to come round and was stretching its arms and legs. After feeling around the base of the jar, it pushed against the glass sides for support as it took its first glimpse of its new surroundings.

'Okayy, soo it'ss anotherr onee off uss,' said creature six to itself. 'It'ss sortt off smalll, quitee skinnyy tooo.'

Creature seven now started tapping and waving at creature eight who seemed more than a little startled at this sudden invasion of its senses.

'Leavee thee poorr thingg alonee. It'ss justt wokenn upp,' screamed creature six. 'Stupidd busybodyy.'

But hey, what was this? The creature in jar eight was also now tapping frantically on its own jar.

'It'ss aa diseasee!' said creature six. 'Probablyy caughtt itt fromm thee humanss.'

Wisps of wiry red hair bounced around with each movement creature eight made. A strange smile appeared on its lips. Its eyes were suddenly alert and bright.

Something stirred in creature six's brain. Something fluttered across its heart. What was it? Who was it? It fell back hard onto the glass floor as the memories started to emerge, flitting in and out of its brain. But not being able to stay just yet, they disappeared as fast as they came. That hair, that dreadful hair. It held the key to all the memories.

As the banging and jumping continued, creature six sat looking up at the jar lid for some kind of inspiration. 'II knoww thiss creaturee, II knoww II doo!'

Then, with a broad smile emblazoned on its face, creature six jumped to its feet, pushing its eyes and mouth against the coldness of the glass.

It waved across to jar eight and called out, 'Bugfacee, iss thatt youu?'

# Chapter Two

In a large oak tree, in the centre of Pilpsville, near what used to be Mrs Cheric's juice bar, sat a young lone green sprite of around ten years. For one of the now dominant species he was actually quite small, but he displayed all the usual sprite features; huge floppy ears, large bulging eyes and a strangely cute mouth. He sat leaning against the central branch sighing deeply, his spindly legs dangly limply beneath him. He gazed around sorrowfully.

Even in the darkened night he could see that the town was a mess. The few shops that were there had been looted and their terrified owners had long since deserted their posts. The juice bar, the most popular of all, lay in ruins. Shattered glass, from the gigantic glass roof and the huge rose tinted windows, carpetted the path outside. Its sign, pulled violently from the front, lay battered and defaced beyond recognition. The multicoloured brick work had taken a beating too with large chunks of enamel used in the destruction of the other shop windows. And the weirdly wonderful talking plants that Mrs Cheric had so lovingly tended lay crumpled, shrivelled and dead on the ground. With the barrier between Pilpsville and Spriteland down, the sprites of Spercham Forest had descended like locusts, destroying everything in their path.

Victor sighed again. When the pilp collectors lived there, the shops were busy, the gardens well kept and the streets clean and litter free. The sprite shook his little head in dismay as he surveyed the land from the safety of his perch.

'How could I have let this happen?' he said quietly to himself. He could only look on as his sprite kin ransacked the white enamel houses, fought over their spoils and chased the family pets. He thought back to the good times he'd shared with his friends, the friends he'd so badly betrayed.

*Smack!*

Something hard caught him on the back of the neck. The sprite rubbed his injury then glanced down below. There, in the moonlight stood his arch enemy, Norbert with his faithful gang. In his hand he held the scrawny neck of a terrified dragonfly. 'ifz wjdups! zpv xbou up qmbz?' He shook his captive above his head so the sprite could see

'Go away, Norbert. Can't you see – I want to be alone.'

'zpv uijol zpv upp hppe gps vt, ivi. zpv opu fwfo ubml pvs mbohvbhf boz npsf!'

'Oh, just leave me alone, will you?' begged Victor.

The last few months had taken their toll on him as he wrestled with his guilt. He'd become somewhat of a recluse, only returning to Pilpsville when he had to. Tonight he'd been summoned to the palace. It was only his second visit to the land since the new leader had taken over. It was then that he was awarded the platinum medal for services rendered. He hung his head in shame. He remembered the event as if it was yesterday, rewarded for pretending to be a friend when he was actually a sprite spy all along. There was no reward in that, just heartache. He'd lost everything. Warm tears trickled down his plump green cheeks and onto the head of the sniggering sprite beneath the tree.

'pi, zpv tvdi b cbcz! uifz tipvme hjwf nf uif nfebm, opu zpv!' Norbert snorted loudly then stopped and looked at his gang members. 'xiz zpv opu mbvhijoh upp?' With that, the other sprites burst into false laughter, fear of reprisal swum in their eyes.

'You can have it,' sniffed Victor. 'Here take the stupid thing!' He flung the medal he'd been clutching tightly in his hand at Norbert's head. 'It means nothing to me,' he spat.

The medal fell to the ground with a thump, throwing up a small puff of dust. Norbert jumped back quickly to avoid having his head badly dented by the heavy metal object. It shone brightly as the moonlight picked at its face.

'zpv tvdi b mptfs,' Norbert shouted as he snatched the medal up greedily from the ground with his free hand, the other hand still hanging on tightly to the petrified dragonfly. With a sneering backward glance,

Norbert and his gang disappeared into the distance, dragging the poor creature along behind them.

From the safety of his branch Victor watched as Norbert sloped off, flipping the medal up and down in his hand, laughing loudly for all to hear. He sank back into his hollow world of self-pity, desperately trying to refrain from crying again. Making a vain effort to compose himself, Victor cleared his throat, rubbed his hands over his face and straightened himself up. He stayed that way for several minutes then sighed heavily and resumed his original position of slumpiness.

'You should be proud,' came a voice from below. 'Those pilp collectors were enemies. Without you, the sprites would not have known where magic dust was kept.' Victor, recognising the voice as his father's, held his silence. 'We could not have got such good terms with the new leader.'

'Some terms, some leader! We are treated like garbage, father, you know it,' said Victor, crossly.

'Ah, but we are treated like clean garbage not like those Grublins!'

'What's it matter? What does anything matter?'

'You must stop all this right now. The leader is waiting, waiting for you. Now climb down and tidy yourself up!'

Victor hauled himself from the miserable comfort of the tree's branch and slid onto the ground below.

He stood quietly as his father walked around him brushing tree grime from his body.

'That will have to do. Now spread your wings and let's go. You know how he hates lateness.'

# Chapter Three

'Why on Mirvellon did you arrange for that sprite to come here at such a late hour?' spat the new leader. 'I can't keep giving out medals and jobs like this.' His voice echoed around the cavernous Great Hall that used to be part of Pilpsville High School. The once white enamel walls were now encrusted with plaque, displaying the first hints of decay. Furniture that had previously filled the open space now found itself thrown unceremoniously into a heap in the back playground. In its place were several sumptuous red armchairs on carpets of dried rose petals. By the huge wooden doors, two guards stood or rather slouched, one either side. The carved windows looked out onto the courtyard where the fallen statue of Ivor the Zealous, champion pilp collector lay in pieces.

The leader, a male pilp collector of about nineteen years, shuffled around grumpily on his throne in the centre of the room. A large canopy had been erected above it in an effort to increase the grandeur.

'To be quite honest, mother, I begin to tire with these creatures.' His mother waved away another tray of blutterscotch tart, much to the leader's disgust.

'Just keep giving out those medals a little longer, darling. Be patient! Everything comes to he who waits.'

'What's that? Another of your stupid human sayings, huh?' snapped the leader, thumping the padded arm of his throne with his fist. Everything about the human world disgusted him and the thought that his own mother had been turned into one, on his father's orders, made his skin crawl.

'Oh, for portal's sake, Arty! I can't just forget it all, you know!' screamed his mother, throwing her hands up in disbelief. This was not the first time the issue had come up. 'I was a human for a long time.'

Arty leapt up and marched across the room towards her. He paced around sniffing the cold air with each step. 'Yes, and I can smell it on you still. That lingering human stench – it's revolting! Almost as bad as that stinking boyfriend of yours!' He stomped noisily towards the exit. His long purple cloak followed obediently behind him.

As the Grublin guards opened the doors, his mother gritted her teeth and yelled after him, 'I'll try that new potion from the sprites before I sleep, okay! Hopefully, this one will do it.'

'Well, it had better. I can't take much more of that disgusting human odour. It's bad enough putting up with their smell!' He motioned towards the Grublins as he spoke. Leaving his mother behind, Arty headed off to his room – the former classroom of that meddling Lichen girl. All traces of her and her former classmates had been swept clean from the room. Although the perches where they sat remained, other classroom equipment had been destroyed and replaced with large tree wardrobes and chests. On the main wall, a huge four poster bed took prime position. All traces gone – except for a small solitary grey bottle which stood on a table in front of the window. A metal engraved sign beside it held the following inscription, 'Grublin inducing potion used on Aggie Lichen'. Oh, how he hated her. Turning her into a Grublin-fairy, along with her friends, was his finest hour. He smiled wickedly as he remembered her fate at his hands. His hands rubbed together as he recalled her last words as she drank the fateful potion. She'd fallen so easily into the trap he'd set – her and her bugfaced sister. What was her name? He screwed his face up as he thought – Myrtle, that was it.

A loud knock at the door shook him from his evil thoughts. 'Yes!' he screamed. 'What is it now?' He spread himself across the bed as he awaited the answer.

The door slowly creaked open and a large head appeared around the door. Now to say the owner of the head was in any way ugly, was indeed an understatement. Each facial feature seemed locked in battle with another. From the three nostrils it possessed a thick greeny mucous trickled down and was quickly wiped away by a snot laden sleeve. It was clear that this creature, a female Grublin-fairy, had a cold – big time!

'It'ss yourr fatherr, ohh mightyy onee.' She bowed lowly as the rest of her body finally entered the room.

'It's my father what, exactly?' shouted Arty.

'Atishooo! It'ss yourr fatherr what'ss askingg forr youu, yourr regalnesss.'

Arty pulled himself to the end of the bed and sat up. He looked the Grublin-fairy up and down. There was something familiar about her. 'Come forward. I know you, don't I?' he said, getting to his feet.

The Grublin-fairy sniffed, wiped its nose then hung its head low. Its eyes swept the floor not daring to look the leader straight on.

'Sorryy, yourr leadershipp. I'mm justt aa lowlyy messengerr. I'mm nott anyonee reallyy.'

'You just seem familiar,' muttered the leader returning to the luxury of his bed. He sunk down on the deep feathery mattress. 'Oh, whatever. Leave me now.'

'Butt yourr fatherr...' sniffed the Grublin-fairy.

'I will deal with MY father in my own time!'

'Yess, yourr kingshipp,' mumbled the creature backing slowly out of the door. 'Anythingg youu sayy, yourr sirnesss.' Within seconds, all that remained of her was a thick dollop of green mucous occupying the space where she just stood.

Arty sat bolt upright and tapped his head, deep in thought. Who was she? You could almost hear the cogs whirring rustily round in his nasty little brain.

He leapt from the bed and ran over to the table by the window. Turning the grey bottle over and over in his hands it suddenly came to him.

'Gertie Cruet!' he shouted, arrogantly. 'Yes, that's who she *was*.'

# Chapter Four

Bugface stared through the glass jars at the strange creature jumping frantically around in jar number six. Bugface was jumping too. The distortions caused by the glass made the creature a funny sight indeed. But that aside, she discovered a warm feeling inside her. Something felt right, something felt good. She knew this creature – but how?

The captive in jar seven continued to act as a go-between, miming and sending gestures from the jar six occupant. It was beginning to tire of relaying the messages, but because it knew both creature six and creature eight it felt it had to continue. Creature six was proving terribly hard work though. At first there was no response and now there was no quietening the thing down.

*Tap, tap. Tap!* Now what did it want? Creature seven looked over and the jar six occupant was miming something again. Creature seven copied the action then relayed it to creature eight.

It began to push against the side of the jar nearest to the edge of the shelf. Then it pointed to the ground. 'Youu want mee too pushh myselff over thee edgee? Aree you madd?'

The jar seven creature, who was in fact a male Grublin-fairy, put his thumbs up.

'That'ss justt the kindd of stupidd thing myy sister wouldd...' Bugface stopped in mid sentence and frowned. 'Myy sisterr?' Peering through the glass jars once more, Bugface took another look at the creature in jar six. A second look deemed the creature to be around fourteen years of age. It was a possibility. She pushed her face so hard against the glass that her lips attached themselves like suction pads. She squeezed her eyes tighter together. Her sister, huh?

Then she started having doubts – real doubts. The occupant of jar six didn't seem to look much like her at all, and weren't sisters supposed to look a little like each other? The strands of stringy hair it still possessed were black as were its tatty clothes. 'And II,' said Bugface, 'have redd curly hairr.' She prised her lips carefully off the glass and paced around, her hands held formally behind her back. A sister? Surely she'd remember her name if it *was* her sister.

Jar seven continued to mime the 'push the jar over the edge' movement, but was clearly becoming bored as each movement lost its sharpness. After a few minutes he shrugged his shoulders and gave up slumping back down on to the bottom of the jar.

In jar six the tiny creature flapped wings up and down to keep them toned for flying. Every few seconds or so she knocked on the glass and pointed to jar seven. 'Comee onn, telll herr it'ss mee, err, thingyy. I'mm herr sisterr,' she shouted.

Jar seven stood up again and tried to lipread what 'Thingy' was saying. He cupped his hand behind an ear then nodded vigorously to indicate that he couldn't actually hear anything. He sat back on the floor of his prison. He ran his hand across his hair, pressing down on the crown tuft which, as always, never laid flat.

'Ohh, comee onn youu stupidd thingg.' Thingy banged hard on the glass at her neighbour. 'Helpp mee outt. Justt keepp showingg herr whatt too doo.' She pushed hard against the jar to show jar seven what she meant. The jar wobbled. Thingy rushed to the back to steady it. The jar wobbled more. Thingy pushed against the glass, panic written all over her ugly face. With each movement the jar moved closer to the edge of the long wooden shelf. In the other jars the creatures held hands over eyes and ears as they waited for the jar's final surge. But now the shelf was vibrating putting the other jars at risk of falling and instead of being innocent watchers, the other creatures were now unwillingly caught up in the events. The wooden shelf shook and twitched as one by one each jar joined in the bobbing chorus. But jar six was most definitely going to be the first to go. It teetered gingerly on the edge rocking backwards and forwards in large rolls. Inside, Thingy braced herself against both sides of the jar with her feet and hands and swallowed hard as the final roll swung the jar straight over the edge onto the floor below.

*CRASH!*

Slivers of shattered glass flew everywhere, pinning themselves to places like transparent darts. As the brightness of the moon picked out their sparkle, Thingy, still somehow clinging onto a remaining shard of the jar, blinked her eyes in disbelief. 'I'm alive! Ohh, myy portals! I'm stilll alive!' She pulled each limb slowly from the glass and staggered shakily to the even surface of the floor. She had little time to compose herself though as above her head the long wooden shelf was beginning to resemble some kind of macabre white-knuckle ride as jar after jar rolled and rocked to its edge. Quickly she flew for cover.

*SMASH!*

Jar seven crashed to basement floor, narrowly missing the hard work bench opposite.

'I've gott to doo somethingg!' Thingy looked around for something soft for the jars to land on. She had to be quick. Soon the humans would hear the noise and come running then there would be no escape.

Above her head, more jars teetered precariously on the shelf's edge.

She scoured around and there in the corner, a pile of faded grey carpet tiles of poor quality and thankfully thin, made themselves known. Pushing and shoving them onto the floor she heaved one along just in time as the next jar fell.

*THUD!*

The jar rolled gently, stopping with a thump as it bumped into a half-used economy pack of wallpaper paste. Instantly an artificial snowstorm erupted as the long discarded packet spurted its contents joyfully into the air.

Thingy shook her tiny wings to free them from the falling paste flakes and returned to the carpet tiles dragging another one into place before the next jar tumbled.

*THUMP!*

Jar eight rolled across the ground then came to a halt swiftly, the impact knocking the lid of the jar clean off in the process. A dizzy, but very alive, Bugface flew out of the top, landing next to Thingy who had returned for the third time to the pile of carpet tiles and was now nearing exhaustion.

'They'ree heavierr thann theyy lookk aren'tt theyy?' she said stating the obvious then taking one of the four corners of the tile Thingy was holding and flying with her to below the shelf.

Thingy nodded and smiled, too tired to enter a conversation at this point. After five more visits, the carpet tile pile gradually diminished and the jar buffer was safely in place.

As the final tile was laid so the last jar fell releasing its captive back into the nightime world of humans.

Thingy sank to her knees, Bugface beside her. She caught her breath and spoke at last, addressing her only sister. 'I can'tt believee it! I lookedd everywheree for youu, Bugfacee! Where weree youu?'

Bugface looked around bewildered. 'Aree youu talkingg to mee, spiderr featuress?' she said, responding badly to Thingy's reference to her.

'Don'tt you recognisee me att alll? I'mm yourr sisterr!' Thingy threw her a huge smile, teeth and all.

'No, you'ree nott! Youu lookk nothingg like mee andd you're rudee, callingg me Bugfacee too!'

'Butt that's whatt I alwayss calll you! Lookk it's mee, er, Thingyy. You knoww mee!' She wrestled desperately with her mind trying to reach in and pull out her real identity.

'Ahh, Thingyy!' Bugface said sarcastically. 'Noww I recognisee youu – nott! Whatt kind off name iss thatt, huh? What'ss yourr real namee?'

'Er, umm, I knoww it soundss a bitt like Meggiee or Figgyy orr somethingg. I-I-I justt can't rememberr.' Thingy folded her arms crossly in a typical Thingy kind of way.

Oblivious to their surroundings the sisters continued to exchange words, the argument growing more heated by the minute. Across the floor, unbeknown to them, a trail of giddy three nostrilled creatures flew woozily towards the moonlit window, squeezing gently between the hinged panes which had conveniently been left slightly ajar. As the escapees flew off shakily into the darkened sky they left behind the unconscious body of the occupant of jar seven. His torso began to twitch and jerk as he finally started to come round. A dribble of saliva wove its way down his chin like a river. On his forehead beads of sweat were wiped away by a badly twisted arm, but the pain of this was nothing compared to the din ringing loudly in his ears. With his good arm he heaved himself up, leaning against the lid of the broken jar and listened.

'Whatt kindd off personn wouldd leave theirr little sisterr – iff I wass your sisterr – alll alone anywayy? screeched Bugface in response to her sister's latest revelation.

'Lookk, I hadd to seee to somethingg else – I'mm nott sure whatt,' yelled Thingy back at her. 'I didn'tt knoww you'dd be bugnappedd, didd I?'

'Ohh, stopp it! Myy head hurtss enough alreadyy,' shouted the creature with the sore arm. He straightened up his glasses to get a better look at the battling sisters. 'Whatt are you shoutingg about, Aggie?'

Thingy looked at Bugface. Bugface looked at Thingy.

'Who's Aggiee?' said Bugface.

The wounded creature hauled himself to his feet and pointed in Thingy's direction. 'Ohh, for portal's sake! Shee is!'

'Ahh ha! That'ss who I amm – Aggiee!' She punched the air with excitement then asked, 'Err, Aggie whoo, exactlyy?'

'Lichen!' said the creature huffily. 'Youu are Aggie Lichen andd she is Myrtle!'

'Seee I toldd you wee weren'tt relatedd ...' started Bugface before being quickly interrupted.

'Myrtle Lichenn, also known ass Bugface and often describedd by herr sister as a tenn year old pain inn the neck!' The creature fell back clutching his arm, mumbling under his breath about his bad luck and his sore arm.

'Tenn and a half, actuallyy,' said Myrtle.

'The same agee as me – actuallyy!' said the creature through gritted teeth. It pushed its glasses onto its nose with a hand.

The creature now known as Aggie poked her tongue out. 'Toldd you soo! Now doo you believee me?'

'Well, itt doesn'tt give youu the rightt to calll me namess,' said Bugface scowling. 'Andd untill I knoww you betterr, I'd preferr it iff you calledd me Myrtlee!'

'Okayy, Bugface!' sniggered Aggie. 'No problemm.'

'Whatt about me?' said a pathetic voice. 'I do all the introducingg and stuff and get no attentionn at all. I've got a broken arm you knoww!'

'Okayy, okayy!' said Aggie flying over to where the poor creature now lay. 'So whatt do we havee here thenn?' She tore a piece of bedding material from one of the jars into a triangle and strapped the contorted limb up as best as she could.

'Ouchh, you don't have to pull it so tightlyy,' he groaned.

'Sorryy, just tryingg to helpp, er – what didd you sayy your namee was?'

'I didn't actually – but I'm Gilbertt – Fred's little brotherr.' Gilbert hung his head sadly.

Aggie and Myrtle looked at each other and then at him. 'Who'ss Fredd?'

# Chapter Five

'Oh, come on, Victor. Time getting on,' said his father in broken fairy tongue. It was his son's preferred language now so he felt obliged to use it.

Victor, now at least ten paces behind, stumbled along the road that led to the leader's palace. His hands dug deep into his pockets, his eyes never leaving the ground.

'It is great honour to be called to palace again,' said his father.

'Why did he have to live there? Why couldn't he have stayed in Grublin City – far away from us all?' said Victor, sulkily.

'With that dreadful smell? Who could blame him for wanting to move back here.'

'But why call me again, huh? Wasn't it embarrassing enough last time?' said Victor.

'This is special occasion, Victor. They make you in charge of the pilp plant tonight, you see if they don't.'

'Don't want to be in charge. I just want to be left alone,' mumbled Victor, dragging his heels.

'You must stop all that! If you sulk before the leader we will all suffer,' said his father. 'I know some sprite who has many used globstoppers. Wait here! I get one to cheer you up, huh?'

'But there's no time, father...'

'I be just a minute. It will make you happy.'

'That's not it, father. I just want...'

Like a shot, his father headed off to a looter friend who held the monopoly on used goods such as globstoppers.

'I just want to be left alone,' said Victor, finishing the sentence anyway. After kicking the ground for a few minutes he finally lifted his head up to look around. It wasn't a pretty sight that met his eyes. Sprites had wrecked most of the houses rendering them virtually inhabitable. Saying that, they were sort of lived in – by Grublins! With all pilp collectors now transformed into a Grublin-fairy workforce there was a greater need for housing. Unfortunately, the leader's 'pick one and live in it' policy caused chaos and there was constant fighting over the houses. It would have helped if they had retained a better part of their memory following the transformation. Then at least they'd have known which house to head for.

There were houses next to an alley which were always exchanging hands for vast amounts of credits. As corner houses they had bigger garden plots where many sprites or Grublins could pitch a make-shift tent or two, and pay the house owners extortionate premiums for the privilege. The corner plots also meant that there was plenty of room for an enamel extension and both houses on either side of the alley came with added rooms attached... and a shed!

Victor twisted around as he took in the sights. Out of the corner of his eye he could see something strange, something very peculiar. A small figure was jumping up and down in the shadows where the alleyway began. He decided to ignore the distraction and looked away to the other side of the street near to the pilp plant where a couple of Grublins were fighting over a sparkly jacket.

'Psst, psst! Over here!'

Victor turned to see the same little figure calling in his direction. The figure beckoned with its hand.

Victor looked around for the subject of the creature's attention, but there was no-one else around. He pointed to himself. 'Me? Are you talking to me?'

'Yes! Quickly. I have something for you,' called the figure ducking back into the deeper shadows of the overhanging roof of the alley house.

Victor moved tentatively towards the alley. Unable to recognise the figure, he drew his suspicions to the forefront of his brain. It didn't look like Norbert, but it wouldn't have surprised him in the least if his old enemy had set a trap for him.

Victor drew nearer. He decided to call the figure's bluff. 'Show yourself first. Who are you?'

The creature withdrew further into the shadows, backing away as it spoke, 'I cannot. I am not of your kind. If I am seen I could lose my life.'

This intrigued Victor. So much so that he let down his guard and walked, as if hypnotised, straight into the shadow of the alley. This would not take long, he thought.

The little figure stopped suddenly and allowed Victor to approach. Now accustomed to the lack of light in the alley, Victor's eyes widened as the creature was revealed in all its glory. Small and well rounded it was, with bearded facial features and grubby clothes to match. It was unlike anything he had seen before. He knew of other beings that shared the world of Mirvellon, but, not being much of an adventurer, he had not travelled far. Was it a piskie? As he moved in further, Victor noticed how it held both hands behind its back as if concealing something.

'You said you had something for me,' said Victor, bending down, trying to looking over the creature's shoulder for a clue. 'Only I can't stay long.'

'Neither can I,' said the creature, and promptly whacked the bewildered sprite over the head with a large blunt instrument cunningly disguised as an old wooden table leg.

******

'Where am I?' Victor tried to move his arm to rub his throbbing head, but found it difficult – due to the rather thick piece of string that held it firmly in place. He cast his eyes around for some point of reference to where he might be. It was a dark, dingy room which smelt earthy – perhaps underground. No natural light entered the room. The only source was from a small oil lamp that stood on a large wooden crate opposite to the chair on which he sat. He rocked backwards and forwards to loosen his bonds, but it was no use – the vast array of reef knots and sheepshanks held his body tightly. 'What do you want? Who are you?' he shouted.

A deathly silence filled the air as he waited anxiously for a reply. 'My father will be looking for me. I-I-I'm expected at the palace,' he added for good measure.

Still nothing – just the same eerie silence as before. But Victor's huge ears picked up something. There was definitely somebody down here.

'Come on! Show yourself. Who are you?'

From behind him came a voice. A gruff, gravelly voice. An earthy type of voice that seemed to be part of the very foundations of the room Victor sat in.

'I'm of the thinking that we will be asking the questions, my little green friend – not you!' it growled.

Victor grimaced with pain as the twisting rope burnt his arm. Part of him wished it was one of Norbert's traps. Compared to this, facing Norbert seemed a far better bet.

'Just tell me who you are – please,' he pleaded, hoping for the sympathy vote.

The shuffling of many feet behind the chair told Victor that his captors were possibly about to show their faces. And within minutes, several creatures had assembled in a line in front of him. In size they were smaller than sprites, Grublins and pilp collectors. The roundness of their bellies portrayed how well they ate and their clothes, although grubby with dirt like their faces, were well made and of similar design. Each wore a brightly coloured felt hat which flopped to one side just covering one of the two pointy ears it possessed. His initial captor, smaller than the others, stood at the end of the line.

Victor tried to straighten himself up so he could examine each one in turn, but with each movement his head thumped. From his resumed slouching position his brain went into overload as he tried to identify what the creatures were.

'Elves,' he said out loud. 'I might have known. Elves! Creeping up on poor innocent sprites like that.'

'No!' shouted one of the creatures.

'Sorry, but are you saying that I crept up on myself and hit me over the head then tied myself to this chair?'

'No! What I is saying is that we are not elves. We are D.A.F.T.,' said the one in the red hat who went by the name of Jud.

'Well,' snorted Victor, 'that didn't take a lot of working out...'

'Dwarves Against Fieving Tyrants!' snapped the dwarf.

'Isn't thieving spelt with a...' began Victor.

'Be quiet, greeny!' screamed Jud peering directly into Victor's eyes. 'You is in no position to tell us how to spell.'

Victor seemed a little taken aback. For small creatures these dwarves displayed quite a ferocious streak. He pulled himself together quickly, recognising that the best form of defence, in this case, was attack.

'So why do you have me?' he yelled back at Jud. 'I'm not a tyrant – far from it. I'm just a...'

'Traitor! That's what you just is – a dirty, stinking traitor,' said the one called Bod, spitting on the floor in disgust. He was the dwarf who had trapped Victor moments before in the alleyway.

Victor swallowed hard to stop the tears from flowing. He knew what he was, but being told by others hurt twice as much. He shuddered as he fought to regain his composure. 'L-L-Look, if I could change it all back, I would – really!'

'A traitor still! Betrayed your friends didn't you, greeny?' said Jud, sneeringly. 'And for what – some stupid medal!'

'YES! YES! What do you want me to say?' said Victor.

Suddenly the dwarves stepped back. They made no further comment, but stood silently watching the empty space behind Victor's chair.

'I said, what do you want me to say?' repeated Victor, frustratedly glaring at the dwarves.

Still nothing. The dwarves were looking beyond him and felt no need to comment further.

Victor struggled to break free once more. He twisted and turned, trying to move the chair with his body. Eventually though, he realised nothing would free him, but his captors. He sighed despondently, 'Tell me. What do you want of me?'

'How about – sorry?' came a voice from behind him. The tone was harsh, but the voice was instantly recognisable.

Deep inside the pit of Victor's stomach, a mixture of fear, excitement and anticipation fought wildly with the remains of that morning's breakfast. He hardly dared to hope who the speaker was. The throbbing of his head seemed to be pushed to one side as he twisted his neck round to see who it was.

He gasped. 'Is that you, Fred?'

# Chapter Six

*CRASH!*

The basement door was thrown open with such force that it hit the wooden banister and bounced back into the face of the person opening it – the human child, Maddie! Before her lay all that remained of her trip to France. Fragments of shattered glass covered the ground like a shimmering carpet.

'I told you I could hear something, didn't I?' she screamed back up the stairs.

The heavy thud of her mother's footsteps thundered across the ceiling.

Maddie jumped down the basement steps two at a time, stopping momentarily at the bottom to work out a path through the shards of glass. She peered around anxiously for signs of life – anything that could be exchanged for hard currency.

'No, stop! Don't go any further 'til I get a broom,' said her mother, looking down from the doorway at the mess. 'We can sweep a pathway through.' She quickly disappeared back upstairs to find a broom.

Maddie crouched down on her knees and squinted across the room. 'I think there's still some alive over there,' she muttered, pointing in Aggie's direction. 'If I can just climb across...' She stood up and stretched out her right leg, positioning the foot in a small glass-free space. Using her arms to balance, she then moved her left leg across to another bare patch. Pausing for a moment, she resumed her squint. There, just a few metres in front of her. Something was moving.

'Hurry up, mum! I can see some near the window,' Maddie yelled. 'Quick or we'll lose them all.'

Underneath the window were all that remained of her prize collection – three ugly Grublin-fairies.

The creatures watched between the slithers of glass as Maddie advanced slowly towards them, closing in on them with each carefully planted step.

'Oh, helll. We'dd bestt get outt of heree,' said Aggie, the panic apparent in her voice. She looked up at the escape route. A cool night breeze blew through the window gap, ruffling her wings.

Gilbert rubbed his arm, his face contorted in agony. 'Well, I can'tt possibly flyy!' he cried. 'Everyy time I tryy to move myy wingss the painn is awfull.'

'You'lll just havee to stayy then, won'tt you – err, Edward,' she mumbled.

'Youu can't justt leave me – and it's Gilbertt.'

'Sorryy,' said Aggie, grabbing hold of her sister's hand, 'butt I needd to gett Bugface outt of heree.'

Myrtle pulled her hand away indignantly. 'The namee iss Myrtle, spindlee legss!'

'Ohh, whateverr! So sorryy ...'

'Butt I helped you so you shouldd help me!' cried Gilbert.

'Sorryy, butt we havee to go.' Grabbing Myrtle's reluctant hand, Aggie swept up towards the window squeezing through the tiny gap.

'We can'tt justt leave himm!' said Myrtle, craning her neck round.

'Sayss who?'

'Butt he's hurtt andd... it's yourr faultt! You made alll the jarss falll offf the shelff.'

'Yeahh, and heroicallyy saved countlesss other livess in doingg so,' snapped Aggie. 'I meann, we don'tt even knoww him.'

'*WE* don'tt even knoww each other, but youu saved mee!' said Myrtle angrily.

'Butt you'ree my...'

'Sisterr, yeah – andd how do youu know thatt, huh?'

'Oh, forr portal'ss sake! Okayy! I give inn. We'll riskk our ownn freedom andd rescue effervescentt Egbertt!'

'Gilbertt!' shouted Myrtle. 'Hiss name is Gilbertt!'

Aggie glared at the ugly Grublin-fairy face in front of her. 'Oh, whateverr! Let's justt do itt.'

They retraced their steps, landing quietly on the tatty red tiled window sill of the basement. As a lower floor room, the window and sill had been neglected for many years. Peeled red paint from the tiles vied with the moss and crumbling plaster for first position in the deterioration stakes. Aggie and Myrtle trod carefully over it all to reach the corner of the pane.

'I can'tt see a thingg,' complained Aggie, using her elbow to polish the glass. 'These windowss are filthyy.'

Myrtle pushed her sister to one side. 'You needd to spitt on it firstt.' Then she used her own arm and elbow to wipe away the many years of grime. 'Ahh, there hee is.'

Aggie pressed her face to the window. 'How'dd he managee to gett under theree?' She pointed to the work bench where Gilbert was hiding behind one of the four legs. 'We'lll have too be quickk. The humanss will spott him soonn.'

'We needd a distractionn,' said Myrtle. 'Somethingg to move theirr attentionn away fromm him...'

'I knoww whatt a distractionn iss, Bugface!'

Myrtle scowled. 'Howw aboutt you goingg round the frontt and ringingg the doorbelll?'

'How aboutt YOU goingg round the frontt and ringingg the doorbell, huh?' Aggie crossed her arms and leant back casually on the window pane.

'Okayy – I'lll go roundd while youu go inn andd gett him. Andd remember – he'ss called Gilbertt!' Aggie watched as Myrtle took off from the ledge and disappeared round the corner of the house. She pushed her ear to the window, listening out for the shrill sound of the bell. Seconds drifted past. No doorbell. Minutes drifted past. No doorbell!

Myrtle's worried face reappeared round the corner of the red house. 'There isn'tt a doorbelll!' she call-whispered.

Aggie prised her ear away from the window in disbelief. 'Welll, use the knockerr, you plankk!'

'Ahh!' Myrtle raised her index finger up in acknowledgement and promptly flew back to the front door.

Repositioning her ear onto the pane of glass, Aggie sighed as she tried to dig into her memory for clues of her life with Bugface. Was this strange little creature really related to her? She had her doubts!

*KNOCK! KNOCK!*

I meann, thought Aggie, she'ss nothingg like me att all. She's stubbornn, stroppyy and sometimess seems justt a little bitt stupidd. Nothingg like mee att all ...

*KNOCK! KNOCK!*

'Ahh! Myy cue.' She peered in, listening intently to what the humans were saying.

'Who on earth can that be at this time of night?' said Maddie's mother who had by now returned to the basement. 'I mean, it's past 9'0'clock!' she added, passing a huge silver plastic broom to her daughter.

*KNOCK! KNOCK!*

Maddie swept away the last pieces of glass that lay between her and Gilbert. 'Aren't you going to get that, mum?'

Mum looked back up the stairs and then across to Maddie. 'I'm not going to the door at this time of night on my own! Not with all these strange creatures about. You'll have to come with me.'

*KNOCK! KNOCK!*

'No way! I can't move from here otherwise this one will escape too!' Maddie leant down to look under the workbench. Something near the back leg caught her eye – Gilbert! 'Come here, you little toad,' cried the child, using the head of the broom to try to hook the terrified Grublin-fairy from behind the work bench.

*KNOCK! KNOCK!*

Outside the window Aggie looked on exasperated. 'Ohh justt openn the pigging doorr, willl you?'

*KNOCK! KNOCK! KNOCK!*

'Oh, come on, Maddie. That knocking is driving me mad! Just lock the blasted window. The pesky thing can't go anywhere.'

*KNOCK! KNOCK! KNOCK! KNOCK!*

'Fine! But if this one gets away you owe me £50!'

Cautiously, Maddie scrambled on to an old wobbly stool, which had been in the family for many years, and pulled the window tight shut. She gave it a hefty push just to make sure it wouldn't open before reluctantly leaving the basement to attend to the *urgent* business at the front door.

Aggie had to act quickly. With the window now firmly shut, she squeezed through the tiny gap between the pane and the hinges ... and stuck fast! Grublin-fairies were bulkier than tooth fairies – fact! Grublin-fairies are more likely to get wedged in window gaps – fact. Aggie was going nowhere – fact!

'Oi, Filbertt. I've comee to rescuee you, butt ... itt mightt take longerr thann I'd hopedd,' she called out to the workbench leg that was furthest from her sight. 'Iff you couldd make yourr way upp here perhapss we couldd help eachh other ...'

Gilbert crawled out from behind the leg, clutching his wounded arm tightly and ran to where the old stool wobbled. Looking up he could just make out the hefty bulk of Aggie's Grublin-fairy frame, although the smell would have drawn him towards her sooner or later!

'Ohh, so you've come back then, huhh! Foundd time out of yourr busy schedule to rescue me, didd you?'

'Welll, yes I didd, Engelbertt. Butt I seemm to have gott myselff kinda stuckk in the processs.' Aggie wriggled about to demonstrate her state of stuckness.

Gilbert swallowed hard. Part of him wanted to scream his name out again and again at this stupid

Grublin-fairy, but he decided to save that for later. Right now, Gilbert's priority was to get Gilbert free! He looked around for something to pull himself up to window ledge level.

'Oi, Bertt – lookk for somethingg to pulll yourself upp to the windoww ledge – some stringg, perhaps?'

Gilbert swallowed harder and mumbled something unrepeatable, to do with string, under his breath. He scoured the floor quickly. Time was running out. The humans could be back at any moment.

'There,' called Aggie, hurriedly. 'Justt overr there byy the shelff.' She pointed with her free arm to a small untidy ball of green garden twine lying in a long discarded spider's web. It was half-hidden under the row of shelves where the jars that imprisoned them once sat.

Gilbert grimaced with pain as he shuffled across the floor to grab the twine. With his good arm, he dragged it towards the leg of the wobbly stool.

'Throww it upp, come onn – I'lll catch itt!'

'I can'tt,' he whinged. 'My poor arm's justt too painfull.' A look of agony slowly crawled across his face as he spoke.

'Fine! Stayy here!' said Aggie angrily, completely forgetting that she was stuck fast and wasn't actually going anywhere. She wriggled frantically, but the only thing that moved was her third nostril which swung from side to side. 'Aaarrrgghh!'

Above them the sound of footsteps echoed as the humans made their way to the front door. They needed to do something – fast.

'Noww look heree, Talbertt,' she began. 'You've gott to pushh your painn aside andd throww the stringg to me orr we're bothh goingg to becomee the latestt additionss to their zooo!'

'I can'tt. It's so soree.'

Aggie took a deep breath to calm herself before calling down once more to the injured Grublin-fairy. 'Justt liftt up the stringg with yourr good armm and swingg it upp here to me – there'ss a dearr!'

'Butt my arm ...'

Aggie could take it no more! 'Justt throw the stringg up – noww!' she screamed.

Finally Gilbert swung into action. All thoughts of pain subsided as he threw the string with all his might straight into Aggie's waiting hand.

She wrapped one end tightly round her hand and let the ball fall back down to the ground. Gilbert tied the rest round his waist and started to climb up the wobbly stool – with one arm.

'Come onn,' said Aggie breathlessly. The weight of Gilbert was more than she'd imagined. 'Gett a movee onn!'

'I can'tt ...'

'Don'tt tell me – yourr arm'ss sore!'

'Welll, it is!' Gilbert grabbed the leg of the wobbly stool between his two legs as he tried to make his way to the summit.

*CRASH!*

Vibrations shook the floor above as the front door was slammed with some force. Raised disgruntled voices rang out as the intention of the bogus caller was realised.

Gilbert clung fiercely to the wooden leg and looked upwards. 'They're comingg back, Aggie. What'lll we do?'

'Climbb, for portal'ss sake, climbb!'

Gilbert stretched out his good arm above him and grasped the string. He swung himself round to face the wall, pushing against it with his feet. Desperately, he tried to pull the weight of his bulky body up.

Footsteps thundered back across the ceiling.

'Come onn, come onn!' called Aggie, tugging madly on the green string.

'It'ss no use,' cried Gilbert. 'I justt can't do it.' He let go of the string and dropped the short distance to the floor. Self-pity oozed from every pore as he broke into a massive sobbing fit.

'Gett upp, Wilbert! Get upp, now!' screamed Aggie, sensing the imminent return of Maddie and her mother. 'Do somethingg or we'lll both gett caught!' She pushed against the glass again with limited success as a few millimetres of Grublin-fairy flesh freed itself from the window's hold.

Gilbert continued to sob uncontrollably.

Aggie prepared herself for the inevitable, accepting

her fate as prisoner number six once more. The human child would have at least something to exchange for her visit abroad. She sighed deeply – then suddenly cried out in pain.

As she turned her head, her face grimacing from her unexpected injury, she recognised the perpetrator immediately – Bugface!

'Heyy, why're you stilll here? You're supposedd to have rescuedd Gilbert!' shouted Myrtle.

'Oooohhh, iff I ever gett outt of here …' said Aggie crossly, the red mark on her arm throbbing from the fierce pinch she had suffered.

Myrtle jumped back as Aggie's hand flew out in her direction. 'Oh, come onn, we've gott to go.' She pulled hard on Aggie's arm which now hung loosely by her side.

'Look closerr, sister dearr – I'm stuckk!'

Myrtle tugged on her arm again to confirm her sister's news.

'Andd as forr your cheeryy friend,' Aggie continued, 'welll, he's stilll in theree – he can'tt get outt!'

'Butt the humanss are onn their wayy backk – and they're reallyy angryy!'

'So pulll me outt then – andd hurryy!'

Myrtle grabbed Aggie's wrist and, pressing her heels down against the crumbling window sill, yanked hard on her arm. Aggie moved a few millimetres, but it was nowhere near enough to make a difference to her predicament.

Myrtle looked in through the window at Gilbert who was still lying on the floor and crying.

'Get upp, you stupidd fooll!' she shouted through the crack above Aggie's head. 'The humanss willl be backk anyy minute.'

Gilbert's head suddenly lifted and he shot an evil glare through the glass straight at Myrtle. 'Howw dare you calll me a fool!' he thundered. As he rose slowly to his feet the pale colour in his face diminished and was quickly replaced by vivid shades of scarlet and crimson. 'Howw dare you!' he screamed again, shaking his fist at the window.

Then he vanished. Just like that!

'Where'dd he go?' screamed Myrtle.

'I kneww there wass somethingg strange aboutt him!' said Aggie.

They'd hardly time to recover from the shock when a terrible smell assaulted their many nostrils.

'Ohh, my portalss, whatt have youu done?' said Aggie holding her nose. 'You stinkk!'

'That's rightt, blame itt on me.' Myrtle covered her face with her hand.

'It'ss me,' said an angry voice.

'Who saidd thatt?' said Myrtle.

'Mee!'

Hovering just behind Myrtle's back was Gilbert, a strained expression across his face.

Myrtle jumped to one side as he fluttered down and settled on the sill.

'Wheree the helll didd you come fromm?'

'Nott sure – I justt remember gettingg really angry thenn some strange wordss appeared in myy head andd 'POP', I turnedd into a green whispyy thing.'

'I thinkk you meann a greenn whiffy thingg,' said Myrtle, fanning her nose.

'Neverr mind alll that,' shrieked Aggie. 'Lookk the humanss are comingg. Quickk, pull me outt!'

Through the window they watched as Maddie and her mother re-entered the basement. They started turning over pots, peering under the bench legs and lifting up the old carpet tiles in search of the missing prize. As long as their attention remained at ground level Aggie might have a chance...

'Aaaaarrrgggghh!' yelled Aggie. 'They'vee seen uss – quickk Bugface, grabb my arm. Er, Milfordd, grab myy leg. Now pulll!'

Inside, Maddie made a dash for the window followed swiftly by her mother. In her sights were three tiny Grublin-fairies, a tidy fortune hopefully – if she could catch them.

She leapt forward to where the wobbly stool had fallen and grabbed it with both hands.

'I'll hold it while you get up,' called her mother.

As the human child climbed, the two younger Grublin-fairies had hold of the older one's leg and arm and were tugging and pulling with all their might – even if it was with only three good arms.

'I'm nearly there,' called Maddie, as she brought her knees up to the top of the stool.

'We'ree nearlyy there,' puffed Myrtle and Gilbert, as they wedged their feet against the glass and heaved.

'Just a few centimetres,' yelled Maddie, standing on tip toes to reach the top of the window.

'Justt a feww millimetress more,' shouted Myrtle, as her sister's bulky body was jerked and hauled unceremoniously through the window gap.

Suddenly there was an enormous splop as Aggie was at last released from the windows grasp.

'YESS! We've done itt!'

# Chapter Seven

It had been two hours since Ferrett Granger had last requested to speak with his son, the new leader. He had made many such requests over the past months, each of which had been simply ignored or had never been delivered.

'There must be some way of getting through to him,' Ferrett mumbled to himself, twisting his long grey beard round and round through his fingers. He paced backwards and forwards as the walls of his prison, a basement room in the grand palace, closed in around him once more as another dark and lonely night fell.

After twenty minutes or so he sunk down slowly onto the thin grey mattress of his prison bed. There was no other furniture except for a small wooden desk with a lift up lid and a carved wooden chair. On the desk sat a pile of dusty unused white paper and a quill pen with ink, also untouched and unused.

Ferrett stared at the blank paper that eagerly awaited his words and signature then cupped his head in his hands. 'Confess? Confess how wrong I was about his mother? No, no, no, no, no!'

He stood up again and walked towards the window, a small hole hacked out of the enamel many years ago. Peering into the darkness at the freedom that lay outside he shook his head. 'I was right to have her turned into a human. She was evil. She would have killed me.' He leapt across the room to the door and screamed through the bars, 'I will not confess, I will not.'

'Then you'll stay in there and rot!' sneered a familiar voice.

'Arty, at last. Is that you – *son*?'

From the dark shadows outside the room emerged the unrepentant figure of the new leader. His eyes looked mockingly at his father as he snarled, 'You call me son? What kind of father are you!'

'I was trying to protect us both. She would have killed ...'

'Nonsense, father! Mother would never harm me. She has only my best interests at heart,' spat Arty, grabbing so hard at the bars that his father jumped back. 'Do you really think I would have gone to such extraordinary lengths to get her rescued if I believed that?'

Ferrett moved slowly toward the bars that retained him, holding his arms wide open in a gesture of honesty. 'If you really think that why am I still here? Surely if you believe so much in your mother you can afford to lose me – and have me turned into a Grublin-fairy like every other pilp collector.'

Releasing his tight grip, Arty turned away.

'Go on,' cajoled Ferrett, 'go and get a bottle of the potion – I'll drink it!'

Arty remained silent.

'What are you frightened of, huh?' his father enquired, pushing his face through the bars as he reached them. 'Being on your own? Not being able to control her? You can't, you know. No-one can!'

Arty turned back and grabbed at his father's face with both hands. 'Shut up, shut up!' he screamed. 'You know nothing – she's changed.' Realising what he'd just said, Arty pulled away quickly and began to walk away.

'So you admit it!' shouted Ferrett after him. 'You know she's evil, you know it!'

The retreating footsteps told him his son had heard enough, but that didn't stop him screaming one last warning, 'You can't trust her, son. You can't trust her!'

# Chapter Eight

Not far, in fact very close to the new leader's palace, in a damp, dark cave just beneath the earth, an interrogation had begun.

'Perfect fairytongue! Amazing, seeing as you could hardly speak a word of it before.' Fred's sarcastic tone singed the back of Victor's head.

'I had to pretend – they made me do it.' Victor strained his neck round trying to get a glimpse of his former friend.

'Rubbish! From what I saw back in Spercham, you knew exactly what you were doing.' Fred sidled up close to the sprite's right ear. 'You left my brother for dead, you scragpit!'

Looking to his right, Victor got his first glimpse of Fred since their last meeting six months ago. He looked a lot older than his fourteen years, although he was nearing fifteen. His hair, although still black, was long and unkempt, and as always the crown tuft stood firmly to attention. The clothes he wore were familiar, but the tears and holes portrayed a hardened life, a life that had changed beyond all belief since the new leader had taken over.

'Call me what you want – I deserve it!'

'You deserve a lot worse,' said Fred, moving round in front of Victor. 'You could have stopped all this happening. You are the cause of all the problems ...'

'Okay – I get it,' cried Victor. 'So kill me – that's what you intend to do, isn't it?' He squeezed his eyes together as if waiting for the inevitable. 'Just get it over with quick ...'

'Oh, shut it will you? You're pathetic!' said Fred. 'Death is too easy an option for you – you're going to put it all right!' Fred moved to the back of the chair and started untying the lavish array of knots that held the captive so firmly.

Peeking with one eye, Victor turned his head as far as he could then, realising what Fred had said, protested loudly, 'I-I-I'm what? Me? How can I ...'

'I'll help – and so will the dwarves. But you are to restore the equilibrium in our world, got it?' And with the last of the knots undone, Fred beckoned to the sprite to stand up.

'I'm to restore the what?' asked Victor, slipping cautiously off the chair to the ground.

'The balance, you fool, the balance.'

The dwarves, who had remained quietly observant during this time, now moved forward and with one on either arm they marched the sprite to the back of the cave. Bod grabbed the oil lamp from the large wooden crate as they passed and moved in front to lead the way.

'So Fred,' said Victor quietly, his little green legs barely touching the ground, 'how comes you're not a Grublin-fairy?'

'He don't like to talk about it,' whispered Jud. 'So be quiet, greeny.'

'No, it's okay, Jud.' Fred, who had been walking a little way behind, caught up with the dwarves holding Victor and began to explain. 'I *was* a Grublin-fairy, in fact I was, I'm ashamed to say, one of those creatures who held Aggie Lichen while her sister administered the changing potion.'

'And you call me a traitor,' mumbled Victor.

'Ssshh,' said Bod.

'At least I only did it because I was under the influence of the potion!' snapped Fred.

'I told you, the sprites made me do it ...' cried Victor.

'Anyway,' said Fred, ignoring his protest, 'I was set to work at the metal works, with Bessie. You remember Bessie, don't you?'

'Yes, the grungy one. Funny squiggly hair too.'

'They're called plaits, imbecile!' sneered Fred. 'So, as I was saying, I was working at the metal works with Bessie. My memory isn't as it was, but I do remember that day, the day I was rescued.'

'You were rescued?' said Victor, who was now listening intently – well, listening as best as he could, considering he was being held up by his arms and his feet were hovering just centimetres above the ground.

Fred waited until they were through the wooden door and had exited the cave before continuing. 'Yes, I was rescued.'

The dwarves released their grip on the sprite's arms and as his feet touched the ground he looked around at where they had brought him. The vastness of the cellar, which it was, made him gasp aloud. It ran for hundreds of metres to the left and right of where they had just entered. But amazing as that may seem, that was not the cause for the sprite's loud gasp. For all along the length and breadth of this white-washed, non-windowed room were small wooden crates piled high, one on top of the other.

Fred tried to distract Victor by carrying on the conversation, 'I told you some time ago that my father did business, of the magic dust variety, with the dwarves, didn't I?'

'Mmmmnnn,' said Victor, fluttering up the side of a nine storey crate pile.

'Well, because of their friendship, the dwarves agreed to risk their own freedom and try to rescue me.'

'Mmmmnnn!' growled Victor as his concentration deepened and he neared the summit.

'Are you listening to me?' Fred looked up at where the sprite had stopped.

'Er, yes.' Victor repeated back what he thought he'd heard, 'Your father rescued some dwarves and set up a magic business with them!' He climbed up and onto the last remaining box. 'Now let's see what's in here.'

Fred shook his head in dismay. So much had changed over the months and although the Victor before him had changed in many ways, elements of his curiosity and self-absorbency still shone through, providing Fred with a ray of hope that perhaps all could be restored.

'Oh no! Have you seen what's in here? Oh no! You're just not going to believe it.'

He also reminded Fred of Gilbert, his younger brother, now a Grublin-fairy somewhere in the former tooth fairy world. Gilbert had a tendency to drag things out too! But Fred and the dwarves already knew what each and every container held. They had been to this particular cellar more often than they cared to remember.

'Fred,' called Victor, 'there's loads of them, thousands of them, perhaps millions ...'

'We knows what they are, greeny,' said Pod. 'We see'd them many times afore.'

Victor fluttered to the floor, disappointed at not being the first to know about the bottles. 'So why are they here and why so many?'

The dwarves looked to Fred for the answer. He was leaning against the door, picking at his nails. 'I'm sorry – did you want to know something? Only the last time I started answering one of your questions you completely ignored me!'

'You mean your father didn't have a magic business?'

Fred furrowed his brow.

'I'm just teasing. I heard everything you said.'

And considering the size of his ears, Fred was inclined to believe him. 'Okay, these bottles are bottles of the Grublin changing potion.'

'Yes, I know that – but why so many?' said Victor impatiently.

'They're for topping up,' said Fred, casually opening up a crate near to him and pulling out a grey bottle.

'Topping up what?'

'Not what – who?' said Fred. 'They are for topping up pilp collectors. Well, they're for topping up the Grublin-fairies.'

Victor looked puzzled. 'But I thought the potion made you stay a Grublin-fairy forever.'

'So did I, but think back six months to when Arty escaped from Mursham Marshes. We spent so much time chasing clues as we searched for Myrtle that none of us paid any thought to Arty.'

'I still don't get it,' said the sprite.

'When we finally came face to face with Arty, no-fairy questioned why he wasn't a Grublin-fairy any more. And yet we all saw Aggie give him the potion before he went to prison.'

'But I thought somefairy must have given him the antidote – like Gertie Cruet!'

'Well, the antidote would have had an immediate effect, but without a top up, the effects of the potion would have worn off anyway after a month or so. And that's why Arty needs all these bottles – to refill his workforce every day and maintain his position as leader.'

'Hold on – are you saying that we are in his cellar beneath the palace?'

'Exactly!'

'Oh, hellfish! He'll have guards and everything down here to protect these bottles ...' Victor tried to get past Fred to go back through the door to the cave, but Bod pulled him back by the ear.

'Be still!' cried Fred, angrily. 'He has no need for guards down here.'

Victor rubbed his ear as he was set back down on a crate. 'But if somefairy got to the bottles ...' he said sulkily, his eyes big and soulful.

'Arty has total control over all creatures in Pilpsville and Grublin City.' Fred perched on the crate opposite to Victor as he continued to explain. 'The sprites, as you know, are working with him as are the Moshtikes, and no other creature from outside these lands would dare to challenge him knowing he could conjure up a huge army from them at the drop of a gnat's wing.'

Victor's face fell into his hands and he let out an enormous sigh. 'So we're doomed, yes?'

'No, you idiot! We're not doomed at all! The dwarves have been digging tunnels from their land to here for the last six months. The cave they held you in was their final excavation.'

Victor looked blank – again!

'Excavation – it means to dig. This was the final part of the tunnel – digging from their land to ours.'

Victor still looked blank.

'Now what?' said Fred, impatiently.

'How come you know so many long words now, Fred?'

Fred sighed and looked at the ground. How could he explain what he'd been through in the last few months since his rescue? He'd learnt so much from the dwarves about mining, tunnelling and the natural wonders underground, and it was true that his vocabulary had grown with this knowledge.

But emotionally he was a wreck. Leaving Bessie behind was the single worst thing he'd ever done in his short life. Pod had explained to Fred afterwards that they had tried to rescue her, but she was still under the influence of the potion. Poor Bessie. What choice did they have, but to leave her when she called for the works supervisor? She had no idea who Fred was or that he was there to help her. 'Poor Bessie!' he said out loud. Victor stared, but said nothing.

Rescuing Fred, Pod had said, was relatively easy. By night the dwarves had taken up watch outside the metal works. They watched through the roof windows as he sweated and slogged away on the factory line, biding their time until the signs that he needed a top up were apparent. They struck just as the Grublin supervisor left the room. A large piece of tape across Fred's mouth, a dusty sack over his head and they were out of the top window with him.

Once back at the dwarve's abode, they began mentioning names and events given to them by his father and slowly, very slowly, Fred began to remember things.

'Fred, Fred! You haven't answered me,' said Victor unable to keep quiet any longer.

'Long words come from knowledge. And knowledge came from these dwarves – my rescuers.'

'And what about Bessie ...'

A clumping noise above their heads gave Fred a welcome chance to change the subject quickly. 'Something's coming. We'd better get out of here.'

'But ...' whined Victor.

'Now!' And with that Fred pushed him towards the wooden door they'd originally come through. Pod and the other dwarves followed quickly.

'But what about the ...' screamed Victor as they fell back into the cave. But before his sentence was finished, the wooden door had disappeared and was replaced with a large clod of earth which fitted the space perfectly. Bod lowered his arms and wiped his hands of specticide, a finely ground powder made from a variety of minerals and gems, and enchanted with an ancient dwarf spell.

'What?' cried Victor in surprise.

'Dwarf magic, spritey, dwarf magic,' whispered Bod in the shocked sprite's ear.

'Wow!' he shouted. 'That's some magic.'

'Ssshhh!' whispered Fred. 'They may still hear us.'

'What now Fred?' asked Bod.

'We should return to the home caves and plan our next move. My father will be waiting for us – and he's longing to meet you, Victor!'

# Chapter Nine

'Berriess, berries, berriess! If I eatt another berryy I'll go madd,' moaned Gilbert pushing yet another elderberry past his disgruntled lips. He winced as the pain in his left arm raced down to his fingertips. Although tightly strapped against his chest, the injury he had suffered at the red house had rendered him virtually flightless. He managed a little stationary flutter though, through gritted teeth.

Myrtle plucked another berry from the bush they were hiding in. 'It'ss not likee we have muchh of a choicee, is itt?'

'He'ss got a pointt thoughh,' said Aggie. 'A couplee of dayss ago we mightt have beenn stuck in a jar, but at leastt there wass a greaterr variety off food – breadd, mouldy breadd, stale breadd …'

'I don'tt believe youu!' cried Myrtle. 'After alll that effortt to get you outt!'

They had spent the past two days dodging the sunlight in sheltered trees and sheds. Sunlight meant burnt, shrivelled wings. Sunlight, therefore, was to be avoided at all costs.

Food came in the form of berries – and not knowing much about human fruits, elderberries – which looked similar to something back home – were the only ones they had dared to try.

'Ughh!' Gilbert spat a bitter berry into his good hand. 'We mustt be able to leave thiss blasted bush now. There hasn'tt been an eveningg patrol this wayy in hours.'

'They couldd be waitingg round the bushh,' Myrtle said peering through the leaves. 'You knoww he won'tt give upp that easilyy. He'll sendd them throughh every hour until theyy find you.'

'Who willl?' said Aggie, holding her nose and pushing another berry home.

'That fairyy – the one Gilbertt toldd us aboutt, the one who hatess you.'

'Butt', said Aggie, the juice of the elderberry dripping down her chin, 'howw do you knoww he won'tt give up easilyy, hhmmm?'

Myrtle rubbed her head pensively. 'I thinkk I'm beginningg to rememberr bits fromm before.'

Aggie pulled a branch towards her and used one of its leaves to wipe her chin. 'Before whatt?' She let the branch spring back into position. Gilbert leapt back in surprise.

'Before Artyy Granger changedd everything,' he said.

'Oh, don'tt listenn to himm,' said Aggie. 'He's alll doomm and gloomm – mostly gloomm!'

A sudden noise outside the bush quietened all three down immediately. Each held their breath as the raucous sounds of the latest Grublin patrol passed by.

'Hee didd whatt?' laughed one.

'II toldd yerr – hee swappedd herr forr aa sett off shinyy panss!' cried another. More shouts and laughter followed.

Far from patrolling the area for stray Grublin-fairies these creatures, two of the original Grublins from Grublin City, had so obviously misunderstood their orders. The grey bottles containing the Grublin potion remained full and firmly attached to their belts as they continued their rounds. They had clearly not been 'topping up' Grublin-fairies as ordered – neither had they been looking for stray ones ...

Inside the bush, the three little escapees waited patiently for the danger to pass. As the last echoes of laughter disappeared, the three moved to the outer edges of the bush to look through the leaves, just catching the backs of the creatures as they flew awkwardly on to somewhere new.

'See, II toldd you he'dd send Grublinss, didn'tt I?' said Myrtle.

'Hmmm,' said Aggie absentmindedly. 'Soo you didd.'

'You'vee agreedd with mee – what's wrongg?' Myrtle fluttered onto the same branch as her sister and settled beside her. 'Telll me – whatt is itt?'

'Speechh – didd you noticee their speechh?' said Aggie, now sitting on the branch with one leg over the other and her right hand cupping her face. 'Itt sounded kindd of – differentt.'

'Whatt are you talking aboutt?' said Gilbert, shuffling along the branch and sitting down beside the other two. 'They soundedd just like uss – you're justt wasting time. Come onn, we should go!'

'She'ss right, Gilbertt.' Myrtle stared thoughtfully at the ghastly grey creature beside her. 'Listenn to me talkingg now.'

Gilbert looked at Myrtle then at Aggie. He shrugged his shoulders in an expression that meant – I don't know what you two are on about!

'Our accentt is changingg!' shouted Aggie. 'And we're startingg to rememberr thingss too.'

'But howw? We haven'tt done anythingg different.' Myrtle swung her legs to and fro, almost slipping backwards in the process. 'Welll apart fromm being stuckk in trees and bushess for two days.'

'You rememberr more thann us, don'tt you?' Aggie looked at Gilbert as she spoke. Her brow wrinkled as she tried desperately to remember what his name was – then it came to her. 'Don'tt you – Gilbertt?'

Gilbert sighed with relief as he answered, 'It's a bitt sketchy, but I do knoww some of the things thatt happened to uss before we were turnedd.'

'You meann turned fromm pilp collectorss to Grublin-fairiess. But thinkk about ourr time fromm then to noww. What's differentt?' Aggie leant forward as she spoke to show she was sincere and needed his help.

'Welll, each night we were sent outt into the human worldd to collect from the pilpp donors – or was that beforee?' He tapped his head then appeared to be counting days, weeks or months on his fingers. 'Actuallyy, I think that was bothh before andd after, so nothing differentt there.'

'Come on, Gilbertt. Think harderr!' Myrtle pinched his hand impatiently.

'Oww! Pinching me is not goingg to help, you knoww.' Gilbert rubbed his hand against his knee to lessen the pain. 'You're beingg just like those Grublinss. They usedd to pinch me if I didn'tt drink that juice ...'

'Whatt was that? Say itt again!' screamed Aggie, clapping her hands together.

'They wouldd pinch me if I didn'tt drink the juice from the grey bottless when they toldd me to ...'

'That's itt, my groanyy little friendd.' Aggie fluttered upwards, twirling around so much that Myrtle began to feel nauseous.

'Oooohh, stop itt, please. Sitt down and tell us whatt you meann.' Myrtle clutched her stomach and attempted to keep the thirty or so elderberries she'd eaten inside rather than regurgitating the whole lot all over her sister.

'It'ss the juice,' cried Aggie. 'We haven'tt been drinkingg it so the effectss are wearing offf

– although that wouldd probably be difficult to see with you – Gilbert!'

'Very funnyy!' said Gilbert, now rubbing his pinched hand against his third nostril.

'Saying thatt – your accentt has changedd a lott, so have yourr looks. You're stilll bug ugly, but thatt third nostrill is definitelyy getting smallerr.'

Gilbert completely ignored Aggie's remark and felt at the nostril with his fingers. 'Whatt do you thinkk, Myrtle?'

Myrtle leant over to look at Gilbert's face and promptly threw up – thankfully over the branch and not over Gilbert.

'It'ss not thatt bad, Bugface!' said Aggie, chuckling.

Myrtle threw her sister a dirty look and reached for a leaf to clean her face. As it touched her features, Myrtle felt around for a while, noticing that her own third nostril had also shrunk. 'What'ss happening to us thenn?'

'Ohh come onn, can'tt you seee?'

Gilbert, clearly bored by Aggie's attempt to string it out, reached over and wiped some vomit from Myrtle's hair.

'Ah yess, very touchingg. Anyway, I reckonn that to keep uss as Grublin-fairies theyy need to make sure we drinkk whateverr is in those greyy bottles.'

'Crikeyy – we'd alreadyy gathered thatt!' said Myrtle, pushing Gilbert's hand away. 'But whatt does it meann – to uss?'

'It meanss ...' Aggie stalled in mid-conversation. 'It meanss that there iss hope.'

'So what'ss next?' said Myrtle.

'Yeah, what'ss the plan?' said Gilbert.

This all sounded a little familiar to Aggie. She bit her lip in thought. 'You usedd to look to me forr ideas, didn'tt you?' she smiled confidently as she spoke. 'I wass your leaderr!'

The other two Grublin-fairies looked at each other for a brief moment and then burst into sneering laughter.

'Ohh, please. You – a leaderr. You didn'tt even remember your ownn name,' said Gilbert.

'That wass justt the juicee!' said Aggie indignantly. She stood up on the branch and brushed herself down. Her face was held high and her voice had just the tiniest trace of arrogance. 'No, II remember somethingg – something aboutt leading you two – andd others. Whyy else wouldd you lookk to me forr answers?'

'Because, stupidd, we are obviouslyy both youngerr thann you, I still feell sick andd he's gott a brokenn arm!' Myrtle continued, 'Althoughh I'm beginningg to thinkk that thiss here branchh could come upp with a betterr idea thann you!'

Aggie took a swipe, narrowly missing her sister's head by just a few centimetres – which also felt familiar.

'So, seeingg as we've establishedd that I'mm in charge,' she paused briefly to allow for any heckling, 'thenn I say we putt my plann into actionn.'

'Whichh is?' said Myrtle with growing impatience.

'Welll, to go andd find oujamaflipp and whatshernamee – of coursee!'

'You meann Fred and Bessie,' said Gilbert.

'Absolutelyy – so II do!' said Aggie. 'They cann join my gangg and helpp to fightt whoever itt is we have to fightt.'

'That'lll be Artyy,' said Gilbert. 'Did I say howw much he hates you?'

Aggie ignored him and got to the plan. 'Rightt, the patroll has justt passed so iff we flapp to the veryy top of thiss bush we couldd make a flyy for it.'

Gilbert and Myrtle glared at her in disbelief. 'Brokenn arm andd feeling sickk – did you hearr?' said Myrtle.

'Welll, we eitherr move, starve orr get caughtt – take yourr choice because I'mm going anywayy.'

'You'dd leave mee – againn?' said Myrtle not quite believing what she was hearing.

'Lookk, it's nothingg personal. I justt have thiss urge to do somethingg.'

'You have thee urge to interfere,' mumbled Gilbert.

'Butt I'm yourr sister andd besides, whatt would Ma andd ...' The sisters smiled and did something quite extraordinary, something they had only done once or twice before in their short lifetimes – they hugged!

'... andd Pa. Ma andd Pa, Bugface! We havee a Ma andd Pa to rescuee.'

Then they very quickly unhugged.

Gilbert looked at them both in astonishment. 'Ohh, my portalss. I've seen it all noww.'

'Oh, shutt up, misery gutts,' said Myrtle, clearly pleased with the security the sisterly hug had provided. For the first time since their escape, she felt a real emotional attachment to the stroppy creature grinning wildly at her.

'Whatt?' laughed Aggie. 'It was justt a hugg. Don't go gettingg any ideass about me likingg you!'

'Does thiss mean we're moving onn – at last,' said Gilbert sarcastically. 'Only there'ss still the matter of my brokenn arm.' To prove his point he squeezed the offending limb slightly then gasped to display the amount of pain he was experiencing.

'Come here, Wilbertt,' said Aggie, smirking.

'Gilbertt!'

'Just teasingg. Come here – Gilbertt. Let me havee a closerr look at thatt arm.'

'No, keep awayy.'

'Come onn. I've watchedd the healerss sort out loads of shoulderss like yourss before.' Aggie fluttered round to the back of where he sat and rested her hands gently on his injured limb.

Beckoning to Myrtle with her head, she pursed her lips together gesturing silence. 'Yess, I've seen thiss done manyy times.'

Myrtle, now fluttering in front of the patient, glared at her, raising her eyebrows ever so slightly.

'Whatt you have here, myy dear,' said Aggie, 'is a dessicatedd shoulder. And there'ss only one wayy to fix thatt.'

Gilbert looked worriedly at Myrtle as Aggie stopped massaging his shoulder. 'How's thatt then?'

The question hung limply in the cold night air as the answer fell sharply into place.

'Aaaaaaaarrrrrrrrggggghhhh!'

# Chapter Ten

Tucked away in a far corner of her mind was a tiny piece of memory fighting to escape. It wanted to scream and shout. It wanted to rant and rave. It tried to flicker, produce a scene, paint a picture, but Bessie was having none of it. She blinked it back before it even had chance to form. Wiping the sweat from her beaten brow, she resumed her position in the factory line and continued assembling the new style pilp detectors as they rolled by on the conveyor belt.

Making no eye contact with her fellow workers, Bessie attached the silver switch then tested it to ensure the all important light came on. Job done, she moved on to another. With her head down and eyes focused, this day was much the same as any other. Not that she'd noticed.

*Hoooooooot!*

The shrill blast of the factory siren signalled the end of the night shift.

# Chapter Eleven

'What do you mean they can't find her?' screamed Arty. 'The only creature I ask them to track and they can't find her?' He punched a cushion in frustration.

Trembling, the Grublin-fairy shuffled forward to offer her meagre reply. The snot-laden sleeve revealed the identity of the messenger clearly.

'Err, itt seemss soo, yourr Lordshipp.' Gertie Cruet bowed her head as she spoke. 'Theyy sayss shee iss nowheree too bee foundd. Thee patrol'ss beenn lookingg forr twoo dayss noww.'

'Well, some Grublin had better find her!' He slammed another punch into another unsuspecting cushion. 'Blast,' he said quietly to himself. 'Without the potion she'll start to remember. She'll start to remember me!'

He swung around and glared at Gertie the Grublin-fairy. Her appearance disgusted him. She was about four years younger than him – not that you'd have known! Disgusting, but at least the streaming cold seemed to have dried up. 'You will go and find her.'

Gertie's mouth dropped open. 'B-B-Butt I'mm justt aa messengerr, yourr regalnesss. II don'tt evenn knoww whatt shee lookss likee ...'

'Silence! You will know her – I assure you!'

'Butt yourr gloriousnesss ...'

'Enough – guards!' From the corridor outside, two palace guards rushed to see to their leader's needs. Arty led them over to the window where he whispered for some time, into their obedient ears. The conservation was brief, but animated. The guards responded with several nods and grunts before pulling away and returning to their previous positions outside the huge door.

'The guards will ensure you have everything you need including your juice. Don't forget to take it every six hours – I think you're due some very soon.'

'Butt wheree amm II goingg? II don'tt knoww anywheree, butt heree, yourr sirnesss.'

'The guards will take you to the portal – the one that leads to the other side ...'

'Arrgghh! Pleasee, I'mm beggingg youu – nott thee otherr sidee.' Gertie dropped to her knees and shuffled over to where Arty stood. He looked down with contempt as she tugged on his trousers. 'Folkss don'tt comee backk fromm theree ...'

'Don't be ridiculous, Cruet! Pilps are collected there every nightsgritch – by Grublin-fairies – of course they come back.' He pushed her away carelessly, but she wasn't ready to give in just yet. She got to her feet and stood directly in front of him and continued her defence. 'Evenn soo, yourr worshipfull ...'

'You are going, Cruet. If anyfairy can find her, you can.'

Forgetting her fears for just a moment, Gertie straightened up. His sudden belief in her – and the need for an urgent top up – opened up a tiny memory in her mind. A memory she had not experienced for some time. She felt confident again. 'Whatt mee? D'youu reallyy thinkk soo?'

'Mmmm, yes! You are just the creature for this job. In fact you are promoted to ... to ... prefect!'

Gertie smiled broadly. 'Prefectt, huhh?' She scratched at her perfectly rounded stomach then looked at Arty quizzically. 'What'ss thatt thenn?'

Arty ignored her completely and continued with his own train of thought. 'You need to find her quickly before she starts ... er, changing.' He mumbled the last part of the sentence, using his hand to cover his mouth.

Gertie's new found confidence wavered. 'Err, sorryy? Didd youu sayy changingg – changingg intoo whatt?'

But before Arty had a chance to answer, the door was thrown open. The news had reached Martha.

'I knew this would happen. I told you to send her to Mursham Marshes didn't I?' She pushed past the new prefect, knocking the loathsome creature to the floor in her hurry.

'I'll cleann thiss bitt off floorr whilee I'mm downn heree shalll II?' Gertie said, almost apologising for getting in the way. She spat on her hand and rubbed vigorously. 'Seemss too bee aa lott off snott onn thiss carpett!'

'Mursham Marshes was not an option, mother,' snapped Arty. 'The inventor refused to work for me unless I gave his sisters their freedom.'

Martha stared at him, as he continued.

'So I allowed them their freedom ... as Grublin-fairies!'

Martha sniffed haughtily. 'But now she's gone!'

Arty glared down at Gertie, the scorn written clearly across his face then answered his mother. 'I have it all under control!'

'How's that then?' Martha curled her lips as she spoke and waited for his answer.

Arty nodded towards Gertie.

'Oh please,' snorted the leader's mother. 'Look at her! She doesn't know what day it is! What good can she be?'

Arty leaned in towards his mother – not too close, she still stunk of humankind, but just close enough to whisper in her ear, 'She'll find her – I've told the guards to water her juice down.'

'What!' said Martha loudly before reducing her tone. 'Then she'll remember everything.'

'Exactly! She'll remember just how much she hated that Lichen brat.'

'Very good, dear, but you forget one thing. Grublin-fairies all look the same ...'

'Similar, mother. They are similar.'

'Yes, yes! So similar that we can hardly tell one from another.'

'Strands of hair tell them apart and clothing ...'

Martha cut in crossly, 'They all look the same to me!'

'Ah, but if Lichen has gone missing she won't have had her potion and therefore ...'

'... she'll be changing back into a pilp collector ... and with Cruet changing back too ...' Martha drummed her hands on the table under the window.

'... Cruet will remember all the old haunts and go looking for her,' said Arty.

Martha's hand swept across the table in fury. The small grey commemorative bottle that had stood there for so long was thrown high into the air, landing with a smack. Spitting on the sign which displayed Aggie Lichen's initial capture, Martha screamed, 'And this time, dear boy, she will be gone for good.'

The metal sign then also found itself thrown across to the other side of the room. Gertie ducked as it flew within millimetres of her right ear. She'd listened discretely to the conversation, so hard that she'd almost rubbed all fibres out of the carpet. She knew they were talking about her, but regular doses of Grublin potion had rendered her brain next to useless.

'Did you hear all that, huh?' said Martha. 'You are going to be our saviour, Cruet!'

'II thoughtt II wass goingg too bee aa prefectt!' said Gertie.

'Yes, dear,' said Arty, 'and a saviour. Now go and clean yourself up. Meet me by the fallen statue of that idiot hero.'

Gertie pulled herself up to full height and saluted. 'Yess, yourr sirnesss.' Then she marched out of the door and out of ear shot.

Martha brushed down her dress and flicked back her hair in an effort to compose herself. In the mirror she admired her reflection and feigned a smile. 'So what will you do with her after she finds that interfering menace?'

'Each day, the inventor gets closer to a permanent turning potion. With any luck, by the time Cruet returns it will be ready. And she can have first taste.'

'Remind me – the inventor – who is it?'

'Albert, mother,' said Arty, 'Albert Lichen – brother of my arch enemy!'

# Chapter Twelve

Far below the palace, close to the cellar which held the vast collection of Grublin potion, was a small make-shift laboratory. Just like the room next to it, the door had been replaced with long vertical metal bars. And, just like the room next to it, a solitary prisoner paced the length and breadth of the room with increasing anger.

'I can't do this any more! I'm going to drink the potion myself and see what he does then,' screamed the prisoner through the bars.

'Now, now, calm down. You will be no good to anyfairy if you become a Grublin-fairy again, now will you?' said the older prisoner next door.

'It's all right for you, Ferrett,' said the younger one. 'He isn't forcing you to work for him – forcing you to develop something that will rid both worlds of pilp collectors forever.'

'I can't see what choice you have, Albert,' said Ferrett addressing the younger prisoner, a teenage pilp collector. 'He does, after all, have your Ma and Pa under lock and key somewhere.'

Albert Lichen began pacing again. He glanced up at the small barred window where the last rays of the two suns danced upon the ledge. The small cell, barely the length of his own height and the width of his outstretched arms, closed in around him as the light faded. He dug around in an old wooden chest, pulling out a previously used candle and a tatty matchbox.

'Looking for candles? Pass one through, Albert,' said Ferrett, pressing his body up to the bars and stretching out his hand to the left to receive the candle from the cell next door. 'That miserable son of mine crushed the last one I had.'

Albert pulled out another candle from the chest and lit it from his own one. The flame flittered around as the draught from the window caught it. He cupped a dirty calloused hand around it and noticing the grime in his fingernails he sighed. Why didn't Arty just leave him as a Grublin-fairy? He wouldn't have had to think about things then. He wouldn't have had to worry about his sisters, his friends and most importantly, Ma and Pa. If Arty's mother had just kept her mouth shut …

'I should never have trusted her,' Albert said out loud.

'Oh no, not again. Albert. We've been through this so many times.' Ferrett took the candle as Albert absentmindedly held it through the bars. 'She misled you all. It's what she's like.'

'But …'

'No buts, Albert. You'll just have to stall for time a bit longer as we agreed. Keep making strange potions for them, just not the right one.' Ferrett settled the candle down on his desk and stared long and hard into its yellowy glow. 'As long as we have time, we have hope.'

Albert sat himself down on his bed then felt under the mattress for the shard of mirror he had stashed there. An unexpected prick to his finger told him he'd found it. He cursed quietly under his breath before pulling the shiny piece of glass out and in front of him. As he looked into the mirror he watched as the blood trickled down his hand, but then his eyes returned to the gaunt features that stared back at him. He looked so much older than his sixteen years. The face that was once full of life was thin and pale with dark shadows under the eyes. His black hair was lank and unkempt with a fringe so long that it fell over both nose and mouth. Albert bit hard on his lip. In a place like this it would be easy to cry – and wouldn't Arty just love that. No, he must be strong.

He stood up and tightened the belt of his trousers another notch. He remembered how pleased he'd been when Ma had bought the dark green trousers for his last birthday, now, as the only pair he had, he despised them.

'Albert – are you okay?' shouted Ferrett, startling Albert out of his thoughts.

'Yes, I'm just going to go over my notes,' Albert replied, clearing a space on his workbench. 'I need to make this next potion last a little longer. It must be believable.' He pulled the tatty blue jumper up around his neck to keep warm then thumbed through the untidy pile of papers.

'That's right, lad, just make it believable to buy us some time,' called Ferrett. 'As long as we have time, we have hope,' he added quietly.

# Chapter Thirteen

Gertie Cruet stood on the steps of the palace feeling somewhat bewildered. The heavy wooden doors were shut fast behind her and no amount of banging on them had made them re-open. She'd been waiting for the leader for well over half an hour. Of course, he'd never had any intention of meeting her – that was obvious. Yet there she'd sat by the fallen statue of Ivor the Zealous; champion pilp collector, waiting patiently. His days of glory had long gone, but the broken statue pieces served well as a place to sit while trying to get into the palace.

Gertie looked up at the building in disbelief. The carved silver pillars were in grave need of repair, but still looked quite magnificent from afar. The words 'Leader's Palace' now took the place of the school motto which had previously been emblazoned across the huge enamel wall. 'Pilpus Victorius' it had once proudly said, although Gertie would not have remembered that anyway. Her mind was so out of focus, so blank of memories – just like the other poor creatures that served the leader, but she retained enough to remember recent events including the mission she'd been sent on.

Why wouldn't they answer her shouts? How could they just leave her out here without any proper preparations?

Go and find that meddling Lichen girl he said. Go now! Gertie got up and kicked the door hard, immediately regretting it as her foot throbbed with pain. Why did *she* have to go? She didn't even know who this wretched Lichen girl was, did she?

She thumped the door again.

A guard appeared at a window above. 'Doo youu knoww whatt timee itt iss? Goo awayy!'

Yes, she did know what time it was – well, she knew it was getting dark and time for bed. And no, she wasn't going away. She hit the door again.

This time a very angry Arty thrust his head out of the window, pushing the guard to one side. 'I thought I told you to go and find that pilp collector, Cruet. Why are you still here?'

'It'ss gettingg aa bitt darkk, yourr highnesss. Can'tt II goo inn thee morningg?' Gertie wrung her hands in desperation.

'No! Knowing Lichen, she will think herself to be safe under darkness so this is the perfect time to search.' He forced a smile then added, 'As my prefect you are the only one I can trust to do the job, so go – and don't come back without her!' Slamming the window, he returned to his huge throne and rearranged the cushion before settling back down to his comics again.

Outside, a disgruntled Gertie picked up the small bag, which had been packed by the guards, and threw it over her shoulder. 'II supposee someonee hass too doo thee jobb,' she said, straightening her back up. 'Andd seeingg ass I'mm thee prefectt, II supposee itt hass too bee mee!' Saying that out loud made her feel much better and slightly more important.

But as she flew away from the palace and towards the edge of town where the portal was, Gertie slowly began to lose her nerve again. Darkness was forming all around her, strange noises came from the trees below and hundreds of night-time eyes seemed to follow her tracks. Over the centre of Pilpsville she flew, past the decaying enamel dwellings that were now homes to Grublins and sprites, and down by the twisted memorial that was once the fountain of eternal tooth. By the time she reached the roots of the sacred oak tree, the suns had almost set leaving her less than a minute to fly through before the portal into the other side shut down for the night. As a Grublin-fairy, her flying was poor and unco-ordinated which, on top of her fear of the other side, slowed her down enormously.

Gertie gave a final push, knowing the wrath of the leader was at stake here. 'Gott – too – movee – fasterr,' she puffed as she pushed herself to her Grublin-fairy limit.

As the roots of the tree passed her by, she sighed with relief, knowing she had actually made it.

She slumped to the side, catching her breath and took a swig of the grey bottled juice that was in her bag.

'Yukk! Thatt doesn'tt tastee nicee att alll.' She spat the offending liquid out on the floor. 'Somee creaturee hass messedd withh myy bagg!' she cried. Then realising it was the only drink she had, continued to sip a little more.

After a break lasting more than half an hour, Gertie pulled her bag, and herself, together and decided to head out of the portal corridor. The light at the end wasn't terribly bright though and her attack of nerves returned.

'II couldd waitt justt aa bitt – noo needd too rushh.' She sighed as she realised there was no turning back and knew that she would, at some point, have to fly out of the portal corridor into the world of men.

'Yess, plentyy off timee soo noo needd too hurryy,' she said, settling back down again. 'Perhapss aa littlee napp beforee II goo.'

But the decision to go or nap was soon taken out of her grey sweaty hands as a loud angry voice echoed down to where she sat.

'Oii, youu! Noo loiteringg inn thee corridorr. Gett upp andd gett outt!'

Gertie couldn't see the owner of the voice so could only imagine that a huge burly Grublin guard had been sent to make sure she completed her task.

Quickly, she got to her feet once more and threw her bag over her shoulder. 'I-I-I'mm upp, sirr andd I'mm offf.'

Forgetting her nerves for just a minute, she flew off towards the far end of the portal corridor. Her wings brushed the sides of the tree roots as she watched the opening grow nearer and nearer. She stopped for a moment. 'Justt catchingg myy breathh, sirr,' she shouted.

She looked out to the world beyond. 'Itt don'tt lookk soo badd,' she said. 'There'ss treess andd cloudss – andd we'vee gott themm backk inn Pilpsvillee.'

Then, on reaching the corridor's end, reality hit home with a bang.

'Ohh, myy portalss!' she cried, pathetically. Clutching the sides of the tree roots for support, Gertie looked out onto the human world. To a small creature who, as a Grublin-fairy, had never ventured into this world, it was a terrifying sight. Trees so tall they almost touched the sky, buildings as high as mountains and creatures of all shapes and sizes running around in the darkness.

Gertie shivered. She'd heard tales of furry creatures called squiggles who would chase their victims for hours then take them to their nests and feed them to their young. She shivered again then reached into her bag and pulled out the small grey bottle. 'Yukk!' she said as she sipped some more of its contents. She took a deep breath, then, after repacking the bottle, she flapped her wings together and bravely took to the skies – well, took to a tree.

Gertie Cruet wasn't quite ready to face the open sky just yet.

'Soo wheree doo II startt?' she said, glancing around from the safety of her branch, hands trembling and clinging to its torso. 'II meann, it'ss nott likee I'vee evenn beenn heree beforee!'

# Chapter Fourteen

'So this is the infamous Victor,' said a voice as Victor entered the darkened room. 'The same Victor who left Gilbert for dead.'

'I-I can explain that,' said Victor, looking around for the owner of the voice.

'The same Victor who betrayed his friends.'

'I-I can explain that too ...'

'I am very pleased to meet you, at last. I trust you have been well looked after in my absence.' Fred's father, Eric Trickle, stepped out from the shadows and walked across to face the anxious sprite.

'Huh?' said Victor, puzzled at this welcome.

'I am pleased to see you because *you* are going to help get us out of this sorry mess, aren't you?'

'Er – yes, sir. I will do all I can,' said Victor, looking around as the lights were turned up. He had spent the past two days locked in a cave cell, now he was in another cave, but this one was more homely. Pictures adorned the walls, chunky wooden chairs and tables were assembled, and a large stove stood in the centre with a pot boiling away on its hob.

Mr Trickle, a heavily built pilp collector, stared him straight in the face. He had waited for this meeting for many months, but hadn't quite been prepared for what he'd seen. In front of him was a very nervous sprite, a youngster, but a lifetime of experiences seemed to be etched on his face. He was beginning to see what his younger son had found so endearing about this creature.

Victor stayed silent, taking in Eric Trickle's rough looks; a bearded face, grubby skin, wide brown eyes topped off with a mane of dark hair which had the all important Trickle crown tuft.

'What are you staring at, spritey?' said Bod, poking Victor in the thigh.

'Leave him be!' said Eric, taking his eyes off Victor and beckoning to another dwarf who stood at the entrance of the room. Fid, as he was called, knew what was required and, grabbing a thick cloth, moved towards the stove to remove the boiled pot.

'You will join us for tea, Victor,' said Eric.

'I don't actually drink ...'

'It wasn't a question!' snapped Fred. 'We drink tea together to show our commitment to the cause – to show our commitment to each other. Can you do that?' Fred slumped heavily into a chair at the table and was quickly followed by his father. The air was tense as they waited for Victor's decision.

Fid silently tipped in several generous spoonfuls of smint tea into a large metal teapot then filled it with boiling water from the pot. Clay beakers were then placed in a circle around the pot, one for each creature present – plus two more. Bod, Jed and Pod took their seats while he finished stirring the mixture.

'*Will* you join us, Victor?' Fid asked, finally sitting himself down.

'Thank you – I don't know what to say. I feel so ashamed, Mr Trickle.' Victor bowed his head and glared at the floor. 'You've made me so welcome. I don't deserve it, I really don't.'

Eric Trickle bent his head towards the sprite and spoke softly, 'I'm not saying that I entirely forgive you, Victor. You left my son for dead. I cannot forget that, but I can understand the pressure you were under from your father.' He glanced over at Fred. 'There were times when I was a little like that with my own sons. You are now in a position to change all that. Now come, take tea and join us.'

Victor gingerly slid onto a chair next to Eric keeping his eyes down. He could hear Fred's deep breathing and felt his eyes bear down on him.

'Fill those beakers, Fid. Fill all of them and call for our missing members – that is, if you are with us, Victor.'

'Yes, of course,' mumbled Victor. He lifted his eyes to meet Fred's. 'I am so sorry,' he mouthed.

Fred's face showed little sign of forgiveness. And when he thought about it, he was a little pigged off with his father's reaction. Since the time of the betrayal, Eric Trickle had seemed consumed with rage, determined to avenge Gibert's near death experience. Yet, here he was now, being so welcoming and reasonable – to a sprite. Why wasn't he angry anymore? What had changed?

As Fred mulled the questions over in his head, the sound of Fid shouting brought him back to reality. The other two members were on their way. He slumped further back into his chair, resting his feet on the bar underneath the table. He knew who was coming.

Victor, beaker of tea in hand, looked towards the door in anticipation. Way down in the pit of his stomach he felt the same sickness he'd had when he'd watched Gilbert drop from that great height in Spercham Forest. Could it be that Gilbert was here? What would he say? He'd rehearsed his speech so many times in his head, but now, when it mattered, he could hardly remember a word.

As the footsteps grew nearer the table's occupants stood up to greet the new guests. Victor stood too. The beaker placed firmly on the table. His eyes now transfixed on the entrance.

And in they came – Stan and Alf Trollitt! The seven year old orphaned twins who had an amazing gift – they were changelings and could will themselves into any shape or body. The twins ran straight over to Eric and *almost* gave him a hug.

'Now boys, what have we been teaching you?'

'Sorry, Eric,' they said together. Then proceeded to give him a very exaggerated bear hug.

'Okay, okay. That will do,' said Eric as he peeled them off his body. 'It's supposed to be a light and gentle hug, remember?' He smiled gently at their efforts.

'Yes, Eric. We will try and remember next time, won't we, Stan?' said Alf.

Stan nodded, but his attention was more focused on the newcomer, Victor.

'Hello, Stan,' said the sprite, trying not to display his disappointment at them not being Gilbert.

'Hello, Victor,' said Alf, prodding Stan.

'Hello, Victor,' said Stan, returning the prod to Alf.

'I hope your family is well.'

Victor felt his face gush bright green with embarrassment. He'd forgotten how very polite the twins were.

'Would you like us to clean up your face?' said Alf. 'You look a little hot and bothered, if I might say.' The twins grabbed a cloth from the table and were poised for action.

Victor had also forgotten how fastidiously tidy they were too – about everything!

'No, no, no!' said Eric, shaking his head in dismay. 'Haven't you two learnt anything? Now, try again.'

Stan threw the cloth back on the table then stood again, with his brother, in front of Victor. 'Er, hem,' he coughed. 'How 'bout me and my brother rearrange your face, huh?'

Victor sunk down into his chair stunned by the quick change in attitude, his face still burning bright green.

Rapturous applause followed, but soon died down when Alf said, 'Actually, we'd much rather give you a good clean.'

'Oh, you've spoilt it again!' said Eric. 'Dear, dear, you may be changelings, but I don't think we'll ever change your characters.'

The whole gathering, except Victor and Fred, burst out laughing, thumping the table with their fists.

Victor looked horrified.

'Don't worry, Victor,' said Eric. 'It's nothing personal. We just needed to try out their training. I thought we were getting somewhere, but I think the best we can hope for is that they tidy someone to death!'

More laughter and fist thumping followed his last remark. Bod slid onto the floor holding his stomach. 'Stop it, stop it,' he squealed, tears of laughter rolling down his cheeks.

Victor, although still a little surprised at the twins, now understood what was going on. And while the laughter continued and the twins sat down, he realised how pleased he was to see them. He didn't dare show it though. Fred was still throwing dirty looks his way and he knew he had a lot to do before Fred would ever trust him again.

'So,' said Fred, pulling his eyes away from the sprite at last. 'What's the plan, father?'

Eric Trickle began to compose himself once more and straightened out his shirt which had risen slightly over his portly belly. 'Er, hem – er, plan, yes.' He took a large mouthful of tea then motioned to Fid. 'Fetch the book, please.'

As Fid rummaged in a small wooden chest, Victor smiled over at the twins who smiled politely back. 'How did you escape from the leader?' he asked.

'Don't call him that!' screamed Fred. 'He's no leader. He's a just a pilp collector like me. He's just Arty ...'

'Calm down, Fred. Let the twins explain,' said Eric as the book arrived at the table. He thumbed through to the right page, folded the corner over then closed the book to listen to the Trollits.

The twins took their beakers in both hands and gulped the tea down noisily, keeping Victor waiting a little longer.

'Well?' said Victor.

'Please be patient, Victor. We need to remember where we were when you last saw us,' said Alf.

'Ah, I've got it,' said Stan. 'It was when Gilbert jumped off that high perch to save his brother, wasn't it Alf?'

Victor cringed. He remembered that moment only too well. How he wished he'd never asked.

Fred glared again, but noticing how uncomfortable Victor seemed, Eric sent him off to find something.

'Carry on please, Stan,' he said, watching as his son left the room.

'We went back through the impenetrable barrier, took Gilbert to the healers, then we looked for Myrtle again ...'

Victor's thoughts ran amok when he heard her name. That was the whole point in them going to Spercham Forest, Spriteland – to find Myrtle.

'... then we went to the mind readers, saw Gertie Cruet, got kidnapped ...'

Victor's brain went into overdrive. He'd missed so much. He could have been part of it all. He could have helped his friends instead of betraying them as he did.

'... then we lost Albert, found Albert with Martha – Arty's evil mother, still no sign of Myrtle ...'

Victor's head felt heavy, beads of sweat formed upon his forehead. He'd heard enough, but still Stan went on.

'... went to the Moshtikes – who were in it with Martha all along, back to Pilpsville which Arty had taken over ...'

Victor felt his breathing get faster and more irregular as Stan drew closer to the end of the sorry tale.

'... Martha teamed up with Arty; Ferrett and Albert were thrown in prison and all members of the gang were given the Grublin-turning potion to drink …'

'A-A-And what about Myrtle?' puffed Victor, wiping his sweaty head on the back of his hand. He clung shakily to the table for support. 'Did you find her?'

Eric looked over at Victor with concern. 'You are clearly unwell, Victor. Stop boys, we'll continue later.'

'N-N-No,' shouted Victor. 'I-I-I must know – did you find her? D-D-Did you find Myrtle?' His head started to hang down now as he struggled to fight off the fever.

'Yes, but she had been turned before anyone could get to her. It was Myrtle who turned Aggie by giving her the Grublin potion.'

'W-W-Where were you two at the time? Couldn't you have stopped them?'

'Come on, we can finish this later,' said Eric, leaving his seat to sit next to Victor. He propped the sprite up, making him ready to move. 'You're burning up, Victor. Enough, Stan, enough!'

'P-P-Please, I must hear what happened.'

Eric nodded to Stan and he continued retelling the events. 'When Gertie Cruet kidnapped us she didn't know we were changelings so we pretended to drink the juice they gave us. When they weren't looking, we just changed into Grublin-fairies.'

Then Alf took up the story. 'We were put with Myrtle in a holding cell until Aggie was caught. But

Myrtle didn't really recognise us as the potion was quickly turning her.'

'We looked after her, right till the end,' sighed Stan.

'Y-Y-You mean – she's dead?' whispered Victor, barely able to contain his grief.

'No, you idiot, she's not dead! None of them are dead.' Fred re-entered the room at the critical point of the story. 'Although they may as well be seeing as they're Grublin-fairies!'

Victor could take no more. His head dropped forward onto his chest, his body was limp and sweaty, and if it wasn't for Eric propping him up, he would have ended up collapsed in a heap on the floor.

'Quick, Bod,' cried Eric. 'Take his legs. Something is very wrong with this sprite.'

Bod was already up when Eric called. 'Take him to my room. The fire is already made up in there.'

'I don't think he'll have need of that, Bod,' said Eric. 'Have you felt his head?'

Bod shook his head. He didn't have a spare hand to do that so he called to Fred. 'Come, feel the sprite's head. Tell me how hot he feels to you.'

Fred had not said a word since Victor collapsed, partly because he felt so guilty at being so unkind to the sprite and partly because he was still so angry. But Fred was mature enough to see that the little sprite was seriously ill and brushed his own feelings to one side.

'He's burning up, father. Isn't there anything we can do?'

Eric looked proudly at his son. It was one thing to be angry, but to put it aside in a time of trouble took great strength of character. Something he saw now in the boy before him.

'Fid,' said Eric, 'what do you think?' He moved slowly towards the door, carefully holding the upper body of the ailing sprite. Fred helped Bod with the legs.

'I'll look at the healing books,' said Fid, rushing to an old bookcase that stood in a corner. Here he grabbed several large volumes, hastily dropping them one by one to the floor. He sat himself down on the floor and began flicking through each book. 'There may be something in them.'

Through the dimly lit, narrow corridor they carried Victor until at last they reached Bod's room. It was more of a mini cave, with alcoves hacked out of the soil walls and tree roots growing through the ceiling. As they lowered Victor gently onto the bed, the little sprite groaned and mumbled. His sweating body now began to jerk and twitch with involuntary spasms.

Against a wall was a wooden stand on which was a china bowl. Bod filled it with cold water from a jug and using a towel, began mopping the invalid's head.

Victor's mumbling got louder as he tossed and turned, his body racked with pain.

'What's he saying, father? What's he mean?' said Fred.

'I think he's saying drink. Perhaps he wants a drink,' said Eric. 'Go fetch some of that tea we were drinking.'

Fred ran out of the room, his footsteps ringing loudly as each foot hit the solid earth in the corridor. It was only a matter of seconds before he reappeared in the room with a beaker of tea.

'Try sitting him up, Fred. See if he wants to take some of it.' Eric placed his hand under one shoulder as Fred took the other. On a count of three they lifted Victor up into a sitting position as Bod threw a couple of comfy cushions behind his back.

'Here, Victor, here's a drink,' said Fred, pushing the beaker of tea close to the sprite's lips.

Victor's mouth opened slightly, just enough to allow a little trickle of liquid to flow in. Almost at once he started coughing, spitting the tea right back out again. He threw his arms around wildly before settling back down to the jerks and twitches he'd had before.

'It's no good. Lay him back down, Fred.' Eric sighed as the sprite started mumbling again. 'I'll go and see what Fid has found out,' he said, heading for the door. 'Perhaps he's ...'

But Eric found his sentence cut short as the dwarf himself burst into the room, a large book tucked tightly under his arm.

'It's poison!' he screamed. 'He's been poisoned!'

# Chapter Fifteen

Aggie Lichen looked out from behind the leaves of the elderberry bush. The same elderberry bush they'd been in for two days and nights.

'Iss it stilll there?' whispered Myrtle, pushing her sister to one side as she took a turn to spy on the bewildered creature, a creature who had been walking up and down the window ledge of a house opposite for the past hour.

'What'ss it doingg?' asked Gilbert. 'I'dd look myselff, if the pain in my shoulderr wasn't so bad.' He rubbed his shoulder and stared into the back of the older of the Lichen sisters.

'Lookk, I triedd my bestt,' said Aggie, turning around briefly to address him. 'It'ss not myy fault you've gott a funny shoulderr now is itt?'

'Yeahh, but it's worse thann before. Now I'll neverr be ablee to leave thiss blastedd bush.'

'Oh, shutt up moaning, willl you?' said Aggie. 'We've gott more than yourr arm to worryy about.' She let the leaves fall back into place and walked back along the branch to where Gilbert sat. The elderberry bush provided perfect cover with its mass of green leaves on the outside, a network of thick branches within and a generous supply of juicy elderberries. As protection from Grublin patrols it had been ideal, but now the novelty was wearing off.

As she slumped down onto a branch, Aggie held her head in her hands and sighed. A deep frown appeared on her brow and she sighed again.

Gilbert picked at the bark on his branch with his good hand. 'Do youu think it's waitingg for us?' he asked. 'Do you thinkk it knows we're heree?'

'Howw can I thinkk about anythingg with you whitteringg on all the timee, Gilbertt Trickle?' she spat.

Normally, Gilbert would have reacted to this with a dramatic sulk or a response such as 'I was only asking, no need to shout!', but on this occasion he sat stunned for 30 seconds then screamed, 'I'm Gilbertt Trickle. Trickle'ss my last name. You rememberedd!'

'Sssshhh,' whispered Aggie, gesturing silence with her finger to her lips, then she added quietly, 'Yess, you're Gilbertt Trickle, you are!'

As Gilbert returned to his bark picking, a tiny smile fought to appear on his normally gloomy face as he thought about his name. Being such a miserable creaturc his facial expressions were usually limited to sulk, sad, fed-up and bored. Smile certainly had its work cut out if it wanted to be part of this elite group, but it was giving its best. Every now and then, it appeared briefly at the corners of Gilbert's mouth, but there was a long way to go before it could be called successful.

Aggie watched him for a while then returned to her thoughts. There was something at the back of her brain, something desperate to get out. She sighed for a third time. This time it was Myrtle's turn to ask the questions.

'Whatt are you thinkingg?' asked Myrtle, climbing down from the leaf spy hole to sit next to her sibling.

'Nott so muchh thinking, more rememberingg,' said Aggie, still deep in remembering. 'Thatt creaturee, well, it lookss kind of familiar.'

'It lookss Grubliny, simplee as thatt!' said Gilbert, returning to his normal morose self.

'Perhaps it'ss a pilp collectorr like us andd not takingg the potion eitherr,' said Myrtle, ignoring the grumpy Grublin-fairy now sat opposite them. 'That couldd explain whyy it'ss walking upp and downn on a windoww ledge inn the middle of the nightt.'

'Hmmm, noww who didd we knoww with a frizzyy brownn mop of hairr like thatt, not thatt there's a lott of it leftt!' Aggie's brow furrowed deeper as she tried to break through the memory barrier that was still in place in her mind.

'Let mee see,' said Gilbert. 'My memory'ss better than yours!' He pushed himself up slowly from the branch and, by holding onto branches with his good hand, moved towards the leaves that had become their spy hole. Myrtle jumped up and pulled the leaves back for him to see.

'Welll! Any idea?' said Aggie, deciding to remain seated.

'Hmmm! I thinkk I might know who it is. Definitelyy an ex-pilp collector. It's er – er, that one who wass at your school. Er, er, Bertie Blewittt!' said Gilbert, feeling very pleased with himself and acting accordingly.

Aggie stood up, climbed over the branches and pulled the leaves back further. 'Lookk, you idiot! It'ss a girl nott a boy. How cann a girl bee called Bertie, for cryingg out loudd.'

Myrtle rubbed her head in thought. 'No,' she mumbled to herself, 'it'ss not Bertie Blewittt – it's, it'ss, it's ...' She started tapping her head with her fingers, getting progressively faster as she came to the answer, 'It'ss Gertie, Gertie Cruett!'

Gilbert and Aggie quickly let the leaves fall back into place. No one said a word. They just stared at each other in silence. Seconds passed and still no movement. Then suddenly Aggie started jumping up and down.

'I knoww her, I knoww her! She'ss one of myy best friendss,' she cried.

'Are youu sure? Onlyy I'm gettingg some differentt kind of memoriess coming throughh,' said Myrtle.

'Oh, trustt you to putt a downerr on everythingg, Bugface!'

'Fine! I justt wanted youu to be suree.'

Aggie looked through the leaves once more, this time with an excitement she could hardly contain.

'She playedd a big partt in myy life as a pilpp collector. I cann feel it.' She squeezed her hands together as she spoke. 'Gertie Cruett is definitelyy one off my closestt friends.' Then she tiptoed out between the leaves.

'Whatt are you doing?' said Gilbert.

'I'mm going too surprise herr,' said Aggie, excitedly.

'Whatt if she'ss not who you thinkk she is?' said Myrtle. 'It mightt be a trapp.'

'You're justt jealouss because I'vee found myy friend,' said Aggie, now completely outside the bush, hovering to keep her position.

'Butt ...' Myrtle's cautionary sentence was left unfinished as Aggie flew off towards the window ledge where her friend Gertie was.

She perched in the tree that was closest to the window ledge and waited as the creature walked up and down one more time. Then she jumped out in front of her and shouted, 'Surprisee!'

Across the way, Gilbert and Myrtle pulled back behind the leaves in fear. Had Aggie completely forgotten the danger she could be putting them all in? It certainly seemed so – and for what? They couldn't really even be sure as to who this Gertie Cruet was, least not until the potion effects had completely worn off.

Back on the ledge, Gertie Cruet's walking had come to a sudden halt by some mad creature leaping out in front of her.

'It'ss me, Gertie, Aggie! Don'tt you rememberr me?'

Gertie just stared, partly because she'd just been frightened half to death and partly because she was still at odds with her memories – memories that were starting to trickle back into her tiny Grublin-fairy brain.

Then a great fear began to take over. She broke into a sweat and, feeling the strange creature was some kind of threat, Gertie began to back away.

'Pleasee, don'tt hurtt mee. II justt beenn sentt heree byy thee leaderr. II doesn'tt evenn likee itt heree. Inn factt II wass justt goingg too goo ...'

'Stopp!' cried Aggie, grabbing the terrified Grublin-fairy just as she was about to slip off the end of the ledge.

'I'mm your friendd, Gertie,' she said pulling her to safety. 'You don'tt have to bee frightenedd of me.'

Back over in the elderberry bush, Gilbert and Myrtle were watching intently. Things didn't seem to be going too well from where they sat.

'Whyy would she try to pushh the creature overr the edge?' said Gilbert. 'I thought itt was her friend.'

'She wasn'tt pushing herr, she wass saving herr from slippingg off the endd,' said Myrtle huffily.

'Grublin-fairies don'tt flapstop as welll as pilp collectorss, you knoww that.'

'Yess,' said Gilbert, raising his eyebrows. 'But I know what your sister'ss like too!'

On the ledge, Gertie had managed to calm herself down a little – well, enough to start asking some questions of her life saver.

'You'ree nott Grublinn, aree youu?' said Gertie, eyeing the creature in front of her up and down. 'I-I-I meann, bitss off youu iss Grublinn, butt bitss off youu iss definitelyy nott Grublinn.' She paused then looked straight into Aggie's eyes. 'Whatt aree youu?'

'I is – I meann, I amm a Grublinn-fairy, butt I usedd to be a pilpp collector. Some off me is still Grublinn – like thiss third nostril, but mostly I amm pilp collectorr.'

'Howw comess youu aree bitss off eachh?' said Gertie, clearly intrigued by Aggie's strange features.

'Welll, I onlyy rememberr bits. I knoww I wass a pilp collectorr. I wass given a potionn and thatt started too turnn me into a Grublin-fairyy.'

'Ohh, reallyy?' said Gertie, reaching in to her bag and rummaging about. She pulled out a grey bottle and after undoing the cap, offered Aggie a drink.

'Noo!' cried Aggie, knocking the bottle clean out of Gertie's hands. 'That's itt! That's the potionn!'

'Whatt didd youu doo thatt forr? II wass toldd too bee suree too drinkk myy juicee andd noww II havee nonee leftt.'

'Butt Gertie, that'ss the stufff that turns uss into Grublin-fairiess,' said Aggie, bracing herself for the next announcement. 'Youu are nott a real Grublinn. Youu are a Grublinn-fairyy, Gertie, justt like uss.' She waved over to Myrtle and Gilbert, instantly revealing their hiding place. 'Lookk, other Grublin-fairiess are overr there. You cann come witth us.'

'Ohh, noo! I'mm onn aa speciall missionn.' Gertie took a short pause before continuing. 'I'vee comee heree too findd aa certainn pilpp collectorr. I'mm thee leader'ss prefectt, youu seee!' she said proudly.

Aggie took a step back as both statements sunk in. 'You aree close too the leaderr?' she said, immediately beginning to regret her hasty move to rekindle their friendship.

'Ohh, yess. II doess alll sortss forr himm. Hee sentt mee speciallyy too findd thiss onee.'

Aggie swallowed hard before asking the next and most obvious question. 'Andd just who mightt this pilpp collector be thenn?'

'Welll,' she said, puffing up her chest as she relayed her orders. 'Thee leaderr saidd nott too comee backk unlesss I'dd foundd 'thatt meddlingg Lichenn creaturee', soo that'ss whyy I'mm heree.'

Aggie's face dropped, her eyes scanned the ground quickly as she tried not to give herself away..

'Doo youu knoww herr?' Gertie asked.

Aggie gulped loudly. She struggled to keep her poise and thought desperately about what to do next.

'Aree youu alll rightt?' said Gertie. 'Youu lookss aa littlee palee.' She bent down so that her face was in line with Aggie's.

'Er, it's justt getting a bitt late andd I reallly should be gettingg along. Gott to collectt pilps forr the leaderr, you knoww.'

'Perhapss II couldd comee withh youu, afterr alll. It'ss aa bitt scaryy outt heree onn myy ownn andd I'mm beginningg too feell aa littlee strangee.' It was clear that the lack of top up potion was starting to have an effect on Gertie.

I can'tt take herr with me now, thought Aggie. She'll jeopardise everythingg.

'Ohh, err. II don'tt feell veryy welll att alll,' said Gertie, holding her head.

Aggie looked over at the elderberry bush where Gilbert and Myrtle were waiting. She could just see the top of Myrtle's head, instantly given away by her mop of red hair.

But she couldn't just leave Gertie here, could she? She was, after all, her good friend – well, underneath the Grublin-fairy exterior, she was. And if she was left alone, a Grublin could come along and top her up with potion. 'And iff Gertie stayed with uss,' muttered Aggie, under her breath. 'She wouldn'tt be looking for 'that meddlingg Lichen girll' and eventuallyy she wouldd turn backk to a pilp collectorr.' She walked along, still mumbling to herself. 'And, thenn she'd recognise mee and we'd hugg and everythingg wouldd be fine.' Decision made!

'I'mm sorryy, weree youu talkingg too mee?' said Gertie, wiping her hand across her mouth. 'Onlyy II couldn'tt hearr youu onn accountt off myy beingg sickk.' She pointed to a small puddle of vomit that was crawling stealthily towards the end of the window ledge.

'I wass just saying thatt you can come andd join us – just untill you feel betterr.'

'Ohh, thankk youu, Mistresss Aggiee.' Gertie bowed low as she spoke.

'Err, no needd for the mistresss bit, justt Aggie willl do. Noww flap your wingss quickly andd hold onto my handd.'

Seeing Gilbert's head pop sharply out of the elderberry bush, she signalled that she was on her way back. Then, seizing Gertie's hand, Aggie jumped off the ledge and soared across to their safe house.

Seeing them approaching, Gilbert held back the leaves of the spy hole to allow them in. Myrtle was standing just inside the bush, her arms tightly hugging an upturned branch.

'This iss Gertie,' said Aggie, as they landed and walked through to the inside of the bush.

The Grublin-fairy managed a little smile. 'II amm pleasedd too meett youu.' As Gertie swept down low into a deep curtsey, Aggie mouthed to both Gilbert and Myrtle, 'I needd to talkk to you.'

'What?' said Gilbert, letting the leaves fall back into place. 'Speakk up, will youu?'

Gertie suddenly stood up completely unaware of what had just happened. 'II saidd II amm pleasedd too meett youu.' And down she went again into a full curtsey.

Aggie took this unexpected opportunity to repeat herself. 'We needd to talkk – quickly,' she mouthed once more.

Myrtle shrugged her shoulders indicating to her sister that she had no idea what she was saying. Gilbert just looked puzzled.

Aggie had no more time to explain so now she just spat it out. 'Cann I have a quickk word withh you two – privatelyy?'

Gertie looked a little put out at this and this made Myrtle feel somewhat uncomfortable.

'Justt wait a minutee, Aggie. We haven'tt introduced ourselvess properly yett, have we?'

Aggie jumped up and down wildly, throwing her arms around shouting, 'No, no, no, we cann do thatt later. Come onn, let's have thatt talkk first.'

'Ignore herr, she's always like thiss,' said Gilbert.

'You don'tt understandd. I mustt talkk to you ...' screamed Aggie.

But Myrtle continued regardless. 'Well, that'ss Gilbert ... and I'mm Myrtle, Myrtle Lichenn, Aggie's sisterr ...'

# Chapter Sixteen

'Albert, are you awake?' whispered Ferrett. 'It's time.'

Albert Lichen swung his legs over his bed and sat up. He had, in fact, been awake for hours. His brain had been churning all night.

'Albert?' whispered Ferrett again. 'Did you hear me? It is time.'

'I'm ready, Ferrett.' Albert stood up, straightened himself out then gently splashed cold water over his face. Grabbing the remaining shreds of a towel, he mopped the surplus water off and ran his hands through his hair, the crown tuft, as always, standing to attention. He took one last look in the shard of mirror that lay on the crowded workbench, snatched the bulging bag that occupied central position and moved towards the door that held him in his metal cage.

'Have you got enough powder?' called Ferrett quietly, his head pushed up close to the bars of the cell next door.

'Yeah, plenty, but you'd better get to the back of your cell, just in case the explosion hits you.'

'You are sure that this will work, aren't you, dear boy.'

'Almost – I mean, I think so,' said Albert, pulling at his chin. 'From all the experiments I've done it's definitely been noiseless, but they were much smaller quantities.' He pulled a little black leather pouch from his pocket and shook it. Something rattled inside. Undoing the cord that kept it fastened, he reached inside and took out a small piece of scrigger which had been roughly beaten into the shape of a funnel.

'Sorry about the lack of scrigger,' said Ferrett. 'Pilp donors seem to look after their teeth better nowadays.' He was referring to the silver material used to fill human teeth.

'It's plenty,' said Albert, pushing the tiny tip of the funnel into the lock on the bars. 'I just hope the guard you got it from will keep quiet.'

Albert sprinkled some black firepowder from the pouch into the funnel and watched as it flowed down into the key hole. He took a piece of string from his bag and after returning the pouch and funnel to his pocket, pushed one end tightly into the lock.

'Move to the back wall, Ferrett. I'm going to light the fuse.'

In the next cell, Albert's long term companion backed away from the door and crouched down in a corner at the back, covering his ears just in case.

Tentatively, Albert lit the fuse then rushed away cupping his hands over his ears. He knew it shouldn't make a noise, but his natural instincts told him different.

He watched intently as the fuse slowly burnt its way down; grey ash fell to the floor as the flame crept further along towards its goal. The pungent smell filled his nostrils, filtering down into his throat ...

*Psssttt!*

'Was that it?' called Ferrett, lifting his head slightly, but retaining his crouched position.

'I think so. Let me just check,' Albert replied. He crawled slowly over to the door, pulling gently on the bars. The door fell open silently. He listened for any sounds from the guards, but there was nothing. He had timed it well and congratulated himself on it. Nothing came between the guards and their 2 am snack ... or their 3am snack. They would be busy for at least 20 minutes – just enough time to escape.

For the first time in six months, Albert stepped outside his cell and for the first time in as many months, he looked upon the face of his companion, Ferrett.

'You okay?' he asked, trying not to show his anguish at Ferrett's scrawny form.

Ferrett heaved himself up from the back of the cell and strode across to the cell door, placing his hands over Albert's. 'I feel a whole lot better for seeing you, dear boy. Now, let's get this door open too and get the hell out of here!' He returned quickly to the back of his cell, leaving Albert to fill the lock with the firepowder.

With the fuse lit, Albert stepped back inside his cell and waited for the 'psssttt' to happen. He glanced at his watch, recording the remaining safe time in his head – 15 minutes, then the guards would return.

'What's happening?' called Ferrett. 'Has it gone off yet?'

Albert stepped back to the cell, pushing hard against the door, but it wouldn't move. 'I'll try again,' he said worriedly, refilling the lock, but in his hurry spilling some on the floor. 'Don't worry, it'll blow this time.' He lit the fuse and stepped away once more, covering his ears just in case.

After waiting far longer than needed, Albert moved slowly towards the cell next door. Ferrett was already on his feet waiting. 'It didn't work, did it?'

Albert leant against the bars, his eyes to the floor as he tried to avoid Ferrett's gaze. 'It just won't budge,' said Ferrett, pushing against the lock.

'We'll try another time,' said Albert, checking his watch. 'There'll be other chances.'

'No, there won't!' said Ferrett pulling Albert's face towards him. 'You must go. Get out and get help.'

'But what about you?' asked Albert. 'I can't just leave you here. We're in this together. We had it all planned ...'

'Albert, you must go. There's just 10 minutes before the guards arrive back,' said Ferrett. 'Make up a bundle and put it in your bed. I'll say you are unwell. That'll keep them away for a while and give you enough time to escape.'

'But they'll take it out on you,' pleaded Albert, desperately. '*Arty* will take it out on you. You know what he's like ...'

'I'm his father – he'll not dare kill me. Now go, quick, before they return.'

As Ferrett suggested, Albert stuffed some things under the bedclothes, prodding them into a shape that just might fool the guards then returned sadly to his companion's cell. 'I will be back for you. I promise.'

They hugged through the bars, neither of them able to look directly at each other.

'Go,' said Ferrett. 'Find Aggie and Fred. They're probably your best chance of turning all this around.'

Albert nodded reluctantly and made for the door.

# Chapter Seventeen

Gertie stared directly into her rescuer's eyes, her eyebrows knotted and puzzled. 'Youu iss thatt meddlingg Lichenn creaturee', yeahh?'

Aggie swung her leg backwards and forwards, trying to think of something clever, something that would put the leader's bloodhound off, but it was Gilbert who spoke before she could even begin to pull a sentence together.

'Whatt if she iss?' he said, somewhat protectively. 'She rescuedd you and brought you here to uss. That meanss you owe her.'

'Butt thee leaderr saidd ...' began Gertie.

'Forgett the leaderr, Gertie,' said Myrtle, now realising what a mess she'd dropped them all in. 'He's a controll freak. He wantss to hurt Aggie.'

'Butt thee leaderr insistedd ...' Gertie went on to give a word for word account of all the things Arty had told her to do and say if she found 'that meddling Lichen creature', pausing for breath only when completely necessary.

Aggie, now still and leaning back against a thick branch, said nothing. She glared hard at the Grublin-fairy, looking deep into her eyes. Behind them lay something dark, something callous which she could now sense. What was it about this creature? If only she could remember.

'Okayy, we give in,' said Gilbert, sensing that this Grublin-fairy was actually never going to give up the chase. He winked slyly at Myrtle, hoping Gertie wouldn't notice. 'We'lll help you take Aggie backk to Arty, I meann the leader.'

Myrtle raised her eyebrows, pulled a face then, after finally getting his message, said, 'Yess, I think you're quite rightt to be obeyingg orderss.'

Aggie pulled her sister sharply to one side. 'Whatt the helll are you doingg? No wayy are you deliveringg me into thee hands of thatt madman.'

'Just playy along with uss,' said Myrtle, prising her sister's hand from her arm. 'Gilbert'ss obviously gott a plann sorted. Besidess, we needd a way to gett back throughh the portall.'

'I wass planning onn going throughh later, whenn the coastt was clearr!' said Aggie, crossly.

'Butt they're alll looking forr us. Rememberr, we've beenn missing forr days.'

Aggie crossed her arms sulkily. 'Okayy, but if thingss get hairy, don'tt expect me to stickk around!'

'I was justt saying,' said Gilbert, as Aggie and Myrtle moved back towards him and Gertie. 'I was just sayingg how we could stop offf for a rest at the old juice bar. I'm sure Aggie willl be able to concoct a refreshingg drink just for you, seeingg as she used to workk there.'

'Didd I?' Aggie whispered to Myrtle, cupping her hand over her mouth.

'Yess,' confirmed Myrtle, 'and you'll needd to remember a feww of your more exoticc recipes if we're goingg to slow her downn!'

More exoticc? Whateverr did she meann? thought Aggie.

Gertie looked around at the three Grublin-fairies, pursing her lips this way and that, then sighing and puffing as she made her decision. 'Welll,' she said, 'thee leaderr didn'tt sayy *whenn* too bringg herr backk soo II thinkk aa littlee stopp offf willl bee okayy. Noww, shalll wee goo?'

'Not justt yet, Gertiee,' said Aggie. 'I justt need too make suree thatt there aren'tt too many Grublinss aboutt. I meann, you don'tt want themm stealing your gloryy, do youu?'

'Ohh noo! Ass thee leader'ss speciall prefectt, II needd too bee thee onee ...'

Aggie left Myrtle and Gilbert to listen to Gertie rambling on again, and creeping outside of the bush, she looked around for any Grublin guards that may have been on patrol.

From what she could remember, they were not too far from the portal exit that would take them back to their own world. Brief glimpses of past nightgritches, when she collected pilps with her sister, slipped into her mind as she flitted quietly from tree to tree. Memories of her friends were more difficult to define though, and as she moved on she wondered if she would ever remember who Frank and Betsy were!

After five minutes or so, she spotted the opening to the long tunnel where the exit lay. It was busy with Grublin guards and Grublin-fairies who were returning back home after collecting pilps.

Aggie pulled back quickly inside a tree as a patrol flew past, barely a breath away, her heart pounding like a hammer. It brought home just how difficult getting through the tunnel would be. She could just make a fly for it, leave her sister and Gilbert behind to face the consequences, but things felt different now. With every minute she was changing, not only physically, but mentally and although the memories weren't terribly quick in coming back, in her mind she felt more pilp collector than Grublin. And hearing a familiar tinkling noise outside proved that her natural tooth fairy instincts were returning. 'Spritess!' she said aloud. 'There were spritess!'

Daring to put her head outside took a lot more courage than she thought. 'Spritess – green, loudd, shrieky,' she said to herself, crawling towards the end of the branch with the most leaves on it. And there, just below where she was kneeling, were a whole bunch of the bothersome creatures. As a Grublin-fairy, she hadn't taken that much notice of them – the potion saw to that, but now she sensed how loathsome they were and how arrogant they'd become.

'Move outta way,' shouted one as his group flew into the tunnel.

'Andd they've learntt our languagee,' muttered Aggie, returning to the safety of the central trunk. 'II must gett back.'

She flew swiftly, avoiding the main path that led to the tunnel, landing carefully back at the elderberry bush where her companions sat waiting.

'Welll,' said Gertie, as she arrived, 'iss itt clearr too goo?'

'Unfortunatelyy, no. There's a lott of traffic headingg towards the tunnell, sprites too – whenn did thatt happen?'

'D'youu meanss themm greenn creaturess withh thee badd mannerss?' asked Gertie.

'Well, yeahh,' said Aggie, checking that Myrtle was all right.

'Thee leaderr putt themm inn chargee off thee pilpp plantt. Theyy getts paidd inn magicc dustt, soo II heardd. Andd becausee off hiss cleverr thinkingg, theyy don'tt attackk uss noo moree,' said Gertie.

'Theyy don't attackk us *anymore,*' mumbled Myrtle under her breath. 'Evenn I know thatt.'

Aggie turned to Gilbert. 'Butt the spritess – they were ourr enemies, weren'tt they?' she said, keeping her voice deliberately low.

Gilbert said nothing, sensing Gertie's eyes upon him. Was she rememberingg things too? He wondered.

'So, we waitt?' Myrtle asked Gertie, breaking her stare and forcing her to respond.

'II supposee wee couldd waitt justt aa littlee longerr. Justt till thee crowdss havee gonee. II don'tt expectt thee leaderr willl bee waitingg upp ... didd II telll youu howw hee selectedd mee too goo onn thiss missionn ...'

Leaving Myrtle to listen and nod in all the right places, Aggie beckoned Gilbert over to some branches away from Gertie's prying ears. He flinched as she helped him to sit down, his arm still strapped tightly to his chest.

'We needd to gett that armm looked att,' said Aggie.

'Not by you, thoughh! You've done enoughh, thank you.' Gilbert shuffled along the branch where they sat, ensuring there was a decent size space between Aggie and his injury.

'Okayy, don't go onn about it. Noww, what's your plann?'

'Plann?'

'Yeahh, you were talkingg about takingg me to thee palace, butt stopping offf at the oldd juice barr ...'

'Thatt wasn't so much of a plann, more of an exactly whatt would happen, kind of thingg.'

'You meann you were goingg to just handd me overr?'

'Welll, I couldn't do much else with my armm like this, now couldd I?'

'Grrrrr! I oughtt to breakk your other armm, Gilbertt Trickle! If yourr brother wass here …'

'If myy brother was here, whatt?'

Aggie calmed herself and thought about what she'd just said. 'If yourr brother wass here,' she said slowly, 'he'dd ask *me* whatt the plan wass, wouldn't hee?'

'Yess, you always did seemm to have the ideas – fromm what I can remember.'

'Were you reallyy going to justt take me to Artyy?'

'No, I wass hoping you'd find another wayy, hoping you'd come up with a plann yourself.'

'Welll,' she said after a few minutes, 'I thinkk I may have a feww ideas, butt you'll have to helpp me filll in the memoryy blanks.'

# Chapter Eighteen

In the dark, dank, depths of the dwarf caves, all eyes were upon Fred. It had been just over an hour since Victor was taken ill.

'What? You think I did this?' he said, pointing at the panting body of Victor. 'You really think I'd stoop so low as to poison him.'

'If the cap fits ...' said Bod, folding his arms and nodding at Jud.

'And you did say you hated him – on more than one occasion ...' added Jud.

'But I wouldn't try to kill him. I just wanted to see him punished,' said Fred, leaning over the ill-stricken creature's head.

'Enough!' said Eric, placing a comforting hand on his son's shoulder. 'No one here is to blame ...'

'No, indeed!' said Fid, holding his book up for all to see. 'It would seem to be a slow acting poison called treeslanch. He could have been given it hours ago, even days or months.'

Fred and Eric pored over the page that outlined exactly what treeslanch did and how to administer it.

'But who would have done such a thing?' gasped Fred, scanning through the possible outcomes of poisoning, depending on strength, which included paralysis and fatality.

'Victor has lots of enemies, we know that. Not just pilp collectors, but among his own kind too,' said Bod, moping the sprite's large green brow with a cool cloth.

'I'd bet anything that Arty is behind it,' said Fred. 'Word has it that he's had enough of the sprite chief's demands for more magic dust.'

'And,' said Fid, 'wasn't Victor the hero of the hour? A gold medal, endless supply of magic dust ...'

'So how do we cure it?' said Fred, watching as Victor's body thrashed and twisted around. 'He's obviously in a lot of pain.'

'Not so sure we can, not so sure we have the knowledge,' said Fid, scratching his head.

'What do you mean?' said Eric. 'There must be something we can do – we can't just let him die!'

Fid ushered Fred and Eric towards the door. 'No more talk of death, please. He may be able to hear you. Let's go back to the stove room and discuss things.'

'But Victor ...' began Fred.

'Jud is quite capable,' said Fid, pulling the door closed behind them.

They marched quickly back to the stove room where Fid threw the large book onto the table. 'We'll have some tea. It will help us to think.'

'We haven't got time for tea!' said Fred, his knuckles pushing against the table where he stood.

'Victor's knowledge of the palace is central to our plans. You have to save him!'

'Jud will give him carveseed oil to sedate him.' He poured some hot water into three beakers, adding a handful of fresh smint tea leaves to each. 'The carveseed oil will keep the poison from entering the heart until we find something, but it will not hold indefinitely.'

Eric took the tea gratefully from Fid's hand and sat down at the table opposite his son. 'So what can we do? Who might know of a cure – the healers are all locked up somewhere below the palace. Even then, they might not be able to help.'

'You'll need someone who can analyse the poison, someone who can create an antedote, someone who can invent ...'

Instantly Fred knew that there was only one person who fitted this description. 'We need Albert!' he said. 'Albert Lichen.'

Eric looked at his son, confused. 'But we've no idea where he is, Fred,' he said. 'And by the time we find him it could be too late.'

'What choice do we have, huh? We can't exactly go round asking for help can we?' said Fred, jumping up from the table. He began to pace the room as he spoke. 'Arty's already put a price on my head – 1000 credits I heard.'

'Fred is right,' said Fid, walking over to Eric. He grabbed his hand, patting it gently. 'This Albert is our only hope, Victor's only hope. You must allow Fred to go.'

'But I've only just got him back,' said Eric. 'What if I lose him all over again?'

'I'll take Bod and Jud with me, father. We'll use the tunnels where we can,' said Fred. 'Knowing how useful Albert is, I wouldn't be surprised if Arty's put him to work so we'll try the palace first.'

Eric nodded reluctantly. 'Send Bod ahead, son. He can scout around though he'll have to keep to the shadows ...'

'Why don't we go instead?' cut in Stan and Alf together. In all the commotion, the two little creatures had just kept quiet – until now. 'We're changelings, remember. We could easily get Fred through to the palace.'

'Oh, I don't think that's a good idea. You'll just slow me down,' said Fred, sipping more tea.

'But we can get you through the town, past the Grublins, past the sprites ...'

'But can you do it without wasting time, without tidying up?' asked Eric earnestly. 'You will need to put all your training into practice. No tidying, no cleaning, no being polite!'

'We promise!' they said in unison.

'What do you think?' said Eric, turning to Fred. 'They might come in useful.'

'Now where have I heard that before?' said Fred, looking straight at the Stan and Alf who were bobbing up and down in anticipation.

'Okay,' said Fred, holding his hands up. 'You can come, but just remember what you've promised. No tidying ...'

'We won't, we won't, we won't,' the two changelings sung, jumping around excitedly.

'Go and pack some bits then I'll take you through the tunnels,' said Bod. 'That way you can avoid some of the town.'

The twins needed no more encouragement. They hugged each other tightly then ran out of the room laughing and giggling.

Fred raised his eyebrows and sighed deeply.

'They'll be okay,' said Eric. 'They're just a little over excited. They've not been out for weeks.'

'I'd probably be better on my own, but ... having changelings around would be useful.' Fred finished his tea then headed to his room to grab some essentials.

Fid watched him leave then sat down next to Eric, leaning in closely as he spoke. 'I don't know if Victor will last much longer. At best, if he survives, he may need constant care for the rest of his life.'

'I know,' sighed Eric. 'There have been many lessons learnt here today, Fid.' He mopped his worried brow with the back of his hand, wiping the sweat on his trousers.

'Sometimes it takes a tragic event to lift the red mist of anger and resentment,' said Fid. 'It also takes great courage to forgive.'

'But we had banked so much on Victor helping us yet now it is us helping him. How quickly things change,' said Eric.

'Perhaps it is a sign that we should look to ourselves for the solution and not to others,' said Fid. 'Perhaps the hero is amongst us already.'

# Chapter Nineteen

Albert looked down at his watch for the fifth time in as many minutes then ran his fingers through his hair anxiously. With just ten minutes until the guards returned to duty, he had to make a move or risk capture again. He peered round the door once more. If only the thieving sprite in the room next door was also aware of his urgent need to be somewhere else! He could try creeping past without disturbing it, but what if it heard him? What if it was so startled it knocked off some of the boxes on the shelves above it? What if?

Albert's plan had been to simply tip-toe to the end of the corridor, leap up the steps to the next floor, slide along the wall until he came to the small window that looked out on the old playground then fly out, over the various items of school furniture that sat there rotting! The only difficult part could be the window which was probably bolted and securely locked. Otherwise, it was a good plan! He had memorised the route when he'd first been brought down to the basement. It had been stuck firmly in his mind for all these months and now, today of all days, a pesky green sprite stood between him and his freedom.

Albert watched through the crack in the door as it shovelled large quantities of magic dust from a box into a tatty sack, a pilp sack, with its hands. Its huge ears twitched around back and forth, listening out for any sounds or footsteps that might result in its capture. It was risking a lot. It was risking its life. Arty had made the stealing of magic dust a serious offence some time ago. Any creatures caught were force fed the Grublin turning potion, adding to his mighty force of Grublin-fairies and increasing his fortune further.

This sprite must be desperate, thought Albert. All the same he wished it would hurry up and go, so that he could continue his escape.

But as the precious minutes passed, Albert decided he could wait no longer. He couldn't risk the sprite making a noise if it was disturbed so in his wisdom decided that jumping straight on top of its back would have a quieter effect! He slapped his hand over the sprite's mouth for good measure – just in case.

'I'm sorry,' he whispered into one of its very large ears. 'I don't mean any harm. I just want to get out of here before the guards come – like you!'

The poor sprite, thinking it had been captured, trembled under Albert's weight and offered its hands behind his back for tying up.

'No, I'm not the guard. I'm trying to escape.' Albert moved his hand away from the sprite's mouth and turned it over so the creature could see who he was.

The sprite gasped at the bedraggled creature that was bent over it. 'You prisoner?' it said, quietly pulling itself into a sitting position.

'Yes and I need to – *we* need to get out of here now.' Albert gestured towards the door then tapped his watch. 'The guards will be back in less than five minutes. Do you know what the penalty is for stealing magic dust?'

The sprite nodded than added, 'Do you know penalty for escapingism?'

He smiled at the sprite's poor grasp of fairy tongue, but understood what he meant. 'If I help you fill your sack, will you help me to escape?'

The sprite didn't need to answer. It started pouring more dust into the sack which filled quickly with Albert's help. As the sprite tied the string around the bulging bag, Albert peeped around the door. 'Quick, give me one end of the string, you take the other. We can fly along the corridor. It'll be quicker.'

With the sack between them, the unlikely pair flew down the corridor then up, stopping midway on the stairs at a small window through which they might escape.

'It has lock,' whispered the sprite, jiggling the padlock around. 'You have key?'

'Er, no. That's the problem,' said Albert, looking around anxiously. 'Can you use the dust to get us out?'

The sprite looked at him puzzled. 'Magically dust only work in human world, you know that.'

'Yes, I was just hoping that as a sprite ...'

'Come, we will go my way,' said the sprite, dragging the sack and Albert towards a door on the next level. 'There is a window in there that is open. I came through it.'

'Of course, we used that when we were late for school ...' He paused as he recalled happier times when the palace had been a school. It looked so different now.

Albert allowed himself to be pulled towards the window and watched as his co-conspirator pushed it open a little wider. Then the sprite climbed up onto the frame, one hand holding the top of the opened window, the other beckoning to Albert to pass the bulging sack. As the sack came near, he wrapped the string tightly around his thin green arm, jumping off the outside ledge and hovering as he tried to ease the sack through.

'It's stuck!' whispered Albert, beginning to panic. His only escape route was blocked by a sack full of stolen magic dust. Things were not looking good.

'Push harder, prisoner, push hard,' said the sprite.

'What d'you think I'm doing?' mumbled Albert, crossly, the sweat pouring off his forehead, but the sack wouldn't budge. Quickly, he pulled out a makeshift knife; bone handle and a rough metal blade strung together, and cut a small hole in the bottom of the sack. He squeezed until a large pile of dust sat on the floor then pushed at the sack once more. At last, it began to move and before long it was out of the window and safely in the hands of the sprite, leaving a long awaited space through which Albert could escape.

He had just raised his leg to climb up to the window ledge when he heard the sound of angry voices coming from the floor below. He froze.

'Come prisoner boy, before they catching you,' called the sprite, shuffling around outside the window uneasily.

Quickly coming to his senses, Albert scrambled up, bashing his knee hard against the wall in his hurry. He bit down on his lip as the pain rushed through him, taking his mind off his panic momentarily. He looked down at the red patch spreading across his trouser leg then painfully heaved himself up onto the ledge and out through the window. Behind him, the curious mix of blood and magic left a telling trail.

Albert flew from the ledge not a moment too soon for there, sniffing with each of their three nostrils, were the Grublin guards. 'Heyy, youu,' screamed one, his head only just visible over the windows edge. 'It'ss nott allowedd too escapee. Thee leaderr willl nott bee happyy.'

The sprite thief yanked hard at Albert's arm. 'Come,' he said, holding the end of the sack up with his free hand to prevent further leakage. 'Follow me, prisoner boy.'

Albert turned quickly, leaving the confines of his prison far behind as the sprite led him away from the palace and into the night.

It suddenly occurred to him that after being imprisoned for so long, he knew very little about the land they were flying over. It was still Pilpsville, but its features had changed beyond all recognition. Buildings still stood in familiar places, but many, like the library, had been torn apart, the white enamel bricks presumably stolen and taken to the pilp plant for grinding. And as they flew over the local store, it was clear it had suffered a similar fate. Its sorry state made Albert sigh inwardly. The sprites, it would seem, had become greedy – and none more so than the one he was flying with!

'Where are we going?' Albert asked, wincing as the sack brushed against his knee.

'I take you to see my friends.'

'Your sprite friends?' queried Albert, grabbing a corner of the sack to share the burden. 'They won't be too pleased to see me – a pilp collector.'

'They do as my brother says,' laughed the sprite, 'and my brother does as I says, so all be good.'

'Your brother? Is he some kind of leader then?'

'Some say leader, some say bully.' The sprite shrugged his shoulders. 'He's just my younger brother.'

A worrying thought popped into Albert's head as he remembered the last encounter he'd had with a bullying sprite. 'Er, your brother – what's his name?'

'Ah, you not know him ...'

'All the same,' said Albert, 'I don't want to appear rude ...'

The sprite laughed loudly as they started to descend. 'Norbert,' he shouted. 'He is called Norbert!'

# Chapter Twenty

'This will lead you directly to the palace,' said Fid, thrusting out his lantern into the darkness that lay ahead. 'You'll need to be quick. It's almost dawn.'

Fred nodded gratefully then, pushing his own lantern out into the tunnel, led the two changelings into the unknown. He turned just once to see the light from Fid's lantern disappear back towards his father then, with an urgency in his wings, moved on.

The twins fought desperately to keep up with his pace, but realising how time was of the essence they never once complained even though their wings throbbed and ached as if they might fall off.

'And if they did,' said Alf, telepathically answering his brother's comment, 'we would not stop to pick them up, would we?'

'No,' answered Stan in Alf's mind, 'because that was part our training – no tidying up.'

'But if we didn't pick them up we wouldn't have any wings – so we wouldn't be able to fly ...'

'So what you're saying, brother, is that we would have to pick them up in that case,' said Stan.

The twins looked at each other, confused, and immediately stopped flying.

'So, picking up this piece of paper which could fly into our face and cause an accident isn't really going *against our training, is it?* Stan bent down, grabbing the offending litter in one hand then grinned widely at his brother.

*'When you put it like that, Alf, no!'*

It took a while for Fred to notice that they were no longer behind him and as he made his way back to where they were now sitting, his temper was at boiling point.

'Why the pigging hell have you stopped? Victor could die at any moment and you have stopped. Why have you stopped?'

'Well,' said Stan aloud, 'we got to thinking that there are times when tidying up should definitely be allowed ...'

'Like this piece of paper – it could have ...'

'I knew you'd do this! Give me that paper, right now!' Fred snatched it angrily out of Alf's hand, screwing it up tightly into a ball and throwing it back into the darkness of the tunnel they had passed. 'Now either come with me or go back and find your stupid piece of paper.' Leaving them with a look of both bewilderment and frustration, he flew off down the tunnel again, his lantern thrust out in front.

*'See what you've done now – you've made him cross with your tidying up again,'* said Stan, reverting to telepathic conversation.

Alf kicked awkwardly at some stones on the ground for a few seconds then said brightly, *'So shall I go and get it?'*

'Oh, yes,' said Stan. 'We can't leave it there to cause an accident, can we?'

So while Alf flew back to retrieve the offending piece of paper, Stan followed Fred albeit at some distance behind.

'Keep up, if you're coming,' shouted Fred crossly, his voice echoing off the tunnel roof.

'Yes, Fred. Sorry to be taking so long,' Stan shouted back. He looked behind to see where his brother was and on seeing a tiny light hurrying towards him was reassured that Alf was on his way back.

As a breathless Alf sidled up next to his brother, Stan couldn't help, but notice the anxious look on his face.

'What is it, Alf?' asked Stan, out loud. 'What is it? What's wrong?' he asked again as he pulled Alf along in an attempt to catch Fred up.

'Look,' puffed Alf. 'Look at the paper.' He pushed the piece of paper, now flattened out, into his brother's hand.

Stan looked worriedly up ahead of them where the light from Fred's lantern shone out in front. 'Not now, Alf. Fred will be very cross if he sees this. Show me later.'

Alf snatched the paper back. 'Look now!' he gasped. 'You must show Fred – it's Albert!'

They stopped suddenly in mid flight then gently fluttered down until they came to rest on a pile of fallen rocks. They looked in amazement at the sketch of Albert that stared out from the wrinkled piece of paper. His face thin and grey, his hair long and unkempt, but there was no doubting it was Albert.

'It says here that he has stolen sacks of magic dust from the palace,' said Stan, shaking his head in disbelief.

'And that he is armed and dangerous,' said Alf adding several disapproving tuts as he read.

'What rubbish!' said Stan as they scanned the poster for further information about the fugitive.

As expected, it wasn't long before Fred came hurtling back down the tunnel, shouting and screaming at the twins for stopping again.

This time, Stan flew out to meet him. 'There's a perfectly good reason for us stopping this time, honestly.'

But Fred's eyes were glaring at the piece of paper Alf was holding aloft, as he stormed towards him. 'You just had to go back and get it, didn't you?'

'It's not what you think,' said Stan, trying to keep up with him.

'Well, enough is enough,' said Fred, opening the door to his lantern. He reached into his pocket and brought out a used taper, lighting it from the lantern's flame. 'This will put an end to your litter hunt.'

He flew quickly to where Alf now stood, letting the lantern fall to the ground as he snatched the paper from his hand and held the taper at its corner.

'Stop!' screamed a familiar voice, halting Fred promptly in his tracks. 'Look at what it says on the paper!'

In shock, he turned to see a small version of his father where Stan had just stood. The changeling's quick thinking brought Fred back to his senses.

Taking advantage of his bewildered state, Alf pushed the poster of Albert into Fred's hand and removed the lighted taper from the other.

'It's Albert,' said Alf, tapping Fred's arm. 'Look, it's got today's date on it.'

'But dawn's hardly broken. How can they get these out so quick?' said Fred.

'Those Grublins turn things out in minutes, just as the leader orders,' said Alf, stamping on the tip of the taper. 'It must have been blown in from above.'

As Stan changed back to his normal self, Fred's eyes slowly looked from him to the poster, opening wide as he recognised the face portrayed in the sketch.

'Oh my wings – it *is* Albert!' he said, allowing a small grin to crawl over his face.

The twins waited patiently as he read through the written information, watching and listening carefully to his sighs and comments.

'It would seem that I owe you both an apology,' he said, folding the paper into four and putting it in his pocket. 'You were right – there are times when tidying up should be allowed and this was one of those times.'

'We won't do it all the time ...' said Alf.

'But if you hadn't, we wouldn't have had this lead. Well done ... and sorry for shouting!'

'So what do we do now?' said Stan. 'There's no point in going to the palace.'

'No point at all,' said Fred. 'We need to get into town. See what creatures there know about Albert.'

'There was a dwarf bolt hole just a little way back,' said Alf. 'We could try that. It might lead back to the surface.'

Alf led the way back to where a large wooden hatch was fixed to the roof of the tunnel. As they hovered below, ears pressed against the hatch, they listened to noises coming from above to gauge which part of town the bolt hole was in.

'Lots of sprites, that's for sure,' said Stan, rubbing his ear and pulling away from the hatch. 'Why do they have to screech so much?'

As Alf and Fred fluttered down to join him on the ground, Stan knew what they had to do.

'Sprites!' he said to Alf. 'We'll have to change into sprites ...'

'Ah, I hate being a sprite. All that screaming really hurts my throat. Can't we be Grublin-fairies ...'

'No, Stan's right,' said Fred. 'The sprites will have more information – remember, it's sprites who crave the magic dust.'

'Albert will be a kind of hero to them, I suppose,' said Stan.

Fred grinned. 'I don't know if he'd see it quite like that.'

'Okay, so sprites it is,' said Alf, closing his eyes tightly, allowing the greenness to flow through his body.

Next to him, Stan did the same and in a matter of minutes, Fred found himself face to face with two new recruits for Pilpsville's sprite population.

'What about you, Fred?' said Stan. 'Pilp collectors stand out like the suns these days.'

'I'll follow you up, but stick to the shadows. Then you can bring me the information as you find it,' he said then added somberly, 'but you must work quickly – time is not on our side.'

The sprite twins nodded and flew back up to the wooden hatch, listening for a break in the noise above.

On their nod, Fred gently pulled out a tiny scroll from his pocket. He muttered Fid's charm under his breath then watched as the wooden hatch dissolved into a mass of wavy lines. 'It's like a dwarf portal,' he said as the twins gasped. 'Now be quick or we'll have all sorts falling into the tunnel!'

The twins pulled themselves together quickly and peered through the hole.

'All clear,' said Stan.

Fred waited as the twins fluttered out through the hole and watched as they flew out into the town above. They hovered, looking around cautiously before beckoning to Fred to fly out. As he flew into the shadow of a nearby building, the twins watched as the bolt hole magically camouflaged itself against the dusty ground blending in once again with its surroundings.

'We'll never find that again,' said Fred quietly as the twins approached.

The twins just shrugged their little green shoulders and stared at the space where the hatch had just been.

'Still, let's worry about that later,' said Fred, displaying a note of renewed optimism in his voice. 'You'd better go and see what you can find out. I'll wait here ...' He looked up, suddenly realising exactly where he was. He should have recognised it immediately, but in its dilapidated state it was hardly surprising that he hadn't. He leant against one of the walls, sniffing at the bricks, remembering nostalgically the many times he had visited this particular building.

'The juice bar,' he sighed peeking around the corner where the official shop sign lay in tatters. 'Our favourite meeting point!'

# Chapter Twenty One

Dawn arrived abruptly at the metal works and with it came the daily breakfast thirst quencher.

'Drinkk juicee,' said the Grublin, thrusting a familiar grey bottle into a sleepy Bessie's hand.

'*DON'T drink the juice,*' said another voice inside Bessie's head. '*Pour it away and pretend to drink the juice.*'

'Drinkk!' growled the Grublin, taking the cap off and pushing the bottle towards her mouth.

'*DON'T DRINK! Just put it to your lips as if you are drinking,*' said the voice, desperately trying to coax Bessie against her will. '*Pretend, Bessie, pretend.*'

Confused, Bessie drank the potion anyway, handing back the empty grey bottle to the Grublin who sniggered knowingly.

The voice in her head sighed heavily, and despite fifty-eight failed attempts to convince Bessie otherwise, promised to return to try again.

# Chapter Twenty Two

'How is it that we've managed to lose yet another Lichen? Huh?' screamed Arty as the curtains were drawn back to reveal another new day.

'Not to mention a huge bulk of magic dust ...' said his mother. 'Or should I *not* mention that?'

Arty snarled at her sarcasm and continued to aim his abuse at the terrified Grublin lying prostrate on the floor of his bedchamber. 'Call yourself a guard? You're no more a guard than I am a Grublin.' He leant over the poor creature's head shouting, 'Now get out before I have one of your nostrils removed and used as a wind sock!'

Needing no further telling, the battered Grublin leapt up and ran from the room, slamming the large wooden door behind him.

Arty kicked spitefully out at an innocent looking table leg whose only offence had been to hold up the table top – on which once lived the bottle and plaque celebrating Aggie Lichen's defeat. It was an easy target.

'First the Lichen girl and now her brother ...' ranted Arty. 'What next?'

'Calm yourself, dear,' said Martha, brushing the back of her hand over his brow. 'The dust trail her brother and that sprite thief left behind will lead us directly to where they are. I'm *sure* he'll be recaptured in no time.'

'I hope you're right. The last thing I need is a Lichen family re-union,' he said, throwing himself on the bed. 'This is making me look ridiculous.'

'You worry too much,' said Martha, reassuringly. 'Gertie Cruet will have no doubt caught up with the sister by now and we still have the parents ...'

'What about the younger sister, Myrtle?' cut in Arty. He stood up and began pacing around. 'What of her?'

'Last I heard she was still pilp collecting on the other side – as a Grublin-fairy,' said Martha. 'So stop panicking – you're beginning to sound just like your father!'

'Which reminds me,' said Arty striding towards the door. 'I want him moved to a high security cell – just in case Albert has any stupid ideas about rescuing him.' He pulled open the heavy door and motioned for two guards to enter. 'Not that one,' he yelled at a poor trembling creature slumped against the wall. 'He and I have just had words! The only thing that he gives me is bad news.'

Two other guards reluctantly stepped forward and entered the room.

Martha watched intently as Arty gave each of them specific instructions, explaining every step in microscopic detail to ensure no further mistakes would be made.

She smiled inwardly at the anxiety in his voice, turning her face towards the window to watch the suns rise. As the rays danced through the glass catching her sleeve, she carelessly brushed away any evidence of magic dust or indeed firepowder.

With a little assistance, his time as leader was coming to an end, she thought, then she could rule with Belcher, her Moshtike love. It was time for a new and more powerful leader to emerge!

# Chapter Twenty Three

'Iff you layy another fingerr on mee, Gilbert Trickle, I'll ...'

'Howw else are we going to make you lookk more Grublinly?' scowled Gilbert, his one good arm plunging into a bucket. 'And it will keep the sunlight from burning you to a frazzle!'

Myrtle sniggered as Aggie's face disappeared under the smearing of mud provided by Gertie Cruet, who disappeared outside of the elderberry bush only to reappear some five minutes later with yet another bucketful.

'Soo, remindss mee whyy we'ss doingg thiss?' said Gertie, rubbing the mud behind Aggie's ears. 'Onlyy I'mm stilll nott suree II understandss.'

Myrtle sighed and tried once again to explain the plan, this time in a much more simplified version. 'Thee mudd willl make uss moree Grublinn colouredd and smellingg, except forr you, ass you stilll are veryy Grublinn coloured and smellingg ...' She waited for some reaction, but on seeing none carried on explaining, 'Thenn we alll go throughh the portal tunnell together ...'

'Butt whyy aree youu pretendingg too bee Grublinss?' said Gertie, rubbing a further handful of mud into the back of Aggie's arms.

'Becausee we aree changingg backk and iff we go throughh lookingg more like pilpp collectors, whichh is whatt *we* really are, thee guards willl take uss awayy and the leaderr won't rewardd *you*, he'lll reward *themm*,' said Myrtle trying to be patient.

'Butt youu don'tt lookk likee pilpp collectorss orr Grublinss. You'ree alll kindd off halff andd halff.'

'Yess, but the mudd will helpp to disguise thatt, won't itt?' sighed Myrtle for what seemed like the umpteenth time.

'Soo thenn wee goess too thee palacee, seee thee leaderr andd gett myy rewardd ...'

'No!' spat Aggie, picking bits of mud from her mouth. 'Firstt we goo to thee juice barr ...'

'Yess, and Aggie will mix you upp some more potion, won't youu?' Gilbert gave her a look, encouraging her to agree. 'So thatt you'll look your best forr the leader.'

Aggie looked puzzled for a moment, but then answered, 'Err, yeah. I'll mixx something upp for you.'

Gertie cocked her head to one side. 'Thenn wee goess too thee palacee?'

'Yepp, then we goess to thee palace!' said Myrtle, kneeling and patting the last of the mud into place at the back of her sister's legs.

'Oh helll,' said Gilbert, gloomily. He looked the other two up and down, and then glanced down at his own body. 'Whatt do we all lookk like?'

'Hopefullyy like Grublinss or Grublin-fairiess,' said Aggie, 'If nott, we're donee for. Andd you're suree we're nott going to end up crispyy, only I havee a little memory off burning my wingss in the human sunlightt ...'

Gilbert groaned, 'Lookk it's the only thing I cann think of. I don't wantt to stay here any longer thann you do!'

Myrtle sighed at their arguing then stood up on the branch then made her way to a large clump of leaves, peering out carefully to the world outside. She beckoned to the others to join her. 'Quickk, it's quitee empty noww.'

As she held the leaves aside, the others filed through, Aggie at the head of them. 'Welll, I kind of knoww where we'ree goingg,' she said, shrugging her shoulders and frowning. 'Doo you?'

Myrtle let the leaves fall back together behind her. She knew it was best not to argue when her sister had her bossy head on. And besides, she probably wouldn't remember her way to the juice bar anyway.

They flew in a line towards the entrance of the exit tunnel which was, in fact, not that far away. Gertie tucked in behind Aggie while Myrtle stayed close to Gilbert, keeping an eye on his injured arm.

As they entered, Aggie realised that they might have stood a better chance earlier when the tunnel was busier. With just a few other creatures returning to Mirvellon, there was more chance of being stopped by the guards than before. She sighed at her own stupidness and cursed at her lack of alert brain cells.

And to make matters worse, something she didn't notice before made the tunnel even more dangerous – posters! 'Have you seen this Grublin-fairy?' they asked.

Aggie groaned and pulled the jumper she was wearing up high to her mouth. 'Just keepp your headss down andd avoid eye contactt,' she said as the others grouped together near her. 'Andd under no circumstancess draw attentionn to yourselvess.'

'Rightt, Gilbert?' said Myrtle, inadvertently smacking her hand against his bad shoulder as she turned.

'AAARRRGGHH! My shoulderr!' he screamed. 'AAARRRGGHH!'

'SSSHHH!' said Myrtle.

'Andd which bit aboutt not drawing attentionn to yourselff was I nott clear aboutt!' barked Aggie, disbelievingly.

It was too late though, the guards were mobilised and heading their way – two Grublins in full military regalia, three sizes too small with hats to match.

'Piggingg marvellous! Justt two minutess in thee tunnell and we're caughtt!' said Aggie turning her face away to conceal her pilp collector features.

Gertie grabbed Aggie's arm, holding onto the leader's prize for all she was worth, and moved her slightly away from the situation. No two-bit guard was going to come between her and that reward.

Aggie, not wanting to make matters worse, surprised herself – and did nothing. This was neither the time or place to squabble with Gertie.

As the guards approached she felt Gertie ease her away even further. Her immediate concern was for her sister, but she'd forgotten just how much like her Myrtle was.

'What'ss goingg onn heree?' said the larger of the two guards, prodding Gilbert's arm with his wooden club.

Gilbert flinched and fought back the tears.

'Err, he'ss injuredd,' said Myrtle in her best Grublin accent. 'We'ree justt takingg himm too seee thee healerr.'

'Won'tt doo noo goodd,' said the smaller guard. 'Healerss won'tt treatt Grublinss. Refusess too.'

'Butt hiss armm ...'

'Leavee himm withh uss,' cut in the smaller one. 'wee knowss someonee whoo fixess armss don'tt wee?' He nudged the bigger Grublin in the ribs.

Aggie, tried to pull away from Gertie's vice-like grip, but Gertie was having none of it.

'Do somethingg, Gertie,' said Aggie, through gritted teeth. 'After alll, you are thee leader's prefectt!'

Gertie glared at Aggie for a few seconds then said, 'Yess, II amm!' She pushed Aggie to one side and flew in between Gilbert and the guards. 'Stepp asidee noww,' she growled in a deep and menacing tone. 'II amm thee leader'ss personall prefectt onn aa speciall missionn. I'ss takingg thesee creaturess too thee palacee soo stepp awayy – noww!'

'Personall prefectt, ayy,' said one of the guards stepping back.

'What'ss thatt thenn?' said the other holding his ground.

'Nott suree, butt itt soundss importantt ...'

'Itt ISS importantt!' said Gertie indignantly. 'Noww goo orr II shalll reportt youu.'

'Butt wee couldd escortt youu – makee suree youu gett theree okayy. Youu knoww there'ss lotss off nastyy spritess andd Grublinss whoo mightt wantt too takee yourr placee – andd iff there'ss aa rewardd involvedd ...' He rubbed his filthy hands together and gave a sneering sideways glance to his Grublin companion.

Gertie turned and looked at Aggie and whispered, 'AA goodd ideaa?'

Aggie sighed in disbelief then mouthed back, 'Noo, a badd idea – a veryy bad ideaa!'

'Noo, wee won'tt bee needingg youu, butt thankk youu forr yourr offerr. II shalll lett thee leaderr knoww aboutt youu. Cann II takee yourr namess?'

'Err, Flobb andd Globb – att thee leader'ss servicee off coursee.' They bowed deeply, backing away slowly then within seconds they were off in search of other offenders.

'Pheww! That wass close,' said Myrtle, watching as they flew off to investigate a loud bang at the far end of the tunnel.

'You didd well,' said Aggie, patting Gertie on the back as she returned to her side. 'You didd really welll!'

Gertie smiled awkwardly and fought against the strange warm feeling of goodness that was swirling around her insides.

'Rightt, to thee juice barr,' said Aggie. 'I couldd do withh an ice coldd girgberry delightt.'

# Chapter Twenty Four

Norbert the sprite paced round and round and round. His large green face was tilted downwards as if searching for an answer amongst the rubble and broken remains of the room. The pungent smell of rotten fruit filled the air.

'So let me get this right,' he said in broken fairy tongue, 'you want my help to find your friends.' He paced again. 'The friends who tied me up in Spercham and left me in the guest tower with that guard.'

Broken glass crunched noisily under his feet sending small shards into the air and into nearby legs.

Albert held firm knowing that any tremor in his voice would portray weakness. 'Well, yes. I mean, we're kind of on the same side now, aren't we? You hate Arty, we hate Arty ...' Albert, leaning against the old serving counter, held his hands out as he spoke to indicate balance on both sides.

'That guard,' continued Norbert, 'you know it took him almost a week to realise he had been tricked. All that time he was poking and prodding with his stick ... and you want me to help you?'

To his left, two other sprites stood nervously. They flinched with every mention of the imprisonment, stroking away at the invisible bruises and cuts they had suffered at the hands of the ill-seeing sprite guard. They looked at each other and shuddered.

Maurice, Norbert's older brother, nudged Albert to respond. 'Say something back. Not let him have last word.'

'Er, well, we had a bad time too, you know,' said Albert, looking to Maurice for encouragement. 'And your friend Victor was the cause of most of it,' he added boldly.

'Ah, Victor!' Norbert stopped suddenly and faced Albert straight on. He walked slowly towards the pilp collector grinning wildly, stopping only when he was within an arms length of him. 'Now there's good reason to join forces – you hate Victor, we hate Victor.'

'So you'll help?' said Albert impatiently.

'You help us find Victor – we help you find your friends,' said Norbert. 'Then it is back to normal. You hate us – we hate you. Yes?'

'Deal!' said Albert. 'So where do we start?' He moved towards the door, eager to start the search that would reunite him with his sisters and friends. In that state of mind, he wasn't quite expecting what came next.

'Right here!' said Norbert.

'Sorry?' said Albert, puzzled and confused.

Norbert let out a loud roar, holding his stomach as he laughed. He glared at his gang members, silently commanding them to join in too, which they all did except for Maurice who wasn't taking orders, but looked on bemused.

'Your friends have been spotted in the crossing tunnel,' said Norbert. 'They are on way here already.'

'So you knew where they were all the time?' said Albert, incensed that he had been so easily tricked into helping this disgusting creature.

'Oh, yes,' said one of others. 'Norbert knows most of what goes on around here ...'

'Except for where Victor is,' cut in Albert bitterly. 'Not so clever now, huh?'

Maurice moved quickly to him, grabbing his arm. 'Be careful, my prisoner friend. You know how nasty my brother can be ...'

Albert looked back at where Norbert stood, not quite so smug now, but surrounded by his fellow sprites. He took a deep breath and swallowed his pride noisily. 'Great trick!' he shouted over. 'You had me completely fooled!'

Maurice patted Albert heavily on the shoulders.

'Come, sit,' said Norbert straightening up a fallen chair and patting its seat. 'Gryff will make you drink, huh, Gryff?'

Gryff looked around at the mess and shrugged his shoulders. 'Gryff will make drink from what?'

'Out of what you can find!' barked Norbert, sending poor Gryff off behind the counter.

Albert sat down cautiously. He knew all too well about the adverse effects of mixing fruits and spices together, especially stirring not shaking rules... An idea shot into his head.

'Wait!' he shouted above the din. 'How about me fixing the drinks, after all my sister did work here at times. We can then drink to our deal.' He wasn't sure what he could make, but this was an opportunity to good to miss!

Norbert laughed again. 'Sure, pilp collector, you do drinks, why not?'

Albert limped round behind the counter, spotting a piece of old cloth which he quickly wrapped around his injured knee. Then he began scouring for any useable ingredients. The cupboards, clinging to the walls by just one fixing, revealed nothing more than a few cubes of sugar and a half-eaten bar of sweetened milk fat, but Albert grabbed both greedily.

He disappeared through the doorway and out back to where Mrs Cheric kept the bulk of her stores. The chiller had been forced open, leaving the contents rotten and decaying, and not immediately recognisable. Albert thought the pile of green slime at the back could have once been sporach leaves and there was a faint possibility that the red slime that had dripped from the shelf to the floor was blastberries. The disgusting stench though, was overpowering. He heaved at the repulsive sight and revolting smell, covering his nose and mouth with his hands he backed away and kicked the door shut.

As he stood there trying to taking in some cleaner gulps of air, he became suddenly aware of a rare moment of quietness in the front of the shop. Whispering had replaced the screaming and shouting. Something was being discussed. Something was being discussed that was not for his pointy ears to hear. Albert sidled up closer to the doorway, taking care not to tread on the rubbish that littered the floor. He wasn't sure of the full details, but the main content of the sprite discussion soon became very clear.

He recognised the voice as Norbert's. '... and when Pilpy's sisters get here, we do them all – revenge. You did well to fetch him here, brother.'

Albert stifled a gasp and moved his head a little nearer.

'Leader's mother set it up – I cannot take all credit,' came Maurice's voice.

Albert was stunned. He thought back to his last few days in prison when he'd made preparations to escape. What a fool he had been! Bribing the guards for the black powder, Ferrett's cell lock sticking, finding Maurice, his 'lucky' escape – it had all been a set up. And now it looked as if both Martha and Norbert would have the ultimate revenge on them all. The trap was set.

'What about Victor?' asked another sprite.

'The one who always moans will know where Victor is,' laughed Norbert wickedly. 'We will torture him until he tells.'

Albert had heard enough. He pulled himself back quietly, away from the doorway, flattening his body against the wall. His head was pounding with anger and fear. He had to do something, but what did he have – possibly enough ingredients to quench their thirst!

But what of adverse effects? There must be something here he could use. Mrs Cheric often disappeared out the back to attend to her stock. He looked around frantically, tapping the remains of the walls with his hands and the floor with his feet. Then he noticed a tiny gap in the floorboards right at the back of the wall, just before where the door would have been to the home quarters. It was just wide enough for a small hand to slip through. Albert bent down, pushing his face towards the hole. He could see nothing, but he felt a slight breeze on his cheek and the sweet smell of flowers filled his nostrils. He'd found the secret store!

He stood back up feeling pleased with himself, but then quickly became aware of a sudden increase in noise in the shop itself and hurried back before investigating further. He popped his head over the counter.

'What are you doing, pilpy? Where's our drinks?' shouted Norbert as a fellow sprite rode bare back on some poor creature they'd just captured.

Albert swallowed hard, desperately trying to hold his nerve. 'Still searching for the right ingredients. You just continue amusing yourself with that dragonfly,' he said. 'Won't be long – and no peeking or it won't be a surprise.'

He disappeared once again and headed out the back to where the gap was. Ensuring that no one was looking, he grabbed a piece of wood for a lever and began pushing, trying to prise the strip of flooring up. But the pressure on the wood was too great and the lever split in half after just three attempts.

She couldn't have gone to all this trouble to get things, thought Albert, nervously picking at the broken lever. Mrs Cheric would have needed quick access to her plants. There must be a way of opening it up. He leant back exhausted, aware of the time he was wasting – and the impatient drinkers out front. He bent over, hands on his knees, his head hanging down despondently – and then he spotted it!

Through the gap in his legs, he saw a switch hidden in the alcove. It had been impressively disguised to resemble an energy port, but at this angle it was so obviously a switch – the switch! Albert turned himself around then reached in, moving the switch lever to the up position. Just as he did, the floorboard with the gap and two others, sprung open to reveal a short flight of steps down to an underground garden. The sudden humidity immediately engulfed him, leaving him both thirsty and sweaty.

'Hey, Pilpy!' came a cry from the shop. 'You take too long. Gryff will give you hand.'

Albert wiped his face quickly before dashing out to the front again. 'No, I'm almost there. I just have to wait for the klupe to settle. No need for help, honestly.'

'Okay, but not much longer, ay – or I might start thinking you slowing things down on purpose ...'

'Just five more minutes and you will have a drink that will stand your hair on end.'

'Huh! Don't go doing that, Pilpy ...'

'Just kidding, Norbert, just kidding.'

As the sprites slid back into tormenting the dragonfly, Albert darted to the back room where the doorway to the secret store lay open. He rushed down the steps, taking in the extraordinary sight that now lay before him. The whole cellar spread out as far as the eye could see with chinks of light flowing in from above. Rows and rows of Mrs Cheric's famous talking plants battled with each other for space, whispering to each other. And more importantly, a large cupboard under the stairs revealed a huge stash of vanilla klupe, the base ingredient for most of Mrs Cheric's wild and wonderful concoctions.

'I shall give you a drink you will never forget, Norbert my friend,' he said under his breath as he poured two cartons of vanilla klupe into two large jugs. He scanned around at the array of plants before him, all begging to be used.

He rushed around gathering girgberries, sporach leaves and blast berries in his hands, throwing them quickly into the jug of klupe. 'Ssshh!' he said quietly as one tried to engage him in conversation. It did the trick and the plant retreated. He spotted the main ingredient, purple pipkin, halfway down a row and carefully crushed the leaves into the klupe. Finally, he came to the most important part of making the drink. If he shook it, the colours would mix, the smell would be blissful and the taste would be divine. On the other hand, if he stirred it the colours would ripple, the smell would be vile, the taste would be repulsive, but the effects on the sprites would be incredible ... especially with his secret ingredient – fire powder!

But what if they asked him to taste it first? he thought. He decided to leave the final stage of the drink until he returned to the shop. It would look less suspicious.

Albert carefully climbed back up the steps, balancing the jugs and a few old mugs he had cleaned out with an old rag. At the top, he carefully re-positioned the floorboards to ensure the secret garden would not be discovered.

The noise that greeted him was louder than ever. From the sound of it, there seemed to be an added attraction. Another poor creature to torment and belittle, thought Albert as he assembled his concoction on a piece of tatty plastic that would serve as a tray.

'Here we are,' he said as he re-entered the battered remains of the shop, 'a freshly made refreshing drink as promised ...'

It was only as he looked up on the word 'promised' that he saw what all the fuss and noise had been about. The dragonfly had been cast to one side and stood trembling near the door as if begging for its release.

Its place had been taken by another creature who was entertaining the sprites by falling over glass and bricks after they had spun it around several times on a tatty swivelling chair.

'Look what we found outside,' cried Norbert.

Albert stared and gulped. 'Er, your drinks are ready,' he shouted above their hideous laughter, trying to hide his contempt for their actions.

But still the sprite's disgusting antics continued. Norbert cackled loudly as the victim fell time and time again onto the floor, cutting and scraping its already bloodied limbs. 'Spin faster!' he ordered. 'Spin faster!'

Maurice, watching from the corner nearest to the serving bar, looked at Albert and tutted. 'Well, prisoner boy, what do you make of that?'

Albert righted a table and put down his tray of drinks. He fought back the urge to comment truthfully, finding solace in releasing their first victim. 'Oh, let's get shot of this dragonfly. It's beginning to smell really bad.'

Maurice shrugged his shoulders.

Opening the door slightly, Albert let the terrified creature slip through the gap and venture out to its freedom.

On returning to the table, he saw that Maurice was already helping himself to a drink. 'Wait!' he screamed, 'No, not just yet! We need it to seal the deal with Norbert.'

'Okay, Okay,' cried Maurice, returning the mug to the table, 'but you gotta get him here first!' he laughed, tapping the table.

Albert watched in horror as the sprite's victim was spun around and around in the chair then yanked to its feet. How they clapped and laughed as the poor thing lost its balance, falling head first into the piles of shattered glass and broken furniture. He had to act – fast!

Albert rushed over to the swivel chair, shouting 'My turn. Let me spin next.' He pulled the creature roughly back into the seat as the sprites looked on bemused. 'Now you'll see what a pilp collector can do!' he cried, then casually brushed against the creature's ear and whispered, 'Stay down. Pretend you've been knocked out, anything, but just don't move.'

After a loud count of three, he spun the chair as hard as he could. It had to be faster than the sprites spin or they wouldn't believe the outcome. To increase speed further Albert flew with the chair, flapping his wings hurriedly, aware of the implications such speed might have. At last he let go, flying dizzily to the back of the room to watch as the sprites gave a deafening cheer.

Within seconds, the chair spun wildly off its axis, throwing its contents hard against the wall. A sickening moan was heard as the creature collapsed in a heap on the floor, a trickle of blood oozing from its nose. Then it was silent and still.

'Hey, Pilpy. You killed him!' said Norbert gleefully patting Albert on the back. 'You one of us now!'

Albert wrenched himself away from the wall, appalled at what he had done, hoping against hope that the creature wasn't dead and dismayed by Norbert's comparison of him to the sprites.

He feigned a smile. 'Yeah, that's how to do it!' He glanced over at the crumpled body, relieved that it was still breathing – just!

'Right, what about drinks? That made us mighty thirsty,' said Norbert as they all gathered around the table.

'Well, let me in and I'll serve it up.' Albert, desperately pushing his feelings aside, elbowed his way through and grasped one of the jugs. The adrenalin soared through his veins as he carefully poured out six mugs of fruit juice, trying not to slop it about too much.

'Ah, not just yet,' he said as Norbert raised the mug to his huge mouth. 'The final touch ...' He grabbed a long slender spoon from the tray and stirred each mug one by one – except his own which he had quickly put to one side as he poured.

'Okay, one two three! Drink up, drink up!' he cried, watching as each of them downed the drink in one large gulp.

'Ugh! Disgusting!' cried Norbert, holding his empty mug upside down. He paused slightly then laughed and added, 'Give us more!'

Albert happily obliged, stirring each one vigorously before handing them over. He took sips of his own unstirred drink to allay suspicion and kept a watchful eye on the motionless body in the rubble.

Then glancing quickly at his watch, he backed away from the raucous sprites, taking refuge behind the counter. If his calculations had been correct, adverse effects would be springing into action at any moment. He tucked his head in tightly, bringing his hands in over his head for added protection – and waited ... and waited ... and ...

'Hey Pilpy! What you doing down there, huh?' screamed Norbert over the top of the counter.

'Ah, Norbert,' said Albert, releasing his hands

from his head. 'I'm just looking in the rubble for any remains of spices for another drink.' He pushed some pieces of glass around for good measure.

The sprite let out an enormous laugh and said, 'You sure you not hiding from ...'

*SPLAT!*

Albert wiped the sprite goo from his face, covered his head once more and tucked in tight.

An astonished Maurice jumped to his feet. 'Hey, what happened to my ...'

*SPLAT!*

Albert, now drenched in sprite goo, stood up just in time to see the other sprites explode.

With the last one gone, he rushed over to where the crumpled body still lay.

He bent over, whispering into the battered and bruised features. 'They're gone now. Open your eyes.'

A sigh and a groan were emitted then slowly the eyes blinked open.

'I'm so sorry. I had to do it!' Albert hung his head in shame.

'It's okay. You had no other choice. Help me up, will you?'

Albert put his hand around a shoulder, lifting the full body weight against his own. He tugged at a fallen chair with his foot and gently sat the creature down.

'How did you find me? Did you know I was in prison?' he asked.

'I need your help,' gasped the creature, ignoring Albert's questions. 'WE need your help – your ideas and inventions ...'

'No problem,' said Albert, beginning to feel a little more at ease. 'I'll be glad to use my skills for some good.'

'Now! I need you to come now!'

'We can't go right now,' said Albert, looking through the broken pane to the outside street. 'Guess who's coming ...'

But the sentence went unfinished as the creature slipped from the chair onto the floor into a state of unconsciousness.

Albert pulled him across his legs. 'Fred! Fred! Wake up. Aggie's on her way!'

# Chapter Twenty Five

'Whatt the hell happenedd here?' cried Aggie, her mouth dropping open as the final word oozed slowly from her lips like a thick slime.

The battered shell of the juice bar stood before them. Where the massive rose-tinted windows had proudly shone out was a huge void. The decaying enamel pillars had barely stood the test of time.

The famous multi-coloured bricks, known throughout Mirvellon for their arousing aromas, were either chipped or vandalised in some way or another. The tag 'Bilkoo' stated that said creature had frequently 'been here' and vied for position with the declaration that 'Vernn luvss Mayy'.

'S'what'ss thiss thenn?' said Gertie, sneeringly. Youu saidd wee weree goingg too thee juicee barr. Youu saidd you'dd makee mee somee moree potionn.' She stamped her feet angrily, crossing her arms in the fashion of a sulky fairychid, a sure indication that the true Gertie Cruet was veering back from the brink of Grublin-fairy hood.

Aggie slumped to the ground. 'Justt shut upp for a minutee will youu?' Her scrambled brain flashed up long forgotten memories of times when the juice bar had played an important role in her growing up, times she had spent with her friends – Betsy and Ted?

'… andd justt whoo aree Vernn andd Mayy?'

'Oh doo shut upp, Gertie. Give Aggie aa momentt.'

'II wass justt sayingg – that'ss alll …'

'Oh my wingss!' interrupted Gilbert. 'Have you seenn inside?' He thrust his head through the space where the window had been. 'What'ss all this purplee goo?' He wiped a handful of slime from the inside wall down his trousers, but not before smelling and licking it first.

'Yuckk! I wishh you wouldn't do thatt. It's so grosss,' said Myrtle pulling a face of disgust.

'Purple pipkinn – stirred,' said Gilbert, completely oblivious to what she'd just said. 'Why wouldd someone stirr purple pipkin – whatt with the adverse effectss and all thatt?'

'How'dd you know it's beenn stirred,' said Myrtle, inadvertently finding herself sniffing at the purple goo.

'Fromm experience,' he said miserably, looking over at Aggie.

Myrtle blushed slightly as she remembered her sister's little mixing mistake.

'Thatt taste will stayy with me forever,' he said, dramatically. 'But there's ann added ingredient, somethingg I can't quite identify …' He scooped another fingerful off and ran it over his tastebuds for a second time. 'Hmmm, couldd be sporachh or turnile or …'

'Spritee!' said Gertie, licking her hand. 'Tastess likee spritee.'

Gilbert wretched noisily and ran to the corner of the building to vomit.

Gertie sniffed her hand before taking a further lick of her fingers. 'Spritee withh aa hintt off ... withh aa hintt off ... firee powderr. Howw oddd?'

'Firepowderr?' said Aggie, pulling herself up and going through the shop door. 'Welll, that could explainn the messs, the splatteringg on the wallss, the gungee ...'

'Yess, I think we get the picturee,' said Gilbert, holding his stomach and wiping away a strand of mucus from his mouth with his good hand.

'Deliberate thenn,' said Myrtle, joining Aggie in the shop.

'Yeahh, would seemm so,' said Aggie, picking her way through the broken glass and dismembered furniture to reach the only real structure left intact – the serving station. 'Stirredd purple pipkinn wouldn'tt be enough to do thiss – it just turnss the victimm purple, butt the firepowderr ...'

'BANGG!' shouted Gertie.

Myrtle and Gilbert simultaneously jumped with fright.

'Thee leaderr,' Gertie continued, 'hass loadss off thiss att thee palacee. Keepss itt stashedd awayy, lockedd upp.'

'Hmmm,' mused Aggie, oblivious to the two startled creatures beside her. 'Isn'tt it illegall to have firepowderr now? I meann, wasn't there a laww passed againstt it's use …'

Gertie rolled some purple goo between her fingers. 'Yess, andd II thinkk it'ss underr doublee lockk andd keyy …'

'Butt,' cut in Aggie, 'what I'mm saying iss that iff the onlyy powder is heldd at the palacee, whoever came heree must havee come fromm the palacee.'

'Just to mixx up a purple pipkinn surprisee?' sneered Gilbert, wiping startled sweat from his face.

'Andd blow upp a feww sprites inn the processs,' added Myrtle, now recovered.

'No, no, no you'ree missing thee pointt,' said Aggie frustratedly. 'Whyy would someonee come heree with firee powder?' she said, the frown on her forehead deepening as she spoke. 'Andd, more importantlyy, who couldd that someonee be?'

'Howw about Marthaa?' said Gilbert.

'Or Artyy?' said Myrtle.

'Orr somefairyy calledd … Albertt?' said Gertie, picking up a tatty leaflet from the serving counter and waving it in the air.

'Ohh my wingss! Give me thatt, Gertie,' gasped Aggie, snatching it from her hand. 'Lett me seee, lett me seee.'

Myrtle rushed to her sister's side, pushing Gertie roughly out of the way so she could get a better look. 'Welll, what's itt sayy?'

Aggie lay the sheet on the counter, smoothing out the many wrinkles with the tips of her fingers. 'Itt sayss 'Find uss here – Albertt."

'Findd him wheree, Aggie?' cried Myrtle. 'Wheree is hee?'

Aggie paced the floor muttering Albert's words over and over again. 'Findd us heree, findd us heree,' she said loudly. 'Welll, what thee hell doess that meann?'

'Perhapss itt justt meanss findd uss heree?' said Gertie quietly, trying to be helpful.

Gilbert glared nastily at her before addressing Aggie. 'He mustt have escaped from thee palace,' he said. 'I wonderr if he knows where Fredd is?' he added quickly.

'He wass at thee palace – with Artyy?' said Aggie, realising what he'd just said.

'I heardd two Grublins mentionn Albert and the palace as we passedd them in the portall tunnel,' said Gilbert, scrutinising the paper closely. 'I thoughtt I told youu.'

Aggie shrugged her shoulders. He could tell her that the sky was green last week and she'd have to believe him. Such was her memory.

'Whatt does itt mean? Wheree does itt mean?' said Myrtle, jumping up and down excitedly.

'Calmm down andd let mee have anotherr look,' said Aggie, snatching the paper back from Gilbert who was left clutching at the air where the leaflet had been.

On closer inspection she saw that the message was written on some kind of underground newsletter. The print was crudely formed with many spelling mistakes and punctuation errors, but the headline was clear – Hero Required. Below this were many references to the dictatorship rule of Arty Granger, the influx of sprites and the terrible treatment of any who did not comply.

'Hero Requiredd, huhh?' muttered Aggie. 'Hero – Requiredd!' she repeated slowly.

'You'ree not thinkingg ...' began Myrtle.

'Welll,' cut in Aggie, flicking strands of her unkempt black hair behind her shoulder. 'Itt seems a bitt of a coincidencee that ourr brother wrote hiss message onn this newsletterr, doesn't itt?'

'Er, dohh! That's probablyy all he couldd find att the timee,' said Myrtle, crossing her arms and raising her eyebrows to the sky.

'No, thiss is a signn,' insisted Aggie. 'A signn that I'mm needed too save thee fairies off Pilpsville.'

'Ohh, get over yourself. He justt wants us to find himm here.' Gilbert pointed to the writing at the bottom of the sheet.

'Whichh is where, exactlyy?' said Aggie.

'Door seven, nearr the alleyy, past thee pilp plantt, across fromm the libraryy, said Myrtle.

'Welll, that's clear as mucuss isn't it?' said Gilbert, sarcastically.

'Shalll II askk aa guardd?' said Gertie, stepping towards the doorway. 'Theree aree lotss off themm flyingg pastt ...'

'Err, no,' whispered Aggie, pushing Myrtle and Gilbert to the floor. 'I'dd forgotten aboutt them.'

'Andd us nott looking very Grublinyy anymore too,' muttered Myrtle under her breath.

'Yeahh, it wouldn'tt go downn too welll,' agreed Aggie, aware of Gertie's puzzled face peering down at them.

'Whyy aree youu hidingg?' she said, pulling at Myrtle's hair. 'Thosee guardss won'tt doo anythingg – nott withh thee leader'ss prefectt heree! I'lll justt askk ...'

'Err, no Gertie,' said Aggie, grabbing the Grublin-fairy's arm. 'Iff they seee us theyy will take uss to the palacee. They won'tt care thatt you aree the leader'ss prefect. Artyy will rewardd them forr all yourr hard workk.'

'Welll, I'mm nott havingg thatt!' said Gertie, marching across to the far side of the shop, kicking up splinters of glass as she moved.

'No, indeedd,' said Aggie straightening up and flattening herself against the wall. She glanced quickly outside then motioned to the others to move next to her.

'Whatt are wee going too do withh her?' whispered Myrtle, nodding in Gertie's direction. 'We can'tt take herr with uss. She'll givee the gamee away.'

'We can'tt leave herr here eitherr can, wee? She iss, after alll, my bestt friend.'

Gilbert rolled his eyes disbelievingly towards the ceiling and decided that he just couldn't be bothered to correct her for the umpteenth time. He merely offered a sarcastic observation. 'Thanks to you, yourr *best friend* knows exactlyy where we're going andd who we're going to meett.'

Tempted as she was to tell him to shut up, Aggie ignored him and scanned the ruined shop for inspiration. There must be somewhere they could leave Gertie, somewhere secure, somewhere soundproof ...

'The cellarr garden!' she said rather loudly before reducing her voice to just an audible whisper. 'I rememberr now. It's justt below uss.'

'Huhh?' Myrtle stared at her blankly.

'It'ss where Mrs Cherub keptt most of the plantss she greww.'

'Cheric, for goodness sake – it'ss Mrs Cheric,' sighed Gilbert, correcting yet another memory slip.

Aggie's tongue protruded ungallantly from the side of her mouth as she cast her eyes in his direction.

'Huhh?' said Myrtle again, oblivious to the tense atmosphere. 'Howw could theyy grow downn there? It'lll be tooo dark.'

'Lightt tunnels of coursee! Did you reallyy think shee only hadd the plantss in the shopp?' said Aggie. 'There'ss a loadd under heree – well, att least theree was. It'ss a perfectt place too keep thee leader's 'prefectt' for the timee being.'

'Andd she'll have something to talkk to. She can bore the plantss with all herr stuff about the leader andd her mission!' said Gilbert.

'Preciselyy,' agreed Aggie. 'Now gett her over heree.'

'Whatt me?' he said, indignantly.

'Yess, call her overr or somethingg,' said Aggie crunching through the glass to get behind the counter. 'Justt give me a minutee to find the switchh and openn the floor hatchh.'

As she moved confidentally to the back area of the shop, she made straight for the alcove. Bending low, she fumbled under the shelf for the hatch switch. Immediately three parts of the floorboards sprung open revealing the steep staircase for the second time that day.

The warm humid air struck Aggie full in the face, taking her breath away. Holding the sides, she stepped carefully down the stone steps which had been carved out long ago.

As Aggie reached the bottom the dazzling scent of the many flowers hit her full on. It was intoxicating. She studied the rows of different specimens, remembering the names of those she had used in

Mrs Cheric's unusual recipes. The plants whispered quietly among themselves. It all felt like a life time ago, and in many ways for her, it was.

The clambering of footsteps and yells behind her brought Aggie abruptly back to her senses.

'Whatt the helll are you doingg?' said Aggie, addressing the pile of legs and arms on the ground.

'Shee made us alll fall,' said Myrtle crossly, rubbing her elbow. 'We toldd her youu were downn here makingg her potionn and she pushedd right past uss ...'

Gilbert was hugging his arm close to his chest, the pain clear in his eyes. He bit down hard on his lip to stop the tears.

'S'where'ss myy potionn?' asked Gertie. 'II can'tt seee itt anywheree. Alll II cann seee iss leavess andd flowerss andd ...' She stood gazing all around at her green surroundings.

'Woww!' said Myrtle.

'Woww!' said Gilbert, clearly distracted by the sight before him.

'Hmmm! While you aree all wowing, I'lll mix upp Gertie's potionn.' The lure of the amazing underground garden provided Aggie with just the amount of cover she needed to mix up some concoction that might keep Gertie satisfied. Under the stairs she found the cupboard full of vanilla klupe which would form the basis of her drink for

Gertie. She pondered for a few seconds, deliberating on what she could add that would keep the leader's prefect both quite and still. It would only be until they rescued Albert and Fred, she told herself. Then she could fly back and smooth things over with Gertie, who by then, would hopefully be reverted to her former self – best friend and pilp collector.

She stirred in petals of hoplash and smint leaves to disguise the yakspit odour. It probably neither looked or smelt like the Grublin potion issued by Arty, but her secret ingredient of scouder would make it taste and smell of whatever Gertie wanted.

Her memory had at last served her well as she thought of Mrs Cheric's clever juice enhancer for when she ran out of certain ingredients.

She walked carefully over to the flower bed where the other three had gathered. Tapping Gertie on the shoulder, she handed over the hastily made concoction. 'Heree you are, Gertiee. Just as II promised – one mugg of Grublin potionn.'

Myrtle and Gilbert both turned and glared at her. 'You can'tt give her thatt!' said Myrtle. 'She'll go alll Grubliny againn.'

'II likee beingg Grublinyy, thankk youu,' said Gertie between slurps, the red of the hoplash petals staining around her mouth. 'Howw elsee wouldd II bee aa prefectt?'

'Ssshh,' whispered Aggie to Myrtle, behind Gertie's back.

'Mmmm,' sighed Gertie. 'I'vee reallyy missedd thiss tastee. Wouldd youu likee too tryy somee?' She offered the last remaining dregs of the drink to Myrtle who immediately pushed the offending liquid back in her direction.

'What noww?' said Gilbert, watching as Gertie trailed her fingers around the inside of the mug to collect the last few drops.

'Justt wait a minutee …' Aggie watched Gertie's movements intensely. 'It shouldn'tt be that muchh longer …' she whispered.

Gilbert and Myrtle joined in the watching game though what they were actually waiting for they didn't know.

Then the mug smashed to the ground. Gertie's eyelids began to flicker wildly, her arms flailed and her legs trembled.

'Anyy minute … now!' cried Aggie, catching the fallen Grublin-fairy in her arms.

'Whatt the hell have you donee to her?' said Gilbert. 'I knoww she's been going on a bitt, but you didn't have to kill herr!'

'Stupidd! She's nott dead! She's just sleepingg,' said Aggie propping Gertie up against the stairs. 'I put somee yakspit in herr drink. It shouldd keep her quiett for a good feww hours.'

Myrtle breathed a sigh of relief. She poked Gertie a couple of times in the stomach just to satisfy herself that the prefect was comatosed. 'So we cann go now, yeahh?' she said animatedly. 'We can go andd find Albertt?'

'Yess, sister dear,' said Aggie, pulling Myrtle up and pushing her up the steps. 'Let'ss go and findd our brotherr!'

# Chapter Twenty Six

Not far from the juice bar, in one of the grander rooms of the palace, sat the leader. The former common room served well as a dining hall. The furnishings were naturally lavish and expensive. A long dark wood table occupied central position, surrounded by an army of chairs, the seats of which were of the finest gold silk. Hangings adorned the walls, depicting various scenes from the leader's extraordinary life, but it was the huge chandelier of 100 lights that dominated the room.

Arty was having an early lunch with his mother. He wasn't really that hungry, but she had insisted that he ate to keep his strength up.

He picked at the beef and onion pie with his fork then pushed the vegetables around the plate and through the gravy. The foul aroma that penetrated his nostrils made him want to retch.

'I had that pie especially flown in from the human world for you. Do at least try it, dear!'

Arty slammed his fork down on the table. 'It smells, mother! It smells of them!'

'Arty,' said his mother, 'just taste it.'

'Give it to my father. I'm sure he'll enjoy it!'

There was a moment of silence as he thought about what he'd just said. In his newly secured prison cell it was highly unlikely that his father would enjoy anything. A tiny seed of regret swam against the waves of anger in his brain, but was soon drowned by the mighty flow of resentment.

'And how *is* your father?' Martha asked, deliberately keeping her eyes low as she cut her own meal into smaller pieces. 'Has he settled back down again after you blocked his only window and cut his rations?'

'He left me no alternative after helping the enemy escape,' he replied, wearily pushing the plate across the table.

'And what about the Lichens? I take it you've got that all sorted now.'

'I'm working on it,' he said. 'I have two of my finest Grublins checking out their every movement. In fact, I'm expecting a report anytime now.'

Bang on cue, there was a knock at the door. A Grublin face appeared as the door opened. 'Theyy aree backk, myy leaderr. Doo youu wishh too seee themm noww?'

'Yes, of course I want to see them now! Send them in!' Arty leapt off his chair and walked sharply across the room. He was met half way by two exhausted Grublins. Their knees trembled nervously as they bowed low before the leader.

'Ah, Corporal Flobb, Corporal Globb,' he said smiling sweetly in Martha's direction. 'What do you have to report then?'

Arty listened carefully as the two Grublins recalled their encounter with his enemy in the exit tunnel.

'So they were both there, huh?' he smiled triumphantly again at his mother. 'And the Trickle boy too!'

Globb and Flobb then explained how they had followed the group to the old juice bar and listened outside to the plans being made.

'So they are to meet up with the brother.' Arty rubbed his hands together with delight. 'Oh, this is even better than I'd have hoped. We shall have them all in one fair swoop!'

'And what of Gertie Cruet?' sneered Martha. 'I thought *she* was supposed to be bringing the Lichen girl back.'

'Sidedd withh thee enemyy, Ma'amm,' said Globb. 'Wouldn'tt handd themm overr soo herr mustt bee guiltyy.'

'Herr keptt goingg onn aboutt aa rewardd orr wass itt ransomm?' Flobb scratched his head. 'Anywayss, wee offerss too assistt inn bringingg themm backk, butt shee sayss noo – definitelyy guiltyy, yourr sirnesss.'

Arty strode over to the vast window, pushing aside the heavy gold velvet curtains which obscured his view of the outside.

'She will be dealt with severely,' he said, turning to face his mother. 'No one betrays me and gets away with it.'

'Talkingg off whichh, yourr leadershipp, thee guardd saidd anotherr wass waitingg too seee youu,' grovelled Flobb. 'Shalll wee sendd himm inn?'

Arty nodded and waved them away.

The two Grublins backed away towards the door, happy to have delivered the good news, but even happier to be out of the leader's company!

As the last of them left, another Grublin was delivered, or more precisely thrown, into the room. His head caught the corner of a chair as he landed. The gash was large and oozed with blood which trickled down the side of his face.

'Not on the rug!' screamed Arty at those responsible. 'Get him up, get him up!'

The two guards who had dragged the poor creature in, now pulled on his arms and heaved him towards the window wall.

The creature shrieked in pain.

'Mind the tables, you oafs,' the leader cried. 'They were made by blind gnomes in a remote village in the outer peaks.'

'Willl thatt bee alll, yourr goodnesss?' asked one of the guards while planting a hefty kick to the prisoner's leg.

'Yes! Yes! Yes! Now get out!'

The guards backed away to the door leaving Arty and his temper to deal with the prisoner.

Martha had said nothing throughout this latest intrusion on her lunch. Maybe because she had bored of Arty's attempts to show his control of the new nation. Maybe because she knew that no blind gnomes actually existed in the outer peaks. But most probably because she recognised the battered prisoner as the Grublin she had bribed to let the Lichen boy escape ...

Arty kicked at the creature's foot. 'What's your name, Grublin?'

The creature slowly lifted its face, and keeping its eyes low, muttered a barely audible sound.

'Speak up, traitor!' screeched Arty delivering a blow to the creature's face. Its head bounced off the wall leaving a small bloodied stain behind. Arty swore under his breath as he hastily wiped at the mark.

'Itt iss Smitchh, highnesss,' muttered the creature called Smitch.

'Well, *Smitch*, is it true that you allowed the Lichen boy to escape?' said Arty. 'Well, did you?'

Smitch crouched in front of Arty. His hands covered his head to offer some protection from the further blows he might receive. He shook violently as each question was asked. He glanced to the side of the room where a nervous Martha still sat eating her lunch. A worse fate awaited him if he answered any of the questions so he decided to stay silent, much to Arty's annoyance.

'Are you stupid or something?' said Arty, grabbing Smitch by one ear. 'I want answers and I want them now!' He slapped the creature hard across the face then stood back smirking as the blood trickled from Smitch's split lip.

A sudden crash at the table caused both the leader and the prisoner to look up. Martha's fist came down hard on the surface once again. 'How I am supposed to eat my lunch like this?' she screamed, feigning her anger. 'There is a time and a place for torture and this is neither!'

'I need answers, mother!' snapped Arty. 'I need them now!'

'Then take the creature to the cells and torture him there, not in here while I am having my lunch!' She knew he wouldn't want to do that, as this, she sensed, was all part of his bid to impress on her that he was leader not her. How could he do that if she wasn't there to watch? But she had to get Smitch out of the room. She couldn't risk this low life telling everything and spoiling her plans. She pretended to casually pick at her pie then added, 'Or why not let me take him off your hands? I'm sure I could get him to talk – but not before I finish my lunch!'

'Fine! Take him. I was getting bored anyway!'

'Guards,' shouted Martha towards the door.

The two guards returned, bowing low as they approached her.

'Take the prisoner down to the cells. Give him food and water. I'll be down shortly – when I've finished my lunch!'

'Food and water!' scoffed Arty. 'Yeah, that'll get him to talk.'

'He's no good dead is he?' said Martha breathing a huge sigh of relief as the creature was dragged screaming from the room. She steadied the spoon as she placed another piece of beef into her mouth. The prisoner would be dealt with her way – a way that would ensure her dirty secret stayed safe ... and while she was in the cells she could pay a visit to another prisoner – Ferrett!

# Chapter Twenty Seven

Eric Trickle tended carefully to his older son's wounds, fighting hard to hide his tears. A badly bruised eye, a broken rib or two and a split lip formed just part of the list of horrific injuries he had sustained at the hands of Norbert and company.

Fred leant back gingerly on the hard headboard of his bed. He squinted as he looked around, pleased to be back in his own room in the dwarf caves.

'I didn't know it was him at first,' said Albert, guiltily. 'I could just hear them tormenting some poor creature.'

'It's okay, Albert,' said Fred, wincing as Eric dabbed his face with antiseptic. 'You did what you could to keep it all to a minimum. I appreciate that.'

'I should have done more,' said Albert, fluffing up a pillow and placing it behind his friend's head.

'It looks worse than it is,' said Fred, settling back into position.

'Fred's right,' said Eric. 'He'll be as good as new in a couple of days.' He stuck another plaster on Fred's battered body, this time on a cut across his cheek. 'Have you checked on the other patient?' he said to Albert.

'Just a few minutes ago,' Albert replied. 'I'm afraid it's not looking good. That last batch of antidote doesn't seem to have worked either. If it's okay with you, I'll return to my room and get started on the next lot.'

Eric nodded, but didn't look up. With Victor lying at death's door in the next room and his own son badly beaten he felt defeated and, for the first time since the troubles had begun, he actually felt like giving up the fight.

'Don't even think about it,' said Fred, sensing his father's despair. He propped himself up on his elbows. 'This fight continues until Arty is removed and all pilp collectors are restored.'

His son's courage jerked Eric's brain back into action. 'You're absolutely right, Fred. The fight goes on.' He stood up to leave, touching Fred's shoulder gently before he went. 'Rest for a while. I'll wake you if there is any news.' He shut the door quietly behind him, leaving Fred to sleep.

He popped his head around Albert's door as he passed by, but, not wanting to disturb a genius at work, said nothing.

Instead, he made his way down to the room where Victor lay. He pushed open the door, hoping that some kind of miracle had taken place, but was once again disappointed. Victor's body was shuddering and shaking just as it had before and his eyes remained closed.

Eric settled on a dark wooden chest that sat in the corner of the room. While it wasn't the most comfortable of places to sit, it provided the perfect position to watch the sprite. He watched sadly as the body convulsed, rejecting Albert's carefully prepared antidote for the sixth time.

'Come on, Albert,' he muttered under his breath. 'We need this next one to work.'

The time passed slowly as he waited and each little noise outside the door made Eric look up expectantly. Every five minutes or so, he stood up to stretch his legs before retaking his seat on the chest. He glanced at his watch frequently, cursing the slowness of the minutes as they passed. But it was a full hour before Albert appeared at the door with yet another syringe full of liquid.

'Well? What took so long?' he asked, getting to his feet again.

'Sorry, but the ingredients took much longer to combine this time,' apologised Albert. 'I've had to pull in a different variety of herbs which has made the base liquid more difficult to control.'

'But will it work, Albert?' said Eric, brushing aside the technicalities of potion making.

'Will what work?' said Fred, limping through the door. Sleep had not done his face any favours, in fact quite the opposite. His features were now swollen so severely that he was barely recognisable. 'Once again,' he said impatiently, 'will what work?'

'T-T-The new batch of the antidote,' stammered Albert, clearly appalled by the sight of Fred's face.

'I'm just about to give it to Victor.'

'And ... *will* it work?' said Eric, helping Fred to the end of the bed.

'We can only hope,' said Albert tiredly. 'I've tried everything, used everything. We will just have to wait it out.' Then he gently took hold of the sprite's left arm and injected a phial of blue liquid directly into a vein.

Ten minutes passed. The convulsions continued much as before. The sweating continued much as before.

'How much longer?' asked Fred tensely, leaning over to mop Victor's fevered brow again. As he moved he grimaced as a sharp pain raced down his back.

'It should start taking effect in the next few minutes.' Albert wiped the sweat from his own head with the back of his hand then slumped wearily into a chair. Exhaustion seeped from his eyes. He had worked solidly on an antidote for the poison since they'd arrived four hours ago. Six batches had proved ineffective, three of which had in fact worsened the sprite's condition.

Albert hoped deperately that batch seven would prove to be the much needed remedy. If it failed, he would have to start again. He sighed heavily at the thought.

Eric stood at the end of the bed looking on. 'Will he pull through?'

Fred shrugged his shoulders. 'He's done all he can,' he whispered, nodding towards Albert who had just dozed off.

Eric took the damp cloth from Victor's head and dipped it in the bowl of cool water. 'I really thought we'd lost him at one point', he said. 'His breathing had slowed down and the rasping in his chest seemed much worse.'

'So what happened?' Fred perched on the end of the bed.

'I really think he knew you were on your way – somehow. Don't ask me how, but this little sprite knew.' Eric tapped Victor's hand tenderly.

'Did Fid come up with any ideas about how the poison got into his system?'

'He's checked him all over – nothing!' said Eric taking a seat back on the old chest.

'Unless he swallowed it …'

'But,' interrupted Eric, 'treelanch's foul taste can never be covered up. You know that.'

Fred leant over Victor's burning body. His eyes scanned for evidence. 'There must be something,' he said, his bloodied fingers tracing over the sprites arms.

'I told you,' said Eric, leaning back against the wall. 'Fid checked him over and found nothing.'

'Then he's missed it,' said Fred, pressing his hand on Victor's chest. 'It has to be here.'

'Forget it, son. Let him be,' said Eric.

But Fred ignored his father's plea and carried on with his own investigation. He moved his hand across the sprite's body, sweeping this way and that; down the side of the legs, under the arms, across the shoulders. Then the palm of his hand stopped suddenly just above the chest, to the right. He lifted his hand off, looked at it then leant in again for a closer look.

'What? What is it?' said Eric, leaping off the chest.

The sudden fuss disturbed Albert. His eyes sprung open and he too rushed to Victor's side. 'What's happened?' he asked.

'There's a tiny hole – just here.' Fred pointed to a faint mark on Victor's chest. After touching the mark with his finger, he thrust his hand in front of his father's disbelieving eyes. 'See! Discharge!'

Sure enough, on Fred's forefinger, a small trickle of yellowy liquid slowly wove its way down to the centre of his hand.

'In the box, Albert! A glass enlarger – quick!' said Eric, anxiously.

Albert threw open the lid of the wooden chest and, after pushing aside various books and maps, he pulled out a cube shaped cardboard box.

'Pass it over, quickly!' said Fred.

Albert tore open the box and passed the enlarger hurriedly to his friend.

Fred placed the instrument over the mark on Victor's chest then drew a deep breath in anticipation, before looking through it.

'Well,' said Eric, impatiently. 'What do you see?'

Fred stepped away in horror. 'See for yourself, father,' he said shakily, then whispered his horrific findings into Albert's ear.

Eric rushed round to the side of the bed where Fred stood and, after steadying the glass, pushed his eye up to the glass enlarger. He shuddered slightly as the image became clear. A tiny hole just as Fred had said and there, just inside it, was a minute piece of silver metal – like a needle shaft.

'A poison cylinder?' asked Fred.

'Could be,' said Eric. 'Albert, pass me the tweezers – hurry!'

'That's not a good idea, Eric,' said Albert, worriedly. 'If you disturb the needle it could slip further into his skin.'

'And if I don't,' snapped Eric, snatching the tweezers from his hand, 'the poison from it could continue to seep into his body.'

'Why not just wait a little longer?' Albert pleaded as Eric pinched the tips of the metal implement together and bent over Victor's heaving chest. 'The effects of the antidote should be starting to kick in now.'

Eric stopped in his tracks and hung his head. Moments later he lowered the hand with the tweezers and turned his head to look at Albert. 'Half an hour then and if there is no change ...'

'... we take it out,' said Fred, finishing off his father's sentence.

Both left Victor's bedside and headed towards the door. Eric looked back. 'Half an hour, mind.'

Father and son walked back to the large room which housed the cooking stove. Their heads hung low, their hearts sad as thoughts of Victor's impending death flooded their minds.

Thoughtfully, Fid had kept the water boiling and smint tea was immediately brought to the pair as they sat at the huge table. The twins were already seated and for once were quiet.

The next ten minutes or so were silent as each mulled over Fred's gruesome discovery and the events of the last few days.

'I still don't understand how you managed to lose them,' said Eric, out of the blue.

'Not now, father,' said Fred, tersely. He really didn't need reminding of his stupidity at mistaking two of Norbert's henchmen for the twins or his inability to remember where the nearest dwarf bolt hole was.

'I mean, you only had to wait for them to tidy something up and you'd have known ...'

'Like I said, father – not really the time.'

Eric looked at his son's swollen features and shook his head. 'I'm just pleased you all managed to get back in one piece – so to speak!'

Stan looked awkwardly at Alf and shuffled around on his chair. 'W-W-We forgot our training again,' he said quietly. 'If we hadn't stopped to sort the ...'

Eric cut in before the guilt ridden changeling could finish, 'I can't pretend that I'm not disappointed with you both.' He spoke in a quiet tone and looked directly at them.

The changelings' faces dropped, and large tears formed and began to dribble slowly down their cheeks. This was the worst thing Eric could have said to them. Why couldn't he have shouted, screamed or yelled? For him to be disappointed was so much worse.

'Fred could have been killed! But,' he said, holding up his right forefinger, 'He might not have stumbled upon Albert so quickly if you had not been distracted.'

'B-B-But you're still disappointed,' whispered Alf, wiping his eye with his sleeve.

'I'm afraid I am,' said Eric.

More sobbing!

'Oh, father! Just tell them it's okay,' said Fred, tiredly. 'They know they were in the wrong.'

'Okay, okay! Wipe your tears.' Eric passed a rough piece of cloth over to Stan who blew his nose loudly before sitting back down. 'We've got more important matters to attend to.'

'Such as Victor,' said Fred.

'And Aggie,' said Eric.

Fred immediately sat up straight. 'Crikey, I'd clean forgot about that. She's on her way to the juice bar, so Albert said.'

'Yes, if I heard correctly,' said Eric, 'Norbert was expecting her and Myrtle ...'

'Don't forget Gilbert!' mumbled Stan.

Eric gave the twins a harsh look and said curtly, 'I would hardly forget my own son, now would I?'

'I just hope she finds the message,' said Fred. 'We left it on the counter ...'

He had no time to finish what he was saying as Albert came bursting through the door. 'Quick,' he called hurriedly, 'You'd better come.' His face was pale and showed no emotion.

'Has it worked? Is he better?' cried Eric, knocking over several cups in his hurry to get up.

'Well?' asked Fred. The chair he was sitting on crashed to the floor as he stood up urgently.

But while Albert wasn't giving anything away, on reaching the bedroom they were pleasantly surprised to find Victor not only awake, but propped up.

Bod stood by, ready to plump the sprite's pillows at a moments notice.

Eric leapt straight to Victor's side. 'Oh my wings. Aren't you a sight for sore eyes?'

Fred said nothing at first, remembering how angry he'd been with the sprite prior to his illness. It felt a bit awkward, but thankfully Victor broke the tense silence between them by speaking first, 'Albert said you found something in my chest.'

Fred nodded. 'It's still in there. We couldn't risk taking it out at that time.'

'It will have to come out though,' said Albert, 'and soon.'

'A little later, perhaps,' said Eric, protectively. 'I think he's been through ...'

But Victor interrupted him, 'It's okay,' he said quietly. 'Take it out, Albert. Please take it out now.'

'No, you really do need to rest,' said Eric. 'I mean, what about the poison? What if more seeps into your system?'

'The antidote should counteract any further problems with the poison,' said Albert.

'Sounds risky,' said Fred.

'I'd feel better knowing that it was gone,' said the sprite. He lay back on the pillow.

Albert picked up the tweezers and enlarger from the stand where the bowl was and leant over the patient.

'I'll be as careful as I can,' said Albert, pinching the tips of the tweezers in readiness.

He took a deep breath and moved the enlarger into position.

The next ten minutes were laden with sighs, heavy breathing and gasps. It was all that Albert could do to keep his hand steady without the added distraction of an audience. Bod mopped his brow as he pushed the tweezers further into the small hole.

He pressed down lightly on Victor's chest to allow the metal needle shaft to be eased more readily from the skin. The sprite winced a little as Albert moved his hand around to grasp the piece of metal which was proving difficult to remove.

At last the tweezers gripped the silver metal allowing Albert to carefully pull it from its skin sleeve. He placed it in his left hand and stared at it, his head shaking to the right then the left.

'So,' said Eric, 'is it a needle as we thought?'

Albert put the enlarger over his hand and shook his head in disbelief.

'What is it?' asked Fred, brushing past his father to join Albert. He bent over the enlarger and gasped.

Victor looked worriedly at Albert then at Eric.

'Perhaps we ought to discuss this outside,' said Eric aware of the sprite's anxiety. 'Then Victor can rest ...'

'Just tell me something, Victor,' said Albert, cutting across Eric's words. 'Did you never feel something sharp digging into you, something over the last few months or weeks?'

'I can remember having some sharp pains, but I don't recall anything pricking me,' said Victor, his brow creased with curiosity.

'No one bumped into you before you started getting the pains?' said Fred.

'No,' said Victor, 'nothing like that.'

Albert and Fred looked at each other thoughtfully. Something didn't fit, something wasn't right.

'Think hard, Victor. Cast your mind back to when you first started getting the pains,' said Albert.

Victor cast his eyes towards the ceiling as he tried to visualise events over the last months. His face grimaced as he recalled some of the sadder, lonelier times he had spent since betraying the very friends who had now saved his life. He thought back to his many arguments with Norbert and his gang. Then his memory brought up an event he would have rather forgotten about completely, a day of total embarrassment. He thought for a moment before reaching his conclusion. It was the answer both Albert and Fred had been thinking about and expecting.

'I remember now! The pains started just after the medal ceremony ...'

# Chapter Twenty Eight

Lying silently on the bed of matted straw, the Grublin-fairy was barely recognisable. Gone were the round faced fairy features and the cute button nose had been replaced by a hideous three nostrilled monstrosity. The pointed ears remained, but were covered with coarse tufts of hair both inside and out. Where plump brown plaits had once hung, strands of greasy hair clung tightly together. But the Grublin-fairy, although exhausted, didn't sleep. She lay staring up at the ceiling of the wooden hut that had become home. Shared with fifteen others, it was hardly a comfortable existence yet she never complained – she didn't know how to!

Being surrounded by a variety of snorts, grunts, mumbles and sneezes would keep even the deepest of sleepers awake, but that didn't trouble her. The creaking of wooden beds and the cold blasts of air that shot through the gaps in the wall gave her no cause to grumble. Even the comings and goings of shift workers throughout the day could be blocked out so that a decent sleep could be had. But these were nothing compared to the scratching, irritating voice inside her head. No, the voice made sure she would not be resting again before the next shift.

'Bessie,' it said, 'do not drink the potion tonight.'

Bessie turned over onto her side, pushed her hands over her ears and began to think of what she had done at the factory so far that day. But the voice was relentless and pressed its message home once more.

*'Bessie, do not drink the potion tonight.'*

Since the voice had first arrived in Bessie's head, some months ago, there had been no let up in its campaign. In fact, the intensity of its messages had increased daily. And in those six months, Bessie had hardly slept which meant she was exhausted when she arrived for a shift at the factory. This hadn't gone unnoticed by Meltiee and she'd paid dearly for the mistakes her tiredness had caused. A keen fan of the whip, Meltiee took his anger out on Bessie's back on more than one occasion.

And although the voice apologised for causing her so much pain, it continued to haunt her.

*'You are Bessie. Aggie Lichen is your best friend. You are Bessie. Aggie Lichen is your best friend.'*

Desperate for sleep, Bessie turned over again to face the wall. Pulling the thin woollen cover over head, she closed her eyes tightly and waited for the next barrage of information.

In the far corner of the hut, the furthest away from where Bessie lay, a Grublin was unable to sleep. Again, it was not the sounds from the hut or the wind or the noises outside that kept it awake. The reason this creature did not sleep was because it needed to remind Bessie, best friend of Aggie, exactly who she was. For this was not a real Grublin lying uncomfortably on a bed of rotted straw, but Edie, long lost aunt of Stan and Alf Trollit.

Since the very public humiliation of Aggie Lichen outside the pilp plant some time ago, Edie had been part of the factory workforce just like Bessie. But there the similarities ended. For unlike Bessie, Edie was not a pilp collector, she was a changeling, just like her nephews. In addition, having previously worked with mind readers and achieved grade two of her bronze telepathic diploma, she was able to enter minds at will. She was Bessie's tormentor. She was the voice inside her head.

Edie could have easily slipped Meltiee's net and escaped from the factory in one form or another. She could have continued her search for the long lost sons of her twin sister, but she remembered Bessie's kindness in Pershador, where the readers lived. It became her mission in life. She would wear Bessie down until she gave into the voice and refused the drink. Then Edie could reveal herself and make plans for their escape. Until then, she would say nothing, not even look at her – not until the time was right.

# Chapter Twenty Nine

Stepping outside the juice bar for the first time on their own made the three Grublin-fairies realise how much they actually needed the leader's prefect. It had been nearly three hours since they had first arrived there, yet only ten minutes since they left Gertie Cruet.

'Welll, go back andd get her,' said Aggie sharply, after Gilbert suggested it had been a foolish move to knock her out with the special concoction. He was obviously feeling better after chewing the chitwig flowers Aggie had given him to lessen his arm pain.

'It's just thatt,' mumbled Myrtle agreeing with Gilbert, 'she was ourr cover. Now we'ree going to havee to get acrosss town by ourselvess.'

'Justt keep to thee shadows and pulll the scarves downn over your headss,' said Aggie. The scarves, courtesy of Mrs Cheric's bedroom drawer, were all they could find at the time and although not fashion statements, served the purpose of covering their increasingly obvious fairy features. 'She mightt be my bestt friend, but Gertiee would just givee us away. Byy the time wee get back she'lll be restored too normal.'

Suddenly Aggie ushered the younger two to the side of the juice bar, pushing them quickly against the wall as a group of sprites approached.

'Phoaww!' complained Gilbert. 'These bricks still stinkk!'

'Ssshh, you idiot,' whispered Aggie. 'Thosee sprites have gone inside.' She flattened herself against the bricks, pulling Myrtle and Gilbert in close to her. 'He's rightt,' she mumbled. 'They do stinkk.'

'What are theyy doing?' said Myrtle quietly.

Aggie slid along to where the window once was and peeped cautiously through then she quickly moved back into position against the wall. 'I thinkk they just mentioned Norbertt,' said Aggie in a low voice.

'Ugh! You don'tt think that those bitss of sprite were himm, do you?' said Gilbert, the disgust in his voice apparent.

'Alll I know iss that we needd to get outt of here fastt,' said Aggie, trying not to show her interest in the sprite's revelation.

'Butt we can'tt fly fast. They'lll knoww we're pilpp collectors. They'll knoww we're changingg back.' The worry on Myrtle's face was perfectly reflected her sister's expression.

Gilbert looked up suddenly. 'I thinkk I have a wayy,' he said. 'I didd it before … it mightt work … I couldd give it a tryy.'

Aggie and Myrtle glared at each other.

'Try what exactlyy?' said Myrtle.

'Doesn'tt matter now, Gilbertt. Whatever it is, tryy it later.' Aggie edged along to the window again to see what was happening inside. The sprites were checking out the lumps of goo and shreds of clothing. There was lots of nodding, squealing and stamping as they began to realise that the gruesome remains were all that was left of their friends.

'The smelll ...' began Gilbert.

'Lookk, I agree with youu. The bricks smelll awful. But we don'tt have much off a choice ...'

'No, me – the smelll,' said Gilbert frustratedly. 'Whatt if I changedd into the smell ...'

'Okay! Keep itt downn,' cut in Aggie as his voice grew more excited and louder. 'You change intoo the smelll and that willl helpp us how?'

'I'll whizzz around, draw the sprites awayy,' he said. 'It'lll give you two a chancee to find the entrance to thee dwarf tunnel.'

'As muchh as it pains me to sayy so, I'm nott leaving you heree on your ownn.' Aggie grabbed his shoulder, making him look directly up at her. 'Unfortunatelyy, you and Bugface aree all I have inn this world andd I'm not aboutt to let either off you out off my sight.'

'Butt if I chase them awayy, I can still get back heree before they will. II travel a lot faster as a smelll.'

'Ohh, okay then,' said Aggie, quickly.

'Heyy, what was alll that about we'ree all you havee in the worldd?' said Myrtle.

'Soundedd good, huh?' Aggie winked at her sister.

'Noo, seriously, it's aa good idea. Justt make sure you'ree back in tenn minutes or wee really will havee to go withoutt you.'

'Aggie!' said Myrtle. 'Youu can't be seriouss!'

'We alll have to makee sacrifices for thee cause, Bugface, besidess, we don't evenn know if he cann turn into the smelll again yet.'

Aggie gently let go of Gilbert's shoulder and left him to mutter the string of words which formed the spell he always used. As he made himself ready she leant across the window again to look inside the building ... and came face to face with a sprite!

'Aarrgghh!' she yelled.

'bbsshhii!' yelled the sprite.

Backing away quickly from the window, Aggie threw herself in front of the two fairies protectively, except one was missing. 'Where's Gilbertt?' she cried, knowing that the sprites would be around the shop corner in a matter of seconds.

Myrtle held her nose tightly. 'He's behindd you!'

Turning around, the familiar greeny yellow wisp was floating around and with it came the familiar revolting smell.

'And he hadd the cheek too complain about thee bricks!' said Aggie, gripping the tip of her nose. She grabbed her sister and shuffled to the back of the building then waited for Gilbert to perform his trick.

Tearing round the corner came Norbert's friends, snarling, spitting and cursing. They expected to find a creature or two to torture. They expected to have an easy fight. What they weren't quite expecting was to be greeted by a thick screen of yellowy-greeny stuff and an awful stench.

In a matter of seconds, the sprites turned on their toes and ran. And following close behind was the alter ego of Gilbert, snapping at their heels. As the sprites ran, so others joined in the mad stampede heading towards the crossing.

'What noww?' said Myrtle.

'We waitt,' replied Aggie, 'but not forr long.'

They leant back against the wall of the juice bar, taking care to keep well out of sight of any other wandering sprites or Grublins. Myrtle picked at the bricks, trying to identify the individual flavours locked within. Aggie ran her hands through her hair nervously. It was growing back at quite an alarming rate. She twisted some strands around her fingers pulling it this way and that. The smell of Gilbert still lingered in the air, but he was long gone.

With no watch to tell the time, Aggie resorted to counting to sixty for each minute.

'How longg has he beenn gone?' asked Myrtle, impatiently.

'... fifty-eightt, fifty-nine, sixtyy! Probablyy about three minutess,' Aggie eventually replied.

'Sevenn more to go thenn,' said Myrtle anxiously pacing up and down. 'Justt seven more minutess and then ...'

'Ohh, be quiet,' said Aggie. 'You'ree putting me off and making me evenn more nervous.'

'Whatt if he doesn'tt make it backk in time?' said Myrtle. 'Willl you really leavee him behind?'

'Itt won't come too thatt,' said Aggie after counting to another minute. 'He'lll be back.'

'Butt what if ...'

'Justt wait – wait andd see!' Aggie edged towards the end of the shop front and peered round. No sign of sprites, no sign of Grublins, no sign of Gilbert!

'Come onn,' she muttered. 'Come onn!'

She felt a sharp tug on her top. Choosing to ignore it, she continued to gaze into the distance. But the tug came again.

'Timee must be upp, Aggie,' said Myrtle, letting go of her sister's shirt. 'What shalll we do?'

After counting to the tenth minute, Aggie knew they had no choice. They'd waited as long as they could – over ten minutes in fact. It was time to leave.

She turned, took her sister's hand and, after looking all around, flapped her wings ready to fly.

'We can'tt just – go!' said Myrtle tearfully. 'Wee can't just leavee him.'

'He clearedd the way for uss to go. Thatt was the plann. If we don'tt make a move noww all those creaturess will come backk,' said Aggie, her feet just off the ground. 'Andd do you thinkk those sprites willl have forgotten aboutt us – no! They willl tell their friendss and before you knoww it ...'

'Okayy, I get the ideaa,' mumbled Myrtle. 'It's just thatt it seems so wrongg.' She dragged the toes of her shoes along the ground in protest as they took to the air.

There was a last look down. The final glance confirmed that Gilbert was not on his way.

Aggie squeezed her sister's hand gently to reassure her as they climbed higher. Myrtle lifted her gaze. Her eyes were watery and as she blinked, a tiny river ran down each of her cheeks. With little else to say, the two pressed on to their destination.

Apart from Gilbert's after smell, the short journey to the other side of town was completely clear, although one or two dragonflies had crawled nervously out of hiding places to enjoy the eerie peace that filled the air.

On approaching the alleyway they hid in the one of the few remaining trees that had not been destroyed, while Aggie had a quick look at the leaflet Fred had left behind at the juice bar.

'The entrancee to the tunnell should be justt near the back.' Aggie folded the paper and pushed it deep into her pocket.

With her sister in tow, she began to descend, aiming for a shaded area behind the houses. They had just landed when Aggie felt a sudden twitch in her wings. She looked around cautiously, pulling Myrtle in behind her. The twitch started again, this time a gentle buzz purred from the wing tips. Aggie put her fingers to her lips, gesturing for Myrtle to stay quiet.

Twisting the tip of her wing back and forth Aggie tuned in her sixth sense aerial to receive a signal. At first just a crackle was heard, then a hissing, then a pop followed quickly by an almighty scream – a sprite scream!

'Gilbertt must still bee working his smellyy magic,' whispered Aggie. She looked around at where they were, checking for a sign that might lead them to the dwarf tunnels that ran beneath them. 'We needd to find the wayy in quickly, beforee he finishes.'

Keeping back in the shadows, each sister glanced around at the surrounding buildings. The walls around them gave nothing away. Apart from moss, the only other thing that clung to the walls was a mass of graffiti.

'This is hopelesss,' muttered Myrtle, her eyes straining for clues.

'Just keepp looking,' said Aggie, who had now decided to slowly examine each building one at a time. 'There mustt be something heree, somewhere.'

But with each minute that passed the two became more nervous and jittery about being caught. Then suddenly a piece of graffiti on the building opposite caught Aggie's eye.

'Whatt was the namee of that secrett dwarf club?'

Myrtle gave her sister a strange look. 'Howw would I knoww if it's supposedd to be a secrett?'

'Thinkk, Bugface! You're thee one with thee memory!'

Myrtle growled softly, but then pulled a face as she raked carefully through her memories. 'I rememberr someone laughing aboutt the name. I don't knoww who, perhaps itt was me or ...'

'Forgett who, just rememberr what!'

' Dashh or raft orr daze or ...'

'Daft?' said Aggie, pointing to the word spelt out in 30cm high letters. 'Wass it daft?'

'Like II just said,' Myrtle replied curtly, 'itt just sounded aa bit silly!'

'No, you twitt! Was the namee of the clubb D.A.F.T.?'

'Oh, welll it sounds funnyy, so yes, II suppose it couldd be,' said Myrtle looking across the way to the building.

The word D.A.F.T., painted in bright blue letters outlined with a crimson red, was positioned on a wall just above a damp circular patch on the ground.

'Whatt do you thinkk it stands forr?' asked Myrtle.

'Doess it really matterr?' sighed Aggie, taking her sister's hand once more. 'Let'ss just make forr that grey spott on the groundd and hope we'ree right.'

But just as they were about to move they heard the sound of angry voices approaching from above – sprite voices. A clattering on the roof tops declared they had landed.

'jg ju xbto'u gps uibu tujoljoh tnfmm j xpvme ibwf ibe uibu dsfbuvsf jo nz iboe. uibu sfxbse xpvme ibwf cffo njof,' cried one of the sprites.

Aggie realised at once that this was probably the group of sprites that had been inside the juice bar looking for Norbert. She pulled Myrtle back quickly into the shadows, retreating to the darkest depths possible.

'uxp xpvme ibwf cffo cjhhfs sfxbse,' remarked another.

Then a third chipped in, 'cvu j ibwf usbdlfe uifn up tpnfxifsf ofbs. uif bfsjbm tjhobm mfe vt ifsf.'

Aggie stifled a sneeze, knowing that any sudden noise would give them away. She turned anxiously to meet Myrtle's worried gaze. With her eyes wide open, Myrtle was nodding towards her sister's wing tip which was twitching away again madly. She might not have known a lot of Spritespiel, but a twitchy wing tip was never a good sign!

Aggie reached behind, grabbing the tip of her wing tightly in her hand, twisting it back and forth until the twitching stopped.

At that precise moment, a groan was heard from the third sprite. 'j mptu ju!' he said. 'j mptu uif tjhobm.'

'But they here somewhere,' said the first one in broken fairy tongue. 'They not be far. We fly down and look, yes?'

Aggie's heart thumped hard in her chest. The quickened beat led to faster breathing which she fought to keep under control. She knew they had no choice, but to make a run for the grey damp patch on the ground. If it wasn't the tunnel entrance, the sprites had them trapped anyway.

Taking a deep breath, she tightened her grip on Myrtle's hand, nodded towards the damp area beneath the D.A.F.T. graffiti and, deciding it was quicker to run, darted across the courtyard like a forest fire.

'Hey,' screeched sprite one, from the roof tops, 'that's them! Get them!'

The sisters ran for all their worth, adding a flutter of wing power to propel themselves along. The grey patch grew nearer with every step – so did the sprites.

The second and third sprite had joined in the chase, shrieking their alarm out with every move of their wings. They swooped down, just metres away from the terrified Grublin-fairies.

With the grey patch now clearly in sight, Aggie heaved Myrtle in front of her and pushed her towards the area. Four metres, three metres two metres ...

'Jumpp,' screamed Aggie, as Myrtle approached the damp spot.

Needing no further telling, Myrtle closed her eyes, wished, and threw her body onto the grey patch immediately in front of her – and promptly disappeared.

Just seconds behind, Aggie drew a sigh of relief and dived in – head first. But her relief was short lived as a sharp tug on her legs revealed that she was not safe just yet.

Half in and half out of the tunnel, Aggie screamed at her sister to pull. Half out and half in the tunnel, sprite one shouted at his friends to also pull.

Feeling as if she might suddenly split in two, Aggie screamed for her brother. 'Albertt, help!' She knew he must be here, in this tunnel, somewhere. 'HELPP!'

Moments later, the buzzing sound of wings filled the air as Fred, Albert, Eric and the twins came rushing towards them. Following hard on their wingsteps were Fid and Bod ... and Victor.

'Quick,' shouted Fred as they arrived at the bolt hole, 'grab her body. Pull her through.'

Albert took one side of Aggie's waist while Eric took the other, and heaved and heaved and ... down she came collapsing in an untidy heap on top of her rescuers – one sprite still attached!

'I'll take care of him,' said Bod to Albert. 'You take the young misses to the stove room.' He smiled then gestured Fid to take the sprite's other arm.

As they disappeared down the tunnel, Myrtle could hardly contain her excitement. 'Oh, Albertt,' she cried, hugging her big brother tightly. 'I've missed youu so much.'

'I've missed you too – both of you,' said Albert, putting a comforting arm around Aggie's shoulder. '... even though you both stink!' he added, referring to the caked mud they were still wearing.

Aggie looked at him strangely. 'You are *myy* brother, aren't youu?'

'Her memory'ss not that goodd,' said Myrtle, squeezing her brother even tighter.

'It's not thatt I've forgotten, it'ss just that *myy* brother would neverr have admitted to missingg me!' Aggie laughed, something she felt she hadn't done for a long time. There had been so little to laugh about lately, but now here she was with her brother, Fred, the twins and ... Victor!

# Chapter Thirty

'So you lost them! Is that what you're saying, is it?' shouted Arty. 'A perfect trap to catch them all and you lost them. I am surrounded by idiots!'

Martha coughed.

'Yes, yes, mother, apart from you!'

'Welll, itt alll gott aa bitt complicatedd,' said Corporal Globb.

'Itt wass thee spritess thatt gott inn thee wayy, yourr sirnesss,' said Flobb, wringing his hands together. 'Theyy weree alreadyy insidee thee juicee barr whenn wee gott theree ...'

'Andd theyy shoutingg andd screechingg ...'

Flobb took up the story again. 'Thenn wee spotss thee oness youu wantedd hidingg roundd thee sidee andd wee weree justt aboutt too jumpp themm whenn ...'

'... outt fleww thee spritess ...'

'... thenn thee smelll, thee awfull smelll,' said Flobb.

'Wee hadd too escapee. Itt wass terriblee!'

'You lost them because of a smell!' screamed Arty.

'Welll, yess, butt whenn thee smelll leftt wee followedd thee spritess backk intoo townn,' said Flobb.

'Wee weree readyy too pouncee andd everythingg whenn ...'

'... pooff – theyy justt disappearedd intoo thee groundd!' Flobb held his hands up to illustrate the moment.

'Things don't just disappear into the ground, you fool. Magic doors, enchanted entrances – something like that,' snapped Martha.

'Didn'tt seee noo doorr, ma'amm. Noo sparklyy magicyy dustt neitherr,' said Globb, bowing low as Martha swept past to join Arty at the window.

'It'll be the dwarves,' said Arty, after a while. 'Enchanted entrances to tunnels will be down to their magic, you mark my words. And they've set up a secret society called dash or bosh or something because they're not happy with me as leader.'

Martha turned away from him and smirked. They're not the only ones, she thought.

'They must be in league with the Lichens.' He marched across to where Flobb stood. 'Do you think you could manage one tiny weeny thing without messing it up?'

'I-I-I'lll tryy, yerr goodnesss,' replied Flobb nervously.

'Put out the word that no dwarves are to be trusted. Arrest any dwarves on sight on the charge of treason. Have you got that, imbecile?' Arty poked the Grublin several times in the chest to ensure he had. Flobb turned, grimaced and, holding his chest where the leader's finger had dented his skin, walked quickly out of the room. Globb followed too, thankful that this time he had missed out on Arty's cruelty.

'So all are lost – including Cruet?'

'Yes, mother,' said Arty. He was starting to bitterly regret ever deceiving the Lichens into rescuing his mother. 'All are lost, but this time *I* will go myself.'

'You! What can you do?' snorted Martha, revelling in her son's inability to capture his enemies.

'I have the perfect bargaining tool – their parents!' Because unlike me, he thought, they adore their mother and father.

'You'll bargain with them? How weak!' Martha sat herself down on one of the comfier chairs in the room, crossing her legs one over the other.

'No, mother. I'll renege on the deal, of course.' Hell, does she think I'm stupid, he thought.

'And then what?' said Martha, polishing her nails with the edge of her skirt.

'I will imprison the lot of them,' said Arty. 'I'll build a bigger prison where the library is and my father can join them too.'

'And you think that will put a stop to the rebellion?' She pulled at the chain around her neck – a gift from Belcher.

'With them all safely locked away – yes!' said Arty.

So naïve, thought Martha. But she said nothing, knowing that her time to take over would come soon. Then Pilpsville would know what a true leader was!

'Guards,' shouted Arty, abruptly interrupting his mother's thoughts.

As the guards rushed in, Arty outlined his plans to them. He wanted Ma and Pa Lichen brought up from the cells and taken to one of the holding rooms at the back of the palace – the headteacher's old office.

'Then take my father to another holding room in the same area and wait for me there.'

The guards saluted, bowed and scraped several times then left the room.

'Er, your father? Letting your father out of that high security cell is a big mistake!' said Martha.

'Oh, shut up, mother!' snapped Arty, who had clearly had enough of her snide remarks for one day. 'At least my prisoners are still alive!'

Martha jumped up and, feigning anger, shouted back, 'I beg your pardon? What are you insinuating? I was just trying to encourage him to talk.'

'My wings, mother! Even poor Smitch didn't deserve an agonising death like that ... and to give him a medal for being brave, well that's just sick!' He sneered at her in disgust. She really was becoming too much, he decided.

'Oh, I see! Some filthy creature dies and the first person to be accused is me,' screamed Martha. 'What a charming son you are!'

'Well, let's think! How about his desperate struggle with the guards when he knew *you* were going to be his jailer?' Arty stormed across the room and grabbed his mother by the shoulders. 'And what about the terrified look in his eyes when he first saw you, huh?' He pushed her sharply. She fell back hard into the chair she was standing in front of.

Martha gasped, shocked at the force he had shown. 'How dare you?' she screeched as he turned his back to walk away. 'I'm your mother! Show some respect.'

'YOU are a liability! That's what you are!' he shouted without even turning to look at her. He carried on walking until he came to the window then stretched his arms out straight with his hands touching the window sill. He stared at the world he had created; dilapidated and burnt out buildings, empty and demolished stores, squabbling Grublins, screeching sprites. This new land wasn't quite as he had imagined it would turn out. In fact, over the last few weeks things seemed to have got a whole lot worse and with the blasted Lichens at large, he had to act quickly before he lost control completely.

At the back of the room, Martha slumped back down in the chair, trying not to let the contented thoughts of Smitch's death impress upon her face. Treeslanch – of course she knew it was on the badge pin. She'd put it there herself although she hadn't quite expected him to go downhill so quickly. He had to go, after all, she couldn't risk him giving into torture and spoiling all her plans, now could she?

A loud knock at the door pulled her out of her smugness. Corporal Globb put his nervous face around the door and announced that the move was complete.

'I have changed my mind, Globb,' said Arty, still staring out the window.

'Err, sorryy?' said Globb, looking puzzled and half expecting a beating. 'Youu wantt mee too takee themm backk?'

'No, bring my father to me. Keep the Lichens under close guard.'

Martha sat bolt upright. 'Y-Your father? Why bring him here? Are you mad?'

Globb offered a shaky salute and turned to leave.

'And,' said Arty, before the corporal left the room, 'escort my mother to her quarters. Ensure guards are placed outside – for her own protection!'

Martha leapt from the chair and ran over to him, pulling at his arms, but Arty stood firm, ignoring her pleas and continued to gaze outside. 'You're making me a prisoner in my own home?' she screamed as two different Grublin guards entered the room. 'You can't do that! After all I've done for you. I've made you what you are today.' The guards seized her arms and began to drag her, screaming and kicking, towards the door, but she was relentless. 'Without me, you are nothing, nothing! Do you hear me? You won't get away with this!'

Arty listened as the door clicked shut, but the screeching and shouting continued for sometime after until, at last, silence fell.

It lasted all of ten minutes, broken by a sudden urgent rapping at the door. A worried Corporal Flobb pushed open the door and stood trembling just behind the leader.

'Y-Y-Yourr f-f-fatherr,' stuttered Flobb, nervously.

'Ah, yes,' said Arty, 'bring him in, Flobb. I have something I need to discuss with …'

'N-Noo, sirr,' interrupted Flobb. 'Y-Yourr fatherr – hee iss veryy illl.'

Arty's eyes widened as he took in what the Grublin was saying. 'He's ill? So get the healer!'

'Butt sirr, theyy aree withh himm.'

'And?'

'It'ss noo usee, sirr,' said Flobb, quietly, 'hee iss dyingg!'

# Chapter Thirty One

'Oh my wingss!' exclaimed Aggie, examining Fred's face closely once again. 'They must have beatenn you half to deathh.' She brushed her hand gently across his brow where the worst plastered gash was.

Since their arrival, most of the conversation had revolved around how Fred's facial features came to be rearranged and Albert's clever disposal of Norbert and his gang.

Myrtle had also explained in great detail how she and Aggie escaped from the human house, and found then dumped Gertie Cruet.

But one topic had been thoroughly avoided and although they were all desperate to hear news of Gilbert, Eric had taken the matter off the agenda until Victor had gone to bed.

'But I'm fine,' he said protesting as Bod ushered him from the stove room. 'I'm not tired at all.'

'You need to rest,' said Eric. 'We'll talk in the morning.'

The sprite sighed heavily as Bod led him down the passage to his room and mumbled under his breath about the unfairness of it all. Bod tucked him up in bed and waited for a few minutes, by which time the little sprite was fast asleep.

As Bod arrived back in the stove room, the conversation had switched quickly to Gilbert.

'So you last saw him at the juice bar?' said Eric.

'Yes, that's when hee turned into the smelll to give us coverr so we could find thee tunnel.'

'Such a little hero,' said Eric proudly.

'I think it's more about showing off his alter ego, father,' snorted Fred. 'He's always been one for the dramatics.'

'Yes, like the timee he threw himself offf that tree branch inn Spercham Forest.' Myrtle shuddered as she recollected the horrific fall.

'And he seemed okay?' asked Eric.

'Well, his arm wass still quite painful, but II gave him a handfull of chitwig petals fromm the cellar garden to dulll the pain,' said Aggie, trying to catch Albert's eye.

He looked up and understood at once. Leaving Myrtle to answer the rest of the questions, the brother and sister slipped away to the kitchen to talk in earnest.

'Have you seen anythingg of Ma and Pa?' Aggie asked, sitting on a stool near the fire. As more memories flooded through her brain, she was desperate for news of her parents.

'I only know that they were kept in the palace, like me. The guards sometimes brought me messages from them, but they became fewer as the months went by.' Albert's face sank as he spoke. He looked at the ground as if the answers Aggie needed might be there.

'Albertt, this isn't your faultt. This is all partt of Arty's revengee on me. If anyone's too blame it's me.' She took a moment, while she was speaking, to look him over. He was so skinny and so pale. His long dark hair fell limply over his eyes. It was not a good look for a teenage tooth fairy.

'Let's not blame, Aggie. Let's just do something about it,' he said, softly. 'We must assume that Ma and Pa are still at the palace. We need to rescue them and escape before he finds us.'

'I'mm sorry?' Aggie said, sitting up straight. 'Did you sayy escape, as in, runn away?'

'Yes, Aggie. Eric wants to fight on, but we must get our parents and go. We can make a new life somewhere – perhaps in the human world ...'

'Aree you mad? Hass prison life done somethingg to your brain?' she screamed. "Hero Required' – that's whatt the leaflet said ...'

'It was just an old leaflet ...'

'It was a signn, Albert. A sign thatt I am needed once againn to save our world fromm the likes of Arty Granger.' She stood up and placed her hands firmly on her hips in typical Aggie style.

Albert took one look at her and laughed loudly. 'Ah ha! There you are! I knew you were in there somewhere! Fred said you'd take much longer to adopt the 'hero' persona.'

'Whyy you ...' Aggie slapped him playfully on the arm.

Albert's teasing broke the ice between them and before long they had entered into a deep conversation where life in prison was explained, the palace layout was described and the basis of a plan began to emerge.

It was some time later that Bessie's name was finally mentioned albeit in a few short sentences. For, as far as anyone knew, Bessie had been taken to Meltiee's metal works and not been seen or heard of since.

'Ma and Pa first,' said Albert, 'then Bessie.'

Aggie nodded. 'Followed by Ferrett and Edie.'

# Chapter Thirty Two

As in most places of work, rumours were rife at the metal works. The Grublins told tales of how the leader was about to take over the human world, according to palace guards. They whispered about the leader's plans to detain all the Lichen family in a newly built, high security prison. With little else to do, but guard the workforce, they believed most of the rumours that were circulated – except for the latest one about the leader's mother.

'Youu liee,' shouted the Grublin to the one seated by the fireplace. 'Thee leaderr wouldd neverr doo thatt too herr.' He spat on his sleeve and wiped away dust from the framed picture of the leader's mother that hung above the fire.

'That'ss whatt Fligg saidd,' said the seated Grublin. 'Hee heardd itt fromm Plitt whoo workss inn thee palacee kitchenn, whoo heardd itt fromm Girtt, onee off thee guardss.'

'Leaderr iss nott likee thatt. S'rubbishh!' The Grublin smacked the seated Grublin round the head roughly with a piece of firewood from the bucket. 'Don'tt bee sayingg anymoree aboutt thiss, huhh?'

The injured creature fell back, landing heavily on his rear in a pile of black cinder ash. 'N-Noo,' said the Grublin, rubbing his head vigorously. 'Ii sayy nothingg moree.' He climbed cautiously back on the stool, cursing under his breath at the Grublins who had passed this particular rumour on to him.

They had barely noticed a third creature filling grey juice bottles in the corner of the poorly lit room.

It had heard the whole conversation, but showed no emotion and just continued with the morning top up drinks.

Arranging the bottles in twelves, it proceeded to place each group into the metal carriers especially made by Meltiee, the factory owner. They were stacked against the wall, four high, awaiting the Grublin collection squad's arrival. One bottle, however, remained with the creature in the corner, tucked deep into a carefully concealed pocket. With a quick glance across the room, it quietly exited through the nearby door, making its way across the open yard to the factory floor.

Slipping around the side of the building, it waited patiently until the collection squad had picked up the last of the metal carriers then joined in at the back as they entered the factory itself.

As each juice bottle was distributed to the workforce, a member of the collection squad watched as the contents were consumed. Thankfully, the whole procedure took some time allowing the juice filler to find the recipient for its bottle. It moved in close to where she stood assembling metal stands for sprite fighting clubs.

Thrusting the bottle into her grubby hands, it made sure she drank every last drop of the potion before replacing the lid and concealing the bottle once more in the deep pocket.

'Whoo aree youu?' it whispered, leaning in to her left shoulder.

The bewildered Grublin-fairy said nothing. Its dark eyes stared at the ground below. Its brow furrowed. Matted strands of brown wavy hair fell over its saddened face.

'Whoo aree youu?' repeated the juice filler, lifting the creature's face up to meet its own eyes.

'I-I-I amm B-B-Bes ...'

'Youu aree Bessiee,' it said, flicking the hair from her eyes.

'I-I amm B-Bessiee.'

'Andd whoo amm II?'

'Y-Youu aree Ediee,' said Bessie.

She's ready, thought Edie to herself. They would go tonight.

# Chapter Thirty Three

'What do you mean?' cried Arty. 'There must be something you can do?' His hands grasped the wooden bedpost tightly while his eyes scanned madly around the former headteacher's room which was now home to Ferret and his illness.

'We've tried everything we have. Nothing seems to help,' said one of the healers backing away from the bed where Ferrett lay. 'It would help if we knew what we were dealing with.'

Arty pushed the healer away angrily. 'I don't understand. He was fine yesterday.' He looked to the guards standing at the door. They nodded in unison.

'Perhapss it'ss somethingg hee atee,' said Corporal Globb, trying to be helpful.

The healers explained, in simple terms, that food poisoning did not produce the effects that Ferrett was suffering. When Globb cocked his head to one side indicating that he didn't quite understand, they tried explaining again.

'Oh, just get him out of here!' screamed Arty.

The guards moved in quickly and dragged the bewildered Globb from the room.

Arty pulled the curtains hard across the window, blocking the remaining daylight out. A small bedside light was switched on, emitting a soft glow in the room.

'Chair!' he demanded, snapping his fingers. Immediately, a large armchair was brought around to the side of the bed by the guards. After pummelling the cushions several times he perched himself on the chairs edge and began picking at his fingernails.

The healers shuffled to the back of the room, whispering ideas and thoughts to each other in search of some solution to the problem.

The convulsions had grown worse in the last hour and despite frequent moppings of his brow with cold water, Ferrett's fever stubbornly remained.

'Does my mother know?' said Arty after a while. 'Does she know he's dying?'

'I believe she was informed earlier,' said the younger healer softly, as she attempted to take another temperature reading from the patient.

'What did she say?' said Arty. 'How did she appear?'

'I'm afraid I do not know,' said the healer, now on the second reading attempt. 'One of the guards told her.'

'Then I shall see for myself,' he said, leaping from the chair. 'Let's see what she knows.'

Pushing the guards aside, he ran from the room, tearing down the corridor until he came to his mother's quarters. On seeing him approach, the guards stood sharply to attention, then opened the door to let him in.

'Ah! At last.' cried Martha as he entered. 'I hope you've come to take those guards away from my door. I have a late appointment to have my nails done in 15 minutes. Shutting me up like this! It's an infringement of my rights ... '

'Your nails!' cut in Arty angrily. 'What about father? He's ill, you know.'

'Yes,' said Martha, grabbing her coat from the wardrobe, 'and what do you want me to do?'

'Don't you even care that he might not survive?'

'In a word – no!' she spat. 'And I'm surprised that you do, after all, weren't you the one who had him imprisoned?'

'That's different,' snapped Arty. 'I don't want him dead, not now.'

'At a more convenient time then,' said Martha sarcastically. 'When it suits you better?'

'I only kept him in prison because you said he was dangerous,' spat Arty. 'You said he needed to be kept under control or he'd spoil everything.'

'And I was right, wasn't I? You have all you ever wanted; wealth, power, control over the pilp collectors. You have it all!' screamed Martha. 'And what do I have – imprisonment!'

Arty slammed his hands down on the dressing table near to where she stood. 'He is dying, mother! They cannot save him.'

'That's what imprisonment does to you. I suppose I'm next.'

'You think I did this – to my own father!' He grabbed the brush from her hand and threw it across the room furiously.

'Who knows what you are capable of!' cried Martha. 'You've turned all pilp collectors into Grublin-fairies with that potion. You allow sprites to roam freely. And I've heard rumours that humans are now aware of our existence. Oh no, I don't think you'll stop at anything to get what you want.'

'Why you ungrateful ...'

Martha jumped up from her chair and ran towards the door screaming, 'Guards, guards! He's going to kill me. Help!'

The door was thrown open instantly and in rushed the two guards from outside.

'Quick,' she cried, 'he wants me dead – he wants us all dead! Do something!'

One of the guards called for reinforcements as the other stood across the doorway, blocking Arty's exit.

'Let me through! I am the leader of this land. Let me through!' he shouted at the Grublin guard.

'II amm sorryy, yourr highnesss, butt II cannott alloww youu too harmm yourr motherr. It'ss justt nott rightt.'

As the guard stood firm, Arty could only watch as his mother skipped down the corridor towards the bedroom where his father lay. She blew him a kiss knowing the effect her action would have on him.

He punched the wall in anger. How could he have let this happen? Didn't his father say not to trust ...

Then the awful truth suddenly dawned on him. He slumped to the ground, head in his hands. 'It was her. She did it,' he muttered.

The second guard, now with reinforcements behind him, stepped into the room and stood over him. 'Sirr, wee needd too movee youu fromm heree.'

Arty looked up slowly. 'I am the leader. I will leave when I choose.'

'Sorryy, yourr sirncsss, butt yourr motherr hass justt orderedd uss too placee youu inn thee cellss. Sayss youu aree aa dangerr too yourselff.' As he spoke, four Grublin guards pulled Arty to his feet and began to march him through the door.

'But she's killing him,' he screamed, kicking out and thrashing his arms about. 'She killed Smitch too.'

'Shouldn'tt sayy thatt, sirr,' said one of the guards. 'She'ss yourr motherr.'

'But she's killing my father. Stop her!' With his feet trailing along the ground, the former leader was dragged down the stairs to his new apartment in the basement – the cell formerly occupied by Albert.

'You can't leave me here!' he screamed as the guards padlocked the metal door. 'He'll die! You have to stop her.' He rattled the metal bars, screaming as they left. 'She'll kill him, just like Smitch.'

But his words were left unheard as the guards returned upstairs to take orders from their new leader.

Kicking the bed and the table leg did little to quench Arty's fury, only hurting his foot in the process. He swept the contents of the table surface angrily onto the floor with his arm, smashing dirty cups and plates onto the filthy concrete floor.

Finally, after breaking the wooden chair against the cell bars, he admitted defeat and threw himself down on the dirty mattress that would become his bed.

As the rage inside him surged again, he fought against it knowing that he must focus if he was to save his father.

'I had these cells built,' he said out loud, hoping to remember a secret way of opening the door. But he knew that he had ordered them to be made completely escape proof. 'So how did Albert Lichen get out?' He jumped up and ran to the cell door, examining the lock where the new padlock hung. Brushing his hand across and through it, he looked in surprise as a black powder appeared on his finger tips. He smelt it. Firepowder! So that's how Albert did it! He must have bribed the guards to get it. But how would they have got hold of it?

Arty backed away from the door as his thoughts gained momentum. He had the only key to the storeroom where the firepowder was kept. It was kept on a chain attached to the inside of his trousers. He patted his pocket. The rattling sound proved the key was still safe.

The only other keeper of firepowder in Pilpsville was Meltiee, the manufacturer of the deadly concoction. To ensure no foul play occurred, they had two locks placed on each of their storerooms. Arty held one key while Meltiee kept the other. The only way to access the firepowder was together, using both keys.

He patted his trouser pocket again, a tinny sound rang out. Ordinarily, this should have satisfied him, but in the circumstances he decided to pull the key out for closer examination. And there in his hand was exactly what he'd dreaded – a duplicate key. 'Stupid, stupid, stupid!' he cried. It looked pretty much the same shape as the original, but as Arty looked closer, the total give away was the poor craftsmanship and the badly inscribed key cutter inscription – *SpreegleSprite*.

'But they'd have still needed the other key,' he said, puzzled. 'Meltiee would not have trusted any creature ... any creature except mother!'

Then his mind rolled and rolled as he pieced the final parts of the puzzle together. 'She must have had it copied and given it to the guards, knowing that Albert would try and escape.' He thought carefully about it. Her only slip-up seemed to be returning the duplicate rather the original key. 'Huh!' he said, 'Making me look a complete idiot. Making it seem that I had lost control.' He threw the key across the room and screamed, 'What a fool I've been, trusting her when all the while she wanted everything, all for herself.'

He sat despondently on the bed, his face to the floor. 'And what did father say to me, over and over again – don't trust her.' He held his head in his hands, shaking it from side to side in disbelief.

A mixture of anguish and a feeling of stupidity then took over Arty's brain as he went through the events that had led to his sorry situation. He took his frustration out again on the cell, this time on the mattress, thumping and punching it hard and often.

He had to get out. He had to save his father, but how?

# Chapter Thirty Four

'So where is he now? Where's Gilbert?' said Victor, sitting up in bed. 'Can I see him? I have to talk to him.'

'He's only just arrived. Give him chance to settle and then you can talk,' said Fred, patting the sprite on the shoulder. 'You'll see him soon enough.'

He left him in the safe hands of Bod who had been nursing the sprite back to health ever since Albert had discovered the antidote.

Eager to get back to the stove room, Fred opened his wings a little to give an extra boost down the corridor, then fluttered gently in, seating himself next to his brother.

'So then what happenedd?' askcd Myrtle. 'Did they know it wass you? Did thcy rcmcmber fromm the last time you stinkedd them out?'

'Well,' said Gilbert, chewing on another handful of chitwig petals. 'I drew them close to the portall, hoping they'd go through. I wove up and down and all around themm.'

'Wow!' said Alf. 'You are so brave getting near to all those sprites and Grublins.'

'Yes,' agreed Stan, 'it must have been very scary with so many near to you.'

'Yeah, yeah, yeahh! What a hero!' said Aggie. 'Noww can we just get onn with it?'

'Well, as I was saying,' said Gilbert, glaring at her. He lowered his voice and in dramatic tones, continued with the story. 'I drove themm to the crossing portal. The wind was fierce and the suns were setting ...'

'No, theyy weren't! It was just this morningg!' cried Aggie, jumping up from the table. 'Oh, I don'tt have time forr this. I have to save our worldd – again. Then there's Ma andd Pa to rescue, not to mentionn Bessie ...'

'Perhaps,' interrupted Eric, 'if you'd just tell it like it was, Gilbert. We really don't have time for *any* exaggeration.'

'Okay,' said Gilbert. 'I drove them to the crossingg. The portal opened ...'

'How can the portal open in the daytime?' interrupted Aggie. 'You're doing it again ...'

'Actually, he's telling the truth,' cut in Eric. 'The sprites have fixed the portal to open anytime, day or night.'

Aggie's face dropped in disbelief. 'Anytime?' she said.

'Yes, anytime. Noww may I continue?' snapped Gilbert, looking straight at her. 'They all flew through the portal.' He paused for a few seconds then added, 'Then they all flew backk!'

'What?' said Albert, who up to now had said very little. 'They all flew back through the portal?'

'Yes!' said Gilbert. 'Once they'd all gone throughh, I left it a few minutes then decidedd to change back and try to lockk the portal behind themm. But before I could do so, they all came flying backk.'

'So that's why Norbert's friendss found us so quicklyy,' said Myrtle, looking at Aggie.

'Why did they come back? What did they see?' said Alf and Stan in unison.

'Not whatt, but who?' said Gilbert. 'After they all flew out I stayed in myy smelly form and wove my way down the portal tunnell – and there she was.'

'And there who was?' said Fred.

'The human! The Maddie childd! The one who had us trapped in the jarss.' Gilbert threw his hands up in the air dramatically. 'Her face – looking through *our* portal tunnell.' He slumped, as if exhausted, onto the table.

'Just pigging marvellouss!' said Aggie. 'I should have known she wouldn'tt have given up so easilyy.'

'There'll be hell to pay now,' said Eric. 'Those humans, they'll stop at nothing to seek us out. This is the end of Mirvellon!'

'We needd to warn every creature inn the land,' said Myrtle. 'But where willl we all go?'

'We can worry about that later,' said Eric, taking control. 'The most important thing is to get as far away from the portal as ...'

'Stopp! Listen to me!' shouted Gilbert above the din, 'I think I may have putt her off.'

It all went quiet once more and all eyes were back on Gilbert. 'I triedd to use the smell against her, but she didn'tt seem that bothered by it. She was more interestedd in all the sprites and Grublins she'd just seenn.'

'So what did you do?' asked Fred.

'I changed back to my fairy formm ...'

'And that stopped her how?' said Albert.

'It wasn't that! It was the dustt,' said Gilbert. 'I blew it in her face. I think it did the trickk.'

'You had magic dust on you?' said Eric.

'There was a tiny bit left in my pocket,' said Gilbert.

'Andd you think it workedd,' said Aggie, a little taken back at Gilbert's quick thinking.

'Well, she certainlyy sniffed it in because she sneezed, but it was only a tiny bitt.'

'A temporary fix is better than nothing,' said Eric. 'It will hopefully give us enough time to sort the problems out here first. You did a good job, son.'

'Yes, welll done,' said Myrtle, patting him on the back.

Even Aggie was forced to agree. Gilbert had thought and acted quickly in a bad situation. She reluctantly admitted that he was a hero.

'But onlyy temporary,' she said, 'just until the dustt wears off!'

After a quick celebration with rose petal wine, the youngest were packed off to bed, leaving the others to make plans.

'Butt why do I have to go noww?' said Myrtle as Pod led them all to the bedrooms. 'And howw come Gilbert gets to stayy up longer?'

Pod swung the lantern out in front. 'He needs some time with Victor. Now hush and go to your room.' He gently prodded her back, urging her to go in the right direction. She did so reluctantly, shutting the door of the room behind her.

In the stove room, plans were already being set for the next day. Eric spread out a large map of Pilpsville across the table. It was an old one from before the take-over by Arty. Aggie looked it over, thinking about better times when Ma and Pa were with them, and Bessie was around. As she glanced up, she could sense a similar feeling in everyone. They really did need to get Pilpsville back to how it was before – only then could they confront the other danger of human invasion.

'So we'll sleep a little now, then go underground to the palace and find your Ma and Pa,' said Fred.

'And the youngsters can stay here with us. They'll be safer that way,' said Eric.

'You mean you're not coming with us?' said Fred, as shocked as the others.

'I need to be here with the dwarves. I'm their only link between the world above and the world below.'

He patted Fred's shoulder. 'If anything goes wrong, I'll be the back up plan.'

'Oh, that's very reassuringg,' said Aggie, sarcastically.

'And what about Arty?' said Albert.

'Let me deal with himm,' said Aggie. 'He and I have a feww scores to settle!'

With all things agreed, each went their separate ways to their rooms. After a good sleep, they would be ready to put their plans into action and, once again, save their world from the evil Arty Granger.

It all sounded perfect – except to Myrtle, Gilbert and the twins who had been listening in to the conversation of the older fairies.

'They meann to leave us here, after all I've done!' whispered Gilbert, a disgusted look forming on his face.

'That's justt not right!' said Myrtle in a low voice.

'And what about us? We have been very useful and did almost no tidying up in the last mission,' said Alf quietly.

Myrtle looked at him, frowning.

'Well, okay, said Stan, wringing his hands, 'we did do a little too much last time, but we definitely won't do it again, will we Alf?'

Alf nodded at his brother. 'And,' added Alf, 'they haven't even mentioned Edie.'

This gave Myrtle an idea, a stupid idea, but an idea nonetheless. 'We'll rescue Edie!' she said, proudly. 'If they can't be bothered, then we'll do it.'

'What about Victor?' said Alf, sheepishly. 'Are we going to take him?'

The three awaited Gilbert's reaction. He hesitated for a moment then produced a small green sprite from behind his back.

'You're friendss again?' said Myrtle, softly.

'Well, we've been talking about thingss,' said Gilbert. 'I'm not sure that we're really friendss again yet.'

Victor looked on sadly, but said nothing.

'But we're going to tryy,' added Gilbert, patting the sprite's back.

The twins glanced at each other and smiled. 'So we all go, yes?' said Stan.

'Yess,' said Myrtle. 'We'll all go – tonightt!'

# Chapter Thirty Five

Far on the other side of Pilpsville, deep inside the filthy hell hole known as Grublin City, stood the metal works. It dominated the sky line with its brown mud brick outline and its enormous signage from which you had no doubt that Meltiee was the owner. The sheer size of the factory alone took in the space of at least thirty Grublin houses. All roads in the city led directly to it, meaning that thankfully, for Edie, the way out of the city was a direct route too.

It would be so much easier to just fly up and out, she thought as she crept across the hut to the bed where Bessie lay sleeping. But Edie knew, along with all others, that this was not an option. The infamous poisonous fumes and gases from the River Grub, on which the city stood, rose and hovered menancingly overhead making any escape that way completely impossible. For them, the only way out was along the grime laden streets and through the closely guarded city gate. Edie gulped as she thought of the task ahead, but knew it had to be this night. She had been weaning Bessie off the Grublin potion for the last two days. Any longer and Bessie would be too alert, less Grubliny and draw attention to herself and Edie. But at least the watered down potion and repetitive thought insertion, seemed to have at last brought Bessie back to some of her fairy senses.

Now all Edie had to do was persuade Bessie to leave with her and then they would begin the long haul back to Pilpsville.

'Bessiee, Bessiee,' whispered Edie, closely into Bessie's ear.

'Leavee me alonee,' said Bessie, sleepily. She slapped both her hands quickly over her ears. She knew the routine. Night after night the voice appeared inside her head, and it seemed that this night was to be no different.

'Bessiee, it'ss mee – yourr Grublinn friendd,' said Edie, shaking her a little.

'Noww Grublin friendd gets inn my headd, ah!' mumbled Bessie, pulling the tatty blanket over her head. 'Lett me sleepp.'

Edie shook her a little harder then pinched her arm lightly when she didn't respond.

'Ouchh!' Bessie sat up, rubbing her arm vigorously where Edie had pinched her. 'Whatt do youu want?' she said, blinking furiously. 'It'ss not timee for drinkss yet. It'ss not evenn morning.'

Edie put a finger to her lip to motion her to be quiet. 'Wee havee gott somethingg speciall too doo tonightt! Wee aree too goo too thee leader'ss palacee too collectt aa speciall ingredientt forr thee bosss.'

Bessie lay back down and said, 'Find anotherr. I amm too tiredd.'

'Butt hee askedd forr youu personallly. Lookk, hee evenn gavee mee hiss keyy too thee storee att thee palacee.' Edie held out the key in her hand for Bessie to see.

This time the Grublin-fairy took notice. 'It'ss bright andd shiny,' she said, sitting up again and brushing her hand across its smooth surface. All Grublins and Grublin-fairies had a thing about sparkly, shiny objects. They collected them as trophies, boasting to each other about their spoils.

'Thee bosss evenn saidd thatt youu aree too lookk afterr thiss keyy forr himm,' said Edie, dangling the key in front of Bessie's eyes.

'Welll, I supposee if that'ss what hee said.' She grabbed the metal object from Edie's hand, stroking it lovingly before placing the cord it was on around her neck.

After helping Bessie get dressed, Edie guided her charge through the darkness and the mass of snoring Grublins to the outside door. It creaked loudly as they pushed it open, but not enough to disturb the sleeping creatures from their heavy slumbers.

'Comee Bessiee, foloww mee,' said Edie, unfolding her short, stubby Grublin wings. She would have liked to have changed into her normal fairy state as those wings were much stronger and faster, but that would have to wait until they were outside the city walls. Being a fairy in Grublin City was a risk no fairy would want to take.

Edie took Bessie's hand and led her towards the factory exit. As a Grublin-fairy, Bessie had never been outside of the factory site. She had spent all her time in the metal works or asleep in the hut. She looked around as they approached the door to leave the factory grounds then joined Edie in the street outside.

'Youu needd too openn yourr wingss, Bessiee,' said Edie, fluttering her own wings wildly. 'Wee needd too gett movingg. Thee bosss saidd itt wass urgentt businesss.'

Unbeknown to Edie, Bessie had never actually flown with Grublin-fairy wings. There had never been a need or a time when she'd had to use them so even the opening of her wings was a new experience.

'Justt pushh, throughh yourr shoulderss, hardd,' said Edie, demonstrating what she meant. She watched as Bessie puffed and panted yet still no wings appeared.

'Okayy, there'ss onee otherr wayy,' she said looking around warily. Time was getting on. They had to get moving. 'Rightt, thiss timee, putt yourr rightt thumbb inn yourr mouthh andd bloww reallyy, reallyy hardd.'

Pop! Out came the wings – short and stubby, but most definitely wings.

'Greatt! Noww givee themm aa flutterr.'

Bessie flapped the wings together quickly and

before long she was tucked in behind Edie, flitting and fluttering as best she could.

They kept to the shadows, avoiding the ale houses where Grublins drunk well into the early hours, bypassing the houses where candles still burnt in the windows. In their current form they would not attract attention, but to be out so late and flying towards the city gate might pose a few problems, and there was the guard to get past yet!

'Keepp inn. Keepp inn,' whispered Edie, hurriedly as a small group of very drunk Grublins emerged from the Gass Portt Innn. She pushed Bessie into a side alley, allowing the Grublins to pass before moving on.

'Whyy do wee have too hide?' puffed Bessie, the effort of new wings clearly taking its toll.

'It'ss speciall andd secrett rememberr?' said Edie. 'Andd itt wouldn'tt bee veryy secrett iff thosee Grublinss foundd outt, noww wouldd itt?'

Bessie shrugged her shoulders then carried on, panting as she flew.

From then on the filthy smog, that rose from the river, provided the perfect cover, swirling around the lamps, weaving in and out of the alleyways.

'Almostt theree,' said Edie, taking Bessie's hand for the last few hundred metres. 'Andd justt onee guardd onn thee gatee!'

With the means to escape firmly in their sight, the two flew on, landing just a metre or so away from the gate.

The Grublin guard was slumped against the city wall, picking his nails with a thin shard of silver metal. He was incredibly overweight which was best demonstrated by the huge beer belly that hung over his brown checked trousers. The long black jacket he wore was at least two sizes too small, riding high up his arms to reveal the sleeves of a blue striped shirt that clearly belonged to a creature half his weight.

As they approached, his third nostril sniffed the air and he steadied himself into an upright position. He was somewhat surprised at having visitors at such a late hour.

'Whoo goess theree?' he said, staring ahead. 'Whatt d'yaa wantt?'

'Wee needd too goo outt forr aa whilee,' said Edie pushing Bessie behind her.

'Noo onee leavess thee cityy att nightt withoutt permissionn, youu knoww thatt,' he said, stretching his arms across the gateway.

'Wee aree onn aa speciall missionn forr Meltiee, noww lett uss throughh!' growled Edie in her best Grublin accent.

'Noo onee leavess withoutt permissionn!' repeated the guard.

'Wee havee too goo too thee palacee. It'ss veryy importantt.' Edie scowled her best Grublin scowl.

'Likee II sayss,' said the guard. 'Noo onee leavess withoutt ...'

'Whatt aboutt aa speciall paymentt?' interrupted Edie, thrusting a shiny silver spoon into his hand.

The guard ran his finger over the surface of the spoon and held it up to the lamplight.

'Hmmm, perhapss II couldd lett onee off youu throughh,' he said, standing aside for Edie. 'Thee otherr willl havee too stayy heree.'

Edie pulled a piece of clean silver foil from the depths of her pocket. It sparkled in the moon's light.

'Veryy nicee,' said the Grublin, snatching it eagerly from Edie's hand, 'butt nott enoughh.'

'Whyy youu ... ' cried Edie.

'Butt thatt,' said the guard, staring at the key around Bessie's neck, 'willl doo veryy welll. Yess, II havee thatt.' He leant forward to grab the key, mesmerised by its smooth, shiny surface which glistened in the light as Bessie moved.

Bessie immediately pushed the key back inside her top, away from the guard's prying eyes.

'That'ss whatt II wantt. That'ss whatt itt willl costt,' said the guard, resuming his position of slumped against the wall.

'Noo! Wee needd thatt ... forr thee, err, missionn,' explained Edie, trying to hide the panic in her voice. 'Thee leaderr iss expectingg uss too bringg itt ...'

A sudden shrill whistle interrupted the tense negotiations. The guard grabbed the communication pipe from the wall, placing it from ear to mouth alternately. ''Yess sirr, itt iss thee dutyy guardd, Splidgee, sirr.' He shuffled in close to the wall, his back turned to them as he continued the conversation with the central guard house. 'I'mm sorryy, sirr. You'ree nott veryy clearr. Didd youu sayy Mrr Meltiee'ss teaa hass beenn stolenn?'

Edie's heart thumped in her chest. She gulped loudly and looked over at Bessie who was just glaring at the guard.

'Aree we goingg back?' said Bessie. 'Onlyy I havee to bee up earlyy to gett to workk.'

Edie smiled then took her arm gently and pulled her towards the gap in the gateway. The guard was now to the right of the gate, scratching his head as he tried to makc scnsc of the urgent call.

'Sorryy – aa stolenn treee?' he said. He tapped the pipe a couple of times on the palm of his hand, trying to clear the line. 'Onlyy II thinkk I'dd havee seenn someonee goingg throughh thee gatee withh aa treee!'

The gap was just wide enough for them to squeeze through although Edie couldn't help thinking that as fairies they'd have slipped through easily. They crept forward, step by step, with Edie keeping a close eye on the guard.

'Noo, noww youu makingg noo sensee att alll, sirr! Cheesee?' he said, looking up to the sky in disbelief. 'Youu ringg mee too sayy someonee hass takenn hiss cheesee?'

Edie edged forward carefully and quietly. She could clearly see the grounds outside. The lights in the far, far distance were those of Pilpsville. The stinking mud from the river gurgled away noisily. Each popped bubble releasing yet another foul smell into the night air.

Then suddenly, just like the stench, an idea hit her. 'Upp,' she said to Bessie. 'Let'ss justt goo upp andd overr!'

'Poisonouss gases upp there,' said Bessie, pulling away from Edie.

'Nott iff wee holdd ourr breathh!' she whispered, taking Bessie's arm firmly. 'Comee onn, Bessiee. Wee cann doo thiss.'

'Butt the guardd ... we mustt go throughh the gatee. It's thee rules ...'

'Hangg thee ruless!' said Edie, looking deep into Bessie's eyes. 'Youu aree Bessiee. II amm Ediee.'

'I amm Bessie. Youu are Ediee. Hang thee rules,' repeated Bessie.

'Rightt, noww holdd ontoo myy handd tightlyy andd takee aa veryy deepp breathh.'

On the count of three, both Grublin-fairies took in a huge lungful of air, then flapped frantically, propelling themselves upwards and in time, over the large gated city wall.

And as they flew off quickly in the direction of the Pilpsville lights, still smarting from the effort of holding so much foul air in their lungs, they were completely unaware of the final part of Splidge's conversation with the guard house.

'AA keyy! Someonee hass stolenn Meltiee'ss keyy,' he shouted. 'Welll, whyy didn'tt youu sayy soo inn thee firstt placee? II havee twoo creaturess rightt heree whoo mayy knoww somethingg aboutt itt!'

\*\*\*\*\*\*

Flying high over the land, Edie hoped Bessie would recognise their flight path, but her memory was still poor with only a few sketchy details scraping through.

'Lookk,' said Edie, 'that'ss Greatt Molaringg upp aheadd.'

'Rightt,' said Bessie. 'Great Molaringg.' She obviously had no idea of where the place was.

'Soonn we'll bee inn Pilpsvillee. You'll seee thee oldd schooll – Arty'ss palacee noww ...'

'Artyy?' said Bessie. 'I knoww that namee.'

'Yess,' said Edie. 'He'ss, err, aa friendd off Meltiee, yourr bosss.'

'Speciall mission, forr the bosss,' said Bessie.

'Yess, wee havee too findd anotherr friendd off Meltiee'ss andd givee himm thee keyy,' said Edie, gently. 'Hiss namee iss Albertt. He'ss, err, *stayingg* withh thee leaderr att thee palacee.' Edie pauscd for a moment, wondering about all the thoughts she'd listened to in the past months. Much was relying on the degree of truth in what she'd heard. 'Hee hass aa roomm inn thee basementt, soo I'mm toldd.'

'Albertt! I knoww that namee too.'

'Soo youu shouldd. He'ss Aggie'ss brotherr. Youu weree veryy goodd friendss withh himm,' said Edie, swooping low over the once sparkling Great Molaring rooftops.

'Who'ss Aggie?' said Bessie.

Edie sighed. Weaning her off the potion was one thing. Getting her memory back was another!

With the buildings of Insisorton coming quickly into view, Edie decided to land before continuing their journey.

'Whyy are wee stoppingg?' said Bessie. 'What aboutt our missionn?'

'We'ree stilll onn trackk. II justt wantt too checkk youu overr too makee suree youu lookk okayy beforee wee seee Albertt.'

What she really meant was that she wanted to see if there had been any changes to her face or body. They still needed to keep the Grubliny appearance just in case they flew into anyone. With two days of watered down potion in her bloodstream, Bessie's body would be starting to revert back to her pilp collector state, yet apart from a shortened third nostril, smaller ears and a sudden growth of brown wavy hair, she looked practically the same as before. And it was dark so hopefully such subtle changes wouldn't be noticed.

Edie checked herself out in the broken window pane of a burnt out shop. How she longed to be out of this filthy Grublin disguise. Soon, she promised herself, soon.

'Rightt!' she said, using a piece of string to tie Bessie's hair back from her face. 'Thee palacee iss justt aa feww streetss fromm heree. Let'ss gett goingg.'

Flying swiftly through the town's streets, it wasn't long before they came to the former high school, now known as the leader's palace.

'Helll!' said Edie, suddenly pulling Bessie in behind a pillar. 'They'vee gott guardss att thee frontt.'

'That's okayy,' said Bessie. 'We justt tell themm we're fromm Meltiee andd …'

'Err, noo. Let'ss nott disturbb themm, afterr alll itt iss ratherr latee,' said Edie, looking around. 'We'll goo aroundd thee backk wayy.'

She waited until the guards were distracted then dragged Bessie round the back of the building, flying low and hard against the shadows.

After catching their breath, they looked up at the windows. They were standing in the former playground, under a rain shed. The whole building was in darkness except for a tiny glow from a basement window.

'Iss that wheree Albert's roomm is?' said Bessie. 'Seems a bitt unfair puttingg him downn there. II mean theree are tonss of roomss.' She pointed to the vast amount of windows that littered that side of the building.

'Perhapss they'vee gott aa feww peoplee stayingg overr,' said Edie, hurriedly. 'Noww II needd youu too waitt heree forr aa momentt whilee II goo andd findd Albertt.' She ushered Bessie to the long wooden seat at the back of the shed. 'Justt stayy putt. II won'tt bee longg.'

She left Bessie happily playing with the key around her neck and flew low across the playground to the basement window. There was a series of eight low windows in a line, all with metal bars installed. In former times, glass had been fitted and the rooms were used for storage, now they served as cells for those who dared to oppose the leader.

Edie cautiously made her move, creeping slowly in the shadows until she reached the dimly lit cell where Albert was imprisoned. Quickly she changed into her normal fairy state and, after shaking herself thoroughly, bent down and put her face to the bars. The light was poor giving few clues to where the occupant was, but on hearing something shuffling about, Edie called softly through.

'Albert? Albert Lichen, is that you?'

Inside the shuffling immediately stopped.

'Albert? We've come to rescue you. That is me, Edie, and Bessie.' Edie pushed her face in closer to the bars, her hands gripping either side. 'We've got Meltiee's key to the firepowder store. We can blow up the Grublin potion store if we can just get our hands on the other one ...'

From out of the shadows a hand appeared grasping a small silver key. 'It's a duplicate, but it should still work,' said Arty. He stepped out slowly, knowing that the sudden shock of seeing him would cause great alarm. He pushed the key through the one of bars of the window.

'Y-Y-You're n-not Albert!' stammered Edie, recoiling and catching her breath. She sat back on her knees, listening to her heart thump noisily as she stared in disbelief. 'I-I s-suppose the guards are on their way, aren't they?' She looked around expectantly.

'No! Please, I need your help,' said Arty. 'My father is dying.' He moved up closer to the bars. 'She's poisoned him, my mother. You need to get Albert, please. He's the only one who might save him.'

'But you're the leader,' said Edie, feeling much braver and moving back to her original position. 'Send some of your Grublins to find him!'

'I *was* leader, but my mother had me thrown in here so that she can rule,' he said.

'What a shame!' said Edie, getting up to leave.

'Stop! Where are you going?'

'Well, since Albert has clearly escaped already and I now have two keys to the firepowder,' sneered Edie, fighting the urge to spit in his face, 'I might as well blow the whole building up ...'

'Look,' cut in Arty, 'I know I've done some really bad things ...'

'Bad!' said Edie, trying not to raise her voice too high. 'You have destroyed our land! You have destroyed our people! I think that's a little more than bad!'

Arty hung his head despairingly.

'Why?' said Edie. 'Is that shame creeping across your face, Arty Granger? Am I to believe you are actually sorry for what you have done?

'It's not about me anymore,' said Arty, lifting his head up again. 'Please, it's about my father. Find Albert for me. He could help him.'

'You don't give a stuff about Ferrett,' said Edie.

'Wanting him out of the way is not the same as wanting him dead!' said Arty.

Just then, Edie became aware of something sneaking up behind her. She fell quickly against the wall, sucking herself in tight to the brickwork. Seeing her move so fast, Arty slid back into the dark shadows of his cell.

'Did you find him?'

'Oh, Bessie, you scared me half to death,' said Edie, clutching a hand to her chest.

'AAArrgghh!' screamed Bessie, backing away from her rescuer. 'Who aree you?'

'Sssshhh! It'ss mee, Ediee,' said Edie, changing back into a Grublin form again.

'AAArrrgghh!' cried Bessie, starting to hyperventilate. 'II hate Grublinss. I rememberr now!

'Ssshhh! You'll stir the guards. Be quiet,' said Edie, changing back into her normal fairy state. 'Come,' she said, dragging Bessie away from the window. 'We need to get out of here. The place will be swarming with guards.'

She pulled a squealing Bessie across the playground, determined to get into the shadow of the rain shed before the palace guards arrived.

'But what about my father?' called Arty as they left. 'Will you find Albert, for me, will you?'

But his question was left unanswered as several Grublins, aroused by Bessie's screaming, appeared around the corner followed by a clearly upset and half asleep Martha.

'Search the grounds. The message from Meltiee's guard said there were two of them,' shouted Martha. 'If they are here, I want them found!'

At the back of the rain shed, Edie stood with her hand firmly across Bessie's mouth. Looking up, Bessie could see the fear in Edie's eyes and knew she had to keep quiet for both their sakes. She signalled for Edie to drop her hand and listened as the search outside intensified.

They huddled together closely, hardly daring to breathe, trembling at the thought of being caught. The dark shadows in the corner of the rain shed would conceal them for a while, but not forever.

The Grublins were getting closer, sniffing the air with their extensive nostrils. Several were crawling along the lower wall of the palace. Others were up in the surrounding trees, clambering around in the branches.

Suddenly, Bessie tapped gently on Edie's arm. She pointed to the far corner of the shed where the sides met then beckoned to Edie to follow. Desperate not to be heard, they gently fluttered across to a section underneath the seating area which was covered over by ivy. Bending down, Bessie pushed the plant aside and crawled through the gap that now appeared. Edie, immediately behind her, found herself emerging into a small crevice carved into the side of the hill that backed onto the playground. After rearranging the ivy again, Edie sat herself down next to Bessie and waited patiently for the guards to complete their search. The hole, complete with tree roots, stones and the rich smell of damp soil, had been used many times by truanting fairies. It provided a safe bolt hole then and now, and as they settled back both felt extreme tiredness come upon them and within minutes were asleep.

\*\*\*\*\*\*

It was some time later when Edie awoke, cursing herself for dozing off at such a crucial time. She roused Bessie, motioning for quiet by placing a finger to her lips. Sleepily, Bessie nodded and sat up, straightening her legs out as best she could.

She looked Edie up and down relieved she was still in fairy form.

Moving towards the mouth of the crevice, Edie parted the ivy and slowly pushed her head through. It was still dark, but dawn wasn't far away. More importantly though, there was no sign of guards or indeed, Martha. She shuffled backwards to where Bessie still sat.

'Right, you understand that I am a changeling?' she whispered. 'I can change into another creature at whim, okay. So, no need to scream!'

'You mightt have toldd me,' said Bessie.

'And what would you have done if I had?'

'Probablyy – scream!' said Bessie. 'Justt don't doo the Grublinn again. II hate Grublinss.'

Lucky we don't have a mirror then, thought Edie. Although she had noticed that Bessie had undergone more changes as the night wore on. Her skin was almost back to a normal colour, the third nostril had shrunk back more and her eyes were definitely less beady.

'Look, I will have to change into Grublin form,' she said, taking Bessie's hand and patting it gently. 'It's our only way of fooling the Grublins.'

'Can'tt we justt stay here a bitt longerr – as fairiess?'

Edie looked at the Grublin-fairy in front of her and coughed. 'Er, no. We need to find Aggie – we need to find Albert too!' She said the last piece of the sentence a little reluctantly, but knew that saving Ferrett was the correct thing to do and Arty was right, if anyfairy could save him it would be Albert.

'Now, I'm going to change. I'll do it very slowly so don't panic.' And true to her word, Edie changed into Grublin form bit by bit. At first Bessie gasped, but then by telling herself that it was purely a disguise, her breathing slowed to a more normal rate.

With Bessie directly behind her, Edie crawled towards the ivy curtain and the way out. Carefully they climbed through, keeping the noise to an absolute minimum, moving one limb at a time. At last they were able to stand up, stretch and take in some fresh air. The next part of the plan should have been relatively simple; creep to the edge of the playground, sneak round to the column at the side then gently take off into the night. But a hand on Edie's shoulder soon put paid to that idea.

'A pair of rogue Grublin-fairies, well I never,' said a low voice.

'We should hand them over to the guards,' said another.

Edie and Bessie froze, not daring to look behind. To be caught at this point when they'd been so careful was disastrous. All plans of finding Aggie and Albert – and saving Ferrett were quickly put to rest. But then Edie realised something – something very important. The creatures behind were speaking fairy tongue – they were fairies!

'Perhapss we should just torture themm!' came a more familiar voice although this one had hints of a Grublin accent. 'See whatt they know.'

Edie took in a breath. 'Aggiee? Aggiee Lichenn iss thatt youu?' She turned around to confront her capturers.

'Oh my wings! It knows you!'

Aggie was about to turn to her brother and protest that she did not cavort with the likes of Grublins when Edie took that moment to change back to fairy form.

'Edie?' said Aggie, as the last elements of Grublin disappeared. 'Is thatt really youu?'

'We were just coming to find you,' said Edie, hugging Aggie, then Fred, then Albert. 'Do you have news of the twins? Have you found them?'

Fred explained that they were both tucked up and fast asleep in the dwarf chambers. It came as such a relief to Edie who then repeated her earlier statement. 'I just can't believe it – and we were coming to find you!'

Aggie appeared a little taken back. 'You were bringingg a Grublin to findd me?'

Bessie looked around for the Grublin Aggie was referring to. She wasn't aware of a third person joining the search, she thought.

'This is not a real Grublin, Aggie. It's a Grublin-fairy,' said Edie. 'Take a closer look. What do you see?'

'A third nostrill, greyish skin, a rather large waistbandd ...'

Bessie looked down at her waist, then at her arms then felt around her face until she found a third nostril. She was just about to scream when Edie's carefully placed hand stifled any noise she was about to make.

'I'mm a Grublin-fairyy?' she said, the sound was muffled, but the others knew exactly what she was saying. Edie hesitated then took her hand away as Bessie added, 'II hate Grublinss.' She started panting, puffing, panicking.

'Bessiee? Is that you?' Aggie's eyes lit up. 'Oh my wingss! Is that really you?' She pulled out a brown paper bag from her pocket and handed it to her friend. 'Fredd suggested I bring one with me, justt in case!'

Unable to contain her excitement, Aggie grabbed Bessie and hugged her tightly. 'I've missedd you so much,' she said.

Bessie pulled the bag away from her face. 'Andd you aree?'

'It's Aggie,' said Edie. 'Remember?'

'Thatt name!' said Bessie. 'Nightt after nightt inside my headd!'

'I'll explain later,' said Edie to Aggie, 'when we're not so short of time.' She'd noticed how Albert was growing impatient, pacing around the inside of the rain shed.

'Do you have a plan?' said Edie.

Aggie was about to answer when the others cut in quickly.

'We need to get Ma and Pa from the cells first,' said Albert.

'Then,' added Fred, 'find the healers and get them to change Martha back into a human child.'

'Er, excusee me,' said Aggie, butting in. 'Those were myy ideas.'

'Forget whose ideas, think about how – how are we going to do this?' said Edie.

'We could,' said Albert, 'try flying up to an open window ...'

'Or,' said Fred, 'sneak around the guards ...'

'Okayy! Now you're just being sillyy,' said Aggie. 'What we need is some firepowderr, like the stuff you had, Albertt.'

'Firepowder!' said Bessie. 'That's partt of ourr mission, thatt is. Takee the keyy from thee boss too the leaderr.' She put a hand down her top and pulled out the key on its cord.

'You have one of the keys?' said Albert.

'No,' said Edie, holding another key aloft. 'We have both of the keys!'

Albert looked on in disbelief. 'Where did you get the other one?'

'Oh, sky above! I clean forgot about him,' cut in Edie pointing to the barred window with the faint glow. 'Arty, he's in the cells.'

'Whatt?' said Aggie.

'Something to do with his mother being leader ...'

'That's what Fid said as we were leaving,' said Fred. 'He'd heard a rumour ...'

'And Ferrett – Ferrett's dying. He needs our help.' Edie turned to Albert. 'He needs *your* help.'

'Dying? But how?' said Aggie. They were all dearly fond of Ferrett. He was a great family friend and had helped the Lichens out on numerous occasions.

Edie shrugged her shoulders. 'Arty thinks his mother poisoned him.'

'Well, somefairy had better speak to him – find out what's going on,' said Fred.

All eyes turned to Aggie. 'I shalll take great pleasure in speaking to thatt ...'

'Easy though, he's not the same fairy. Something has changed in him.'

'Probablyy the shock of his motherr getting the better of him,' said Aggie under her breath as she crept across the playground to the cell window.

The others waited quietly in the shadows, going over the plans for the rescue of Ma and Pa Lichen. With Albert's knowledge of firepowder and both the keys, they should have them out of the cells in no time then they could blow up the Grublin potion store. There was just one tiny flaw in the plan – how were they going to get to the firepowder store?

This was something Aggie planned to ask Arty – once she'd finished ridiculing him! She bent down on her knees and called through the bars. 'Guesss who?'

From the darkness, his face worn with worry, came Arty. 'Have they cured my father? Is he better?

Aggie was stunned. This was not quite the reception she had expected. 'Don'tt you recognise me, huh? Don'tt you know who I am?'

'Of course I do! You are the bane of my life,' he said sadly. 'But that's not important now. Please, my father – is he okay?' He grabbed the bars with both hands, startling Aggie and making her pull back from the window.

She had been building up to this moment for so long. Confrontation is what she expected, trickery and revenge too; a lengthy battle of wits in which she, the hero, would defeat the Arty the Tyrant. Instead she found herself face to face with a mere shell of a fairy whose only concern was his ailing father.

Now she felt utterly confused and completely deflated. How could she be a hero now? She looked into the former leader's face, determined to get a reaction. 'So noww you care about your father andd he's dying – so you say,' she said scathingly. 'How do I knoww that this is not just another of your spiteful trickss – like turningg me into a Grublin-fairyy?'

'Please, Aggie. Speak to your brother.'

He'd never called her Aggie before and the shock sent her flitting back across the playground to the others.

'SSShhh, keep it down,' whispered Edie. 'There are still guards out front.'

Aggie acknowledged Edie's warning and kept her voice deliberately low. 'You're rightt,' she puffed. 'He's changed.' She turned to Albert. 'You needd to help Ferrett while we findd Ma and Pa.

'You sure about this – your arch enemy?' said Fred.

Aggie sighed. 'Ass sure as I can be. Now you and Albert go andd talk to him about Ferrett's illness and the firepowderr. Us three will go looking for Ma and Pa.'

'But we don't know where they are,' said Edie.

'They'lll be somewhere in that basementt,' said Aggie.

'Aree we goingg on ourr mission noww, Addie?' said Bessie, looking at her puzzled. 'Onlyy we've beenn here aa long timee and thee boss willl be wantingg his keyy back!'

'Yes, butt the mission has changedd a little,' said Aggie, raising her eyes to the sky. 'We're goingg to find two other friendss of Meltiee's first.'

'Oh, okayy,' said Bessie, 'but rememberr, I havee to bee at workk in the morningg. I can'tt stay tooo long.'

'Yes, dear,' said Edie, ushering her along the edge of the playground. 'We'll have you back at the factory in no time!'

Leaving Albert and Fred to talk to Arty, Aggie, Bessie and Edie fluttered over to the playground to the back of the palace, sliding gently along until they came to the corner. Aggie signalled to the others to wait. Looking round, she could see two guards in front of the wooden doors. Two more were posted in the grounds near to the fallen statue of Ivor the Zealous.

She slipped back from her viewing position and reported her sightings to Edie.

'I can't see howw we get past all of themm,' said Aggie in a low voice. 'Especially with her alll half Grubliny!' She cast her eyes in Bessie's direction.

With Bessie at such a crucial 'in between' stage of changing back to pilp collector form, they had no control over what she said or did. She was completely unpredictable!

'I could go in as a Grublin,' said Edie quietly.

'No, not on your ownn,' said Aggie. 'I can't risk losing you againn.'

'Aggie! It's what I do,' said Edie. 'Let me use my powers to help.'

Aggie looked worriedly at Bessie who was playing with the key again. 'Whatt about her?'

Edie pulled a face. 'We could hide her in the rain shed crevice again.'

'No, she mightt get caught. She's so confusedd.' Aggie thought for a moment. 'She can go with Albertt, after all, she does have the other key.'

'Oh crikey! I'd clean forgotten to give him that one,' said Edie. 'Mind you, they'll have to wrestle her for it!'

Aggie smiled for the second time that day. She turned to Bessie and said, 'I'm going to take you to Albertt. He might want to borrow your key. Iss that okay?'

'Is itt for thee mission?' said Bessie, curling her hair around her finger in a familiar way. 'Onlyy if it'ss for thee mission, butt I mustt have itt back. Thee boss willl be lookingg for itt.'

Aggie took her hand and flew swiftly to the barred window where Fred, Albert and Arty were in deep conversation.

'Ah,' said Albert. 'I'm glad you're here. We'll need that key, Bessie.' He leant over to take it from her neck.

Bessie pulled back. 'It'ss my keyy. I'm lookingg after itt for thee boss.'

'It's for the missionn, remember,' said Aggie, as she took off to rejoin Edie.

'Hey,' call whispered Albert, 'you can't leave her here.'

Aggie ignored him and flew quickly back to Edie who was peering cautiously around the corner again.

'It look like the guards are about to change,' she said, pointing to another group of four Grublins marching in from the far right of the building.

'Thiss is our chance then,' said Aggie, 'while they are distractedd.' She took Edie's arm. 'You'd better change back to Grublinn form quickly, before they finish changing over.'

And in seconds, Edie the fairy was gone. In her place stood Edie the Grublin, complete with the appalling stench that came with the role.

Aggie held her nose and waved her forward. 'Go when you're readyy. I'll follow behind.'

Edie waited patiently until both the guards on duty and the guards for the changeover had come together in the courtyard. Fluttering low, she disappeared around the corner with Aggie tucked in behind her. They stopped behind a pillar which offered cover. Edie nodded and they flew on until they reached the great door. It was firmly closed. Only a strong tug on its handle would get it open, Aggie knew that from her school days. She pulled Edie back behind another pillar.

'That doorr will make a right noise as you pull the handle. It'lll give us away,' she whispered. 'You'll have to take me in as a prisonerr. That way, the Grublins won'tt suspect us.'

Edie shook her head. 'It's too risky. They might want to question us.'

'Lookk, they're too busy fussingg over the guard change,' said Aggie. 'Let's do itt!'

Reluctantly, Edie stepped out from behind the pillar and walked up to the door. She pulled hard on the round handle, twisting and turning it at the same time. It opened with a loud creak as the rusted hinges made themselves known.

The Grublin guards looked up in alarm. 'It'ss okayy,' shouted Edie, putting on her Grublin accent, 'II havee prisonerr forr thee neww leaderr.'

The guards seemed unsure at first, but then one waved her on, leaving the entry to the palace clear.

Once inside and having shut the door again, Edie changed back. She looked around. Having never been inside before, she hadn't a clue where she was going.

'The stairss to the basement are at the end of the back corridor. We'll needd to cut through the halll to get there,' said Aggie.

Unsurprisingly, the palace was empty and dim. A few side lights had been left on, but otherwise the place was one of darkness and shadows. This suited Edie and Aggie perfectly. The last thing they needed was to bump into a Grublin and explain why they were creeping around the building in the middle of the night!

The place had changed tremendously although the layout had been kept the same. The once dingy foyer was filled with a comfy seating area and a huge chandelier hovered overhead. In front of them were the school offices, and as they fluttered by, Aggie could see that these too had been refurbished. Memories poured into her head, stirred by the visual clues that surrounded her. 'Ohh my wings! I remember standing outside this roomm and waiting for Mr Fettock,' she said quietly then wondered where exactly the old head teacher was now.

Edie tugged her arm gently. 'While I'm pleased about your memories returning, let's not get carried away.'

Aggie nodded and continued to lead the way to the hall, a large room in the centre of the building.

Passing the old classrooms, she was tempted to look inside, but the need to find her parents urged her on.

'The halll is just there,' she said, pointing out the Great Hall doors that lay ahead. They moved swiftly along, keeping their eyes open for any movements. At the hall doors, Aggie twisted the handle and pushed. The vast room had changed beyond all belief. Gone was the exercise equipment and the wooden seats used for morning assembly. Gone were the tatty moss curtains that had hung for decades at the high windows. The huge room had been converted into a ballroom with large velvet chairs and sumptuous cushions. Chandeliers, like the one in the foyer, hung from the ceiling. And although dark, Aggie could just make out the red colour scheme as a chink of moonlight played on the wall. In normal circumstances, 'WOW' would have been a good response, but knowing what was at stake, they fluttered quickly across and out through the opposite door.

'What was thatt?' said Aggie on hearing a creaking noise.

'Just the door,' said Edie, letting it fall back on its hinges.

Aggie looked around suspiciously. The main corridor was where the head teacher's office and the staffroom used to be. As one door lay slightly ajar, she could see that these had been transformed into elegant bedrooms. They moved quickly past.

Being such a large building, there were still quite a few doors to pass in the former school before they would have sight of the basement stairs.

Then all at once, the lights went on and an unwelcome figure stepped out into the corridor.

'Looking for something?'

They looked up and saw, at the very end of the corridor, the new leader, Martha and her Moshtike love, Belcher. To the side of her were five bedraggled creatures, shivering and shaking. Each was gripped tightly by a filthy Grublin guard.

Aggie and Edie couldn't believe their eyes – Myrtle, Gilbert, Victor and the twins! They'd been left with the dwarves, safely tucked up in bed – so they thought.

'What are they doing here?' whispered Edie.

Aggie shrugged her shoulders and pulled a face demonstrating that she hadn't a clue! 'They're supposed to be asleep – safe in the caves and asleep!'

'Surprise!' laughed Martha, pulling at Myrtle's top. 'Now what would you give to have them back, huh?'

'Leave them alone, Martha,' shouted Edie. 'This is nothing to do with them. This is between you and Aggie.'

'Rubbish!' she cried. 'They are just as much a danger to me as she is!'

'They're frightenedd! Let them go,' screamed Aggie, scanning their terrified faces.

'No, you're quite wrong,' she growled. 'They're very pleased to be here, aren't you, dears?'

The terrified creatures feigned smiles to keep her happy, but Aggie could see through to their pain.

'See, how they smile,' laughed Martha loudly. 'I've not harmed them at all – yet!'

'She's crazy!' whispered Edie. 'Completely bonkers!'

'What do you wantt?' cried Aggie, fighting to keep the anguish from her voice.

'I'll do you a swap,' Martha said, placing an arm around Gilbert's shoulder. He flinched as she touched him – partly through fear, partly because his medication had worn off and the pain had returned.

'Your life for theirs, Aggie Lichen,' she added.

Edie glanced over at Aggie then looked back at Martha. 'How do we know you'll keep your word?'

'You don't!' said Martha. 'Now do we have deal or not?'

Aggie looked across at Edie. 'Whatt choice do we have?' she said to her.

'But she'll go back on what she's said. You know what she's like,' said Edie, deliberately keeping her voice low.

'Andd if I don't give myself up to her, she'll hurt the otherss.' Aggie looked across at her sister. 'I can't let that happenn!'

'Yes or no?' snapped Martha, holding Victor up by the scruff of his neck.

'Yess,' said Aggie. 'We have a deall.'

Martha gave the order to release the five petrified creatures, to the guards then suddenly yelled, 'Stop!' The guards grabbed the crying youngsters back again. 'Don't forget to give them their 'bravery' badges before they go,' she sniggered, looking up into Belcher's eyes.

Each Grublin produced a metal badge from its pocket and pinned it to their captive's chest.

One by one the little creatures yelped in pain as the metal pin pricked their skins.

'She's truly mad,' said Edie. 'Fancy giving them a bravery award. She's lost it completely.'

Aggie couldn't speak. Something in her mind was screaming at her, shouting at her to dig deep into her memory, yelling at her from a higher plane. 'Something's nott quite right here,' she said at last, staring at the five creatures now fluttering towards them.

'Well, of course it's not right!' said Edie. 'What fairy in their right mind ...'

'No, the badgess ... why on Mirvellon did she give them badgess?' Aggie said as the five grew closer.

She looked at Myrtle's face as she approached then at Gilbert's. They were crying, but grimacing also as if in pain.

'What is itt?' she said as Myrtle landed, hugging her tightly. 'What's hurtingg?'

'My chestt hurts,' she sobbed. 'It feelss like it's on fire.'

As the guard Grublins were making their approach to arrest Aggie and Edie, Martha called out, 'Come along! We made a deal! Your life for theirs.'

Knowing that they didn't have much time, Aggie took Myrtle's hands and looked into her face. 'Showw me exactly where it hurtss.'

Myrtle pointed to the placc on her chest where the badge sat pinned to her top, just below her collarbone to the right. Aggie pulled the top away slightly to reveal a tiny speck of blood where the pin had caught her. Then it came to her like a large sledgehammer.

'Poisonn! Oh my wings, she's poisonedd them with Treeslanch, just like Victor!'

Edie's face turned pale. 'It can't be. It's too quick.' She gently took Gilbert's injured arm as she spoke. 'Treeslanch is a slow acting poison ...'

'Not when it's mixed with furrell leaves,' said a voice.

The Grublin guards flumped to a flystill. They had not expected reinforcements to appear. They hovered in the air, confused.

'Albert!' cried Aggie. 'Did you findd Ferrett?'

'First things first,' he said

Albert threw her a bottle of the total cleanser he'd found in the cells below. 'It will clear every trace of Grublin from your body. You'll be completely back to normal and in control although your memory will still take some time to return to normal.'

Eagerly, Aggie twisted off the lid, drinking it down noisily.

# Chapter Thirty Six

'That's better,' *I* said. 'Now I feel completely me again!' I threw the bottle to one side.

'Well, as complete as you can do – with gills!' said Fred who was right behind Albert. He was gripping Bessie's arm tightly.

'Oh, pigging hell, not those again!' I said, feeling around my neck. 'Perhaps there were advantages in being a Grublin after all!'

'They're the least of our worries,' said Albert, bending over Myrtle.

'Guards, get them!' cried Martha, showing no sympathy for the dying creatures.

The guards immediately snapped out of hover mode and charged towards us all.

'Oh dear,' cried Martha, mockingly as she watched the Grublin guards descend. 'Are the poor little things allergic to metal?'

'No, mother,' came a voice from behind her, 'like most things in this land, they are allergic to you!'

Arty grabbed his mother's arms and began tying them together with a piece of cord. As he did, he cast his eyes to the far end of the room and shouted, 'GUARDS, STOP!'

The poor bewildered Grublins halted in mid-air once more and hovered, awaiting further instructions.

'Belcher, help me!' she screamed. 'We can rule together just as we planned.'

Seeing the anger in Arty's eyes, Belcher backed away. 'I just wanted to be with you, Martha – not rule. This is all too complicated.' He turned to fly.

'Don't you dare leave me, you ungrateful savage,' she screamed.

Without looking back, Belcher headed towards the Great Hall, but his final destination was probably back to the safety of Belcham Bog.

Martha composed herself quickly and began struggling with Arty, trying to loosen her bonds. 'How did you get out?' she snapped.

Arty dangled the two keys in front of her. 'You may have taken my key, mother, but your duplicate still worked with Meltiees.' He looked over at Fred. 'With a little direction he was able to find the firepowder store and blow the cell lock.'

'Guards! Guards!' she screamed at the top of her voice. 'Guards! Arrest this fairy. Arrest him now!'

The Grublin guards stopped immediately and looked round. The sight of Arty tying his mother up clearly startled and confused them.

'Who'ss inn chargee noww?' said the larger one.

'I am!' said Arty and Martha together.

'No!' said Ferrett, emerging from a room to the left. He held onto a healer to steady himself. 'Neither of you have any claim on this land.'

'Cann wee goo thenn?' said the large Grublin, looking at the other Grublins with him. 'Onlyy iff there'ss nothingg forr uss too doo ...'

'Soon, but we need your expert guarding for just a little while longer then you will be released from your duties completely.' Ferrett slumped down hard onto the floor.

'Father!' cried Arty, leaving Martha propped against a large window. He rushed to Ferrett's side then called over to Albert. 'Has he had it? Has he had the antedote?'

The healer put her hand on his shoulder. 'Help me get him back to bed. He should not be up so soon.'

'So he's had it?' questioned Arty. 'And it's working?'

'Albert has given him the cure, but it will take time for the poison to be completely neutralised.'

Arty looked over at Albert and nodded his head in thanks.

'You'd better go with him,' I said to Fred. 'Keep an eye on him in case he tries to escape.'

'But Gilbert and Victor ...' he said, leaning over the creatures lying on the floor.

'I'll see to them, Fred. I need you to stay with Arty.'

Reluctantly, he flew down to the room where Ferrett lay recovering, looking back at his brother as he reached the door.

'It'll be okay, Fred,' I called, bending over Gilbert. 'We've caught it quickly.'

He nodded and disappeared inside the room.

'What about her?' said Edie, pointing to a trussed up Martha, still propped against the window. 'What shall we do with her?'

'Oh, I think the healers might have a plan for her,' I said. 'Er, Grublin guards, could you take her through to the Great Hall? I think it's a very suitable place for a leader to be dealt with!'

Leaving the guards to drag Martha through to the Great Hall, Edie and I turned our attention to the five little creatures on the floor.

'What were you thinking of?' said Edie, hugging Stan and Alf tightly. Tears fell freely from her eyes as she looked at her nephews for the first time in many years.

'We were going to come and rescue you,' said Stan.

'But when we got to Grublin City we didn't have anything shiny for the gate guard,' said Alf, 'and then Meltiee arrived ...'

'... and he was really angry. Then he remembered who we were,' said Gilbert, now feeling a little better after Albert's pain relief top up, 'and had us flown to the palace ...'

'... and then that Martha held us in a room,' said Victor. 'She was going to swap all of you for all of us.'

Then Myrtle took up the story. 'She said that Albert would be made to complete his permanent Grublin potion and that you, Aggie, would be the first to try it.'

'Well, that's just not going to happen now,' I said as Albert administered the last of the antidote to Victor who, having already been poisoned only required a small top up.

'She's too late anyway,' said Albert, patting his pocket. 'It's already done and I won't be practising on Aggie – well, as long as she doesn't annoy me!' He looked over and laughed.

I started to poke my tongue out in response, but at that point, a high pitched scream pierced the air and at the end of the corridor where the basement steps were, two familiar figures flew towards us.

'Oh, my wings! My babies!' cried Ma, trying to hug us all at once. 'I can't believe it! You're all okay.'

'Have you been alright?' I said, as Pa pulled me away for a separate squeeze.

'We've been down there for months. We knew Ferrett and Albert were nearby, but we were kept at the far end.'

'Oh, that Arty has got a lot to answer for ...'

'No,' interrupted Pa. 'We weren't badly treated at all, in fact, we were given everything we wanted. The 'cells' were really just two large fully furnished rooms for us to live and sleep in.'

'It was quite strange,' said Ma. 'Arty used to come and talk with us – when his mother wasn't around.'

'But didn't she object to the way you were living?' I said, watching as Myrtle wrapped herself round Ma's waist.

'No, we were hostages,' said Pa. 'We were only being held until she had you and the others ...'

'Then,' cut in Ma, 'I expect we would have ended up like the rest of Pilpsville ...'

'... as Grublin-fairies,' I said, shuddering at the thought.

'These little ones need to rest,' said Ma, taking Myrtle's hand.

'We're not sleepy,' yawned Gilbert. 'It's just the poison.'

'Poison? What poison?' yelled Pa.

'They'll all be fine,' said Albert, pulling Stan and Alf to their feet. 'But it is very late and you do need to sleep it off.'

'Could we just clean those door handles before we go?' said Stan, obviously feeling a lot better. 'They've got really dirty fingerprints all ...'

'No! Come with me down to our rooms,' said Ma. 'It's warm and comfy there.' She turned to Myrtle adding, 'Then perhaps you can tell me what's been going on and what this poison's all about, huh?'

As Ma led the little group away to the safety of her rooms in the basement, Ferrett appeared at a doorway, a healer at each side. Fred followed with Arty, his hands tied together with a thin cord.

Slowly, they made their way down the corridor to meet us. Holding him between them, the two healers flew Ferrett down to where we stood.

'Shall we go?' I asked as Fred and Arty joined us. They nodded together although Arty was unable to meet my gaze. I fluttered to the rear of the group, watching Arty's every move. I couldn't believe that we had finally made it to this point and the villains, the cruel tyrants who had left our land in tatters, were at last caught and restrained.

In the Great Hall, Martha had been tied to one of the huge red thrones. She was screaming and thrashing about, trying to loosen her bonds.

Arty was led to a small chair in the corner of the room where he sat down quietly.

'Guards, bring her forward,' said Ferrett, now seated on a heavy gold chair, padded out with thick red cushions.

The Grublins untied Martha from the throne, dragging her across to where the healers stood waiting.

'We'll take it from here,' said Fred as he and Albert grabbed her arms. They held her steady while the healers worked their magic. As the words were spoken, Martha wriggled desperately to get free.

Ferrett nodded to the Grublin guards who accepted their freedom gratefully and headed out of the door.

'You can't do this to me. I'm in charge,' she screamed. 'Guards! Guards!'

'I think you'll find that the Guards have all left the building,' I said. 'In fact, I suspect that all Grublins will soon be leaving Pilpsville and return to Grublin City!'

'Arty! Help your mother!' she cried. 'Don't let them send me back.'

With Pa and me standing so near, there was little Arty could do even if he wanted to. He looked down at the floor, avoiding her gaze and stayed silent.

One of the healers produced what looked like a clear bauble from her pocket. 'You will be kept within this bubble until you are returned to your human home. Once the bubble is burst, you will become a human once more and remember nothing.'

'No, you can't do that to me,' she screamed, trying to pull her arms away from her captors. 'It was him! Arty made me do it. I just wanted to settle back down with Ferrett.'

'Oh, please, Martha! You tried to kill me!' said Ferrett, the pain clearly showing on his face.

'A genuine mistake. I didn't know the poison was on the tiepin I gave you.'

'Mother,' said Arty, looking up at her, 'you killed Smitch the same way! They know that.'

'Well, we didn't, but I think that has just sealed your fate,' I said, stepping back to allow the healer to come forward with the bubble.

'Take Arty back down to the cells,' said Pa to Albert. 'A son should not have to witness the punishment of his own mother.'

As Martha screamed and cursed at every fairy around her, the final words of the spell were uttered. Within seconds she faded, becoming a multi coloured wisp that entered the bubble in the healer's outstretched hand. Swirling around, it settled moments later and reformed into a tiny version of Martha. Her tiny fists banged on the inside of the bubble, but nothing could be heard. She would remain safely inside until Ferrett took her through the portal, back to her human home.

After watching the bubble disappear inside Ferrett's pocket, we all turned to Arty – who had vanished!

'Where'd he go?' said Albert.

Pa examined the cord left on the floor. 'I think we were all so focused on Martha ...'

'... that he was able to slip out,' said Ferrett.

'But I thought you were watching him,' Fred said to me.

'And I thought I told you to take him down to the cells!' said Pa to Albert.

A heated argument then followed with each fairy blaming the other. Accusations ranged from not watching him carefully enough to allowing him to escape. I had to step in if he was going to be caught any time soon.

'I know where he'll be,' I said quietly. 'Give me the potion, Albert. I'll put an end to this once and for all.'

'But that will change him into a Grublin forever,' said Ferrett as Albert threw the bottle over.

'I thought that was what we all wanted.' I stood and observed the silence. 'I'll take that as a YES,' I said, walking towards the door.

'I'll come with you,' said Fred.

'No, I need to do this on my own.'

I left them all standing there still silent, perhaps shocked at what I intended to do, but something drastic had to be done to rein in Arty and his tyrannical ideas. He may have changed, but who could say what he might attempt with his mother gone and his father healed. No, a butterfly cannot change its spots ...

I flew through the corridor to the basement steps then fluttered down them to the cell where Arty was.

He was sat quietly on the bed, his knees under his chin with his arms wound around them.

'I wonder,' he said as I came in. 'I wonder if things would have been any better if I had been on my own. You know, without mother.' He paused then added, 'I just wanted a mother like you – some kind of family.' He looked up at me smiling. 'You have it all; Ma and Pa, a brother and sister – a family.'

'But you had Ferrett,' I said propping myself against the table. 'He cared about you.'

'But I was brought up as his nephew. I didn't even know he was my father.'

'He was just trying to protect you from what your mother had done to you both,' I said.

'It could have all been so different though, and watching you with your family made me so jealous, so angry.'

'Y-You watched me?'

'All the time ...' he said sadly. 'But you never seemed to like them much. You called your sister names, you stalked your brother, you lied to your Ma. It just didn't seem fair.'

'You saw all that?' I said, surprised.

'Bits and pieces, yes.'

'That's what families do, though. We argue and fight, but we still care.'

'I know that now. Seeing my father so ill made me realise that.' He picked at his fingers, awkwardly.

'He's okay now though,' I said.

'Yes, thanks to Albert. If only I hadn't brought her here in the first place ...'

'Ma says that we can't live our lives through 'if only'. Besides, it's all been sorted out ...'

'Except for me!' he said, looking at the bottle I was holding. 'Albert finally found the formula for permanent Grublin changing then. How ironic! A solution to everything – so I thought.'

I hid the bottle behind my back, a little embarrassed.

'It's okay. I know you have to do it,' he said. 'It will make you the hero of the hour!'

I took the bottle out, unscrewed the lid ...

# Chapter Thirty Seven

An amazing sight greeted us all as we stepped out onto the newly erected platform. In front of us stood hundreds of pilp collectors, in various states of post Grublin-fairy, waving and cheering as we took our seats.

The newly elected leader, Ferrett Granger, limped across to the podium where his long speech had been carefully placed. The effects of Treeslanch still racked his body, but with the healer's help he was able to control the worst of it.

'My dear friends,' he began. 'We are gathered here to celebrate our freedom from tyranny and thank those who have once again risked their own lives for ours.' He looked around at where we were all sitting and smiled. I couldn't help, but notice a little sadness in his eyes though. For while we were all being hailed heroes, he had lost a son.

'It was only Arty,' whispered Myrtle, as he turned back and continued his speech. She had also noticed his sadness. 'You'd think he'd be pleased.'

'Oh, just shut up, Bugface,' I said, pretending to straighten my skirt.

Ma looked over, holding a finger to her lip. My fault again! Sitting on the seat next to her was Eric. He shuffled around uneasily. We all knew he didn't really want to be there. He only came to see his sons collect their medals then he would disappear down the nearest bolt hole to be with his dwarf friends who were organising the fireworks for the evening celebration.

It was some while later that Ferrett finally finished talking and the award ceremony began at last.

Medals were given out to Myrtle, Gilbert – arm now fixed by the healers – Victor and the twins. Then Edie and Bessie stepped up to receive theirs. Bessie, still a little Grubliny, grabbed the shiny medal preferring to hold it in her hand than have it pinned to her chest.

The final awards went to Albert for his ability to create the Treeslanch antedote, to Fred for his determination and then my name was called.

As the last fairy to collect their medal, I received the biggest cheer and the loudest applause. I had waited so long for this moment and dreamt of a large gold medal for months and months. Yet, as I looked up to the pilp plant chimney stacks, where a lone figure sat crouched, watching over the whole proceedings, I couldn't help feeling a bit of a fraud.

But I smiled and waved at the crowd, and with the shiny gold medal attached firmly to my new black top, I took my seat again.

The ceremony continued with the swearing in of Ferrett's new assistant – Mr Fettock, now fully recovered from his own personal Grublin-fairy ordeal and ready to serve the population. He gave a short speech on how he would be honoured to serve under Ferrett and took the opportunity to remind everyone that the schools would be open very soon. His face swung round in our direction displaying the all too familiar smile that meant there was no escape – not even medal winners avoided school.

In the concluding speech, Ferrett gave a stark warning about a possible human invasion and the dire consequences it might bring. For now, they had been kept at bay by Gilbert's quick thinking, but what the future held no one knew. Ferrett had given the population a lot to think about.

As the crowd began to disperse, I glanced up again to the chimney stacks only to see a sparkling flight trail leading away from Pilpsville, towards the wild lands at the edge of Mirvellon.

'Do you know,' said Bessie, nudging me, 'for a minute I thought I saw Arty Granger up there.'

'Bess, I think your mind is still a bit muddled from being a Grublin-fairy!' I laughed and patted her back. 'Come on, let's go and join the party. We don't want to miss the fireworks – all that Grublin potion being blown up should be quite a spectacle!'

And taking one last look up above, I grabbed her hand and flew off with her towards the palace to join the new leader and the grateful residents of Pilpsville.

******

I awoke suddenly that night. At first I thought it was because of the strange surroundings – I'd never slept at the leader's palace before. I looked around at the beautiful furnishings, pulling up the thick velvety blankets under my chin. It would soon be converted back to a high school then normality would kick in big time! But after trying for another half hour, I still couldn't settle back to sleep. Then I listened as my stomach rumbled and put it down to hunger. I switched on the side light and crossed the floor to find the kitchen. The carpet was soft beneath my feet, the tufts catching between my toes. I pulled the door open as gently as I could, but it was heavy and needed quite a tug.

As the wood hit my toe, I tried desperately not to scream, but as the pain soared through my body it must have triggered something in my brain. My memory suddenly exploded, flashing through all that had happened before, after and during Arty's reign. It was then that I finally realised what was troubling me.

'Oh, my wings! GERTIE CRUET!'

P.S. To translate from Spritespiel,

Just take the previous letter

in the alphabet!

# Aggie Lichen; Pilp Collector

## Part One of the Mirvellon Trilogy

Aggie Lichen faces the same dilemmas as any other thirteen year old. But while other teenagers are doing their homework or watching T.V., Aggie flits from house to house in search of prize pilps. That's where Aggie is a little different. You see, Aggie Lichen is a pilp collector – a tooth fairy!

One nightsgritch – a tooth collecting evening – Aggie is attacked by a bright, mysterious light. Is is a low flying glow-worm or something more sinister? Unknown to them, Aggie and her gang have just thirty days to save their kind, but time is not on their side ... neither are the sprites or the Grublins.

## Out now!

ISBN 978-09550192-0-3

# Arty's Revenge

## Part Two of the Mirvellon Trilogy

Heroes and heroines appear in many disguises. Some wear capes, others have masks but rarely do they have their very own wings!

Six months after saving Pilpsville from the evil Arty Granger, Aggie Lichen hopes for nothing more than a good night's sleep and a shiny gold medal. But after her younger sister disappears, the medal still seems a long way off as Aggie and the gang are forced to face their old enemies, the sprites and the Grublins.

And word has it that Gertie Cruet's not too pleased either ...

## Out now!

ISBN 978-09550192-1-0